MEN OF INKED, BOOK THREE

# RESIST ME

www.chellebliss.com

CHELLE BLISS

USA TODAY BESTSELLING AUTHOR

# COPYRIGHT

# THE MEN OF INKED SERIES

*To all the people who said, "Don't do it."*

*I say, "Go fuck yourself!"*

*Dream big and reach for the stars.*

# CHAPTER 1
# FLASH

IZZY

"I DON'T LIKE the idea of you going to Bike Week, Izzy," Joe fumed, slamming his beer on the worktable and glaring at me.

"I'm not a fucking child anymore, Joe. You can't tell me what to do." I stared at him, holding his gaze. I'd always been the little sister, the one everyone wanted to protect. When I was a child, I'd found it flattering, but now? Now it was just a fucking pain in my ass.

"We're not saying you're a kid, babe. Too much bad shit happens during Bike Week. It's not safe for you there. We're just looking out for ya." Michael leaned forward, running his fingers across the back of my hand.

"I can take care of myself. It's just for the weekend. Flash will be with me. I'm not going alone." I sat back, tilting my head to watch their reaction. I knew it wasn't going to be pretty.

"Flash?" Joe asked with wide eyes. "I thought I told you to stay away from that dumbass prick." He ran his hand down his face before squeezing the bridge of his nose. "It was bad enough you brought him to Thanksgiving dinner. I hate that asshole more than I ever did."

"Fucking unbelievable, Izzy." Michael shook his head.

"There's nothing wrong with Flash. He's harmless, but he'll look out for me."

1

Flash wasn't a pussy, but he wasn't a Gallo man either. I didn't give a shit. He was a friend and we hung out when he came through town. We had never been a couple, but he knew how to please me in bed. I liked being with him. He was uncomplicated and not looking for a relationship. He breezed into my life from time to time and exited just as quickly.

"Izzy," Joe warned. "He was a good kid, but now he's prospecting to get into the Sun Devils MC. I know what shit goes down in a club. I've spent enough time at the Neon Cowboy to know what the life is all about. What the fuck do you think Tommy would say if he knew you were going there with Flash?"

I loved my brothers. I truly did. But for shit's sake, they could be overbearing.

"I don't know what he'd say because I haven't seen him in over a year. I'm not Flash's old lady or his whore. We're going as friends. I'm going and you two can't stop me. He'll protect me." I smiled, crossing my arms.

"Flash is a fucking pussy." Michael hit the table with his fists. "Mia could protect you better than him. Jesus Christ, Izzy, why are you so damn hardheaded?"

"Didn't you two teach me how to protect myself?" I glared at them.

"Yes," they answered in unison.

"I can handle myself. I know how to kick ass and bring a man to his knees." I tried to hide my smile. I knew the double meaning wouldn't be lost on them. "I'll be good."

"It's not your behavior we're worried about, baby girl," Joe growled, cracking his knuckles. "Michael and I can't risk jail because we have to kick some fucker's ass for touching you."

"Speak for yourself, old man. You're still pretty fucked up from the accident, but I'm always down to kick ass, brother." Michael laughed. "Anthony is going to be fucking livid when he hears this shit."

I smiled at them. "He already knows, so shut it. I love you both and appreciate everything you've done for me, but I'm an adult. Have a little faith in me for once. Who's the first person

2

you two run to when shit goes bad?" I arched my eyebrow and laughed. "Me. You're always coming to me for help. I'll be fine." I waved my hands. "Don't try and stop me. I promise to be safe and not go anywhere alone while I'm in Daytona. I'll stay with Flash and won't do anything stupid." I stood, completely done with the conversation.

"You'll call us every day," Michael insisted, giving in. He knew he wasn't going to win this battle.

"Text," I replied. "I'll text you every day while I'm gone, but that's all you're getting." I headed toward the front desk to cash out my tips.

"Fine." Michael sighed, shaking his head. "Don't like this shit one bit."

"Not my problem," I called out from the front of the shop.

"Women are a fucking pain in the ass," Joe said to Michael, and they both laughed. "And shut your fucking mouth. I'm healed from the bike accident, dumbass. I can kick your ass right now to prove it too."

"I don't hit the disabled." Michael laughed.

My boys. Their banter and laughter made me smile as I grabbed my money and slammed the drawer closed. I had everything I wanted in the world: four fantastic brothers, one that was MIA—Tommy—a flourishing business, a growing clientele. And I was totally unattached.

What more could a girl ask for?

# CHAPTER 2
# FLASH IS A DUMBFUCK

IZZY

ROLLING into Daytona was an unforgettable experience. The entire beachfront was lined with row after row of bikes, babes, and badass boys. Flash and I checked into the shitty, seedy-ass hotel, but at least it seemed clean and had a bed. I chuckled when I caught a glimpse of the old coin-operated machine that caused the bed to vibrate. We'd find a way to make that useful.

After throwing my bag down on the floor, I collapsed on the lumpy mattress. The vibration of the three-hour bike ride still hadn't left my system as I stared at the brown spot on the ceiling.

"Hey, baby." Flash crawled on top of me, crushing me with his weight. "I want to taste you before we head out." He planted soft kisses on my neck before biting down on the tender flesh of my ear.

I moaned, tangling my fingers in his hair. "You know how I like it," I whispered, pulling on his scalp. "Do me good." I pushed his head down my body, not wanting to waste any time.

"Don't I always?" He licked his lips as he unbuttoned my jeans.

"Mm-hmm. Usually." I smirked as I lifted my ass, allowing him to slide the denim down my legs.

Flash was a beautiful man. He didn't resemble the scrawny kid I used to play kickball with at recess. His blue eyes, killer smile, and chiseled body made my mouth water. I was sure I wasn't the only girl out there who enjoyed his beautifully bent cock—not broken, just curved. It wasn't too wide or thick, just total perfection. Each stroke hit just the right spot, and I'd never found another one since. It was the reason I always welcomed him in my bed.

He threw my jeans across the room before he nestled between my legs. "No panties," he mumbled as he kissed the skin on my lower abdomen. "Landing strip too. You know how I like it."

"Just for you," I lied.

It was the start of bikini season in Florida. I wouldn't be caught dead with stubble or razor burn. I pulled my knees up, planting my feet flush with the comforter, to give him better access.

He inhaled, a gleam in his eye. "You smell better than I fucking remember. You have the sweetest pussy, Iz. Fucking fantastic." Sticking his tongue out, he flicked my clit as he gripped my hips, holding me in place.

A jolt of pleasure shot through my body as I arched my back, pushing my head into the mattress. Warmth cascaded across my body as he latched on to me, sucking my flesh. Letting my knees fall toward the bed, I lay before him, spread eagle and wanting more than his mouth.

His hands slid under my ass as he squeezed it roughly, kneading it with his fingers. He sucked and licked my core while he stared in my eyes. Our gazes were locked as he rubbed his fingers against my opening.

"You're so wet, baby. I can feel how much you've missed me."

"Stop talking, Flash." My body was overly sensitive from the long bike ride. The slightest touch of his lips sent tiny shockwaves down my legs, causing my toes to curl. "Make me come and maybe I'll let you stick your cock in me."

"I'm taking that shit," he muttered against my flesh as he thrust two fingers inside me.

I cried out, the pleasure too intense as he latched on to me.

He rhythmically sucked and finger-fucked me until I screamed through the breath-stealing orgasm.

"It's my turn now, Izzy." Flash patted my thigh as he sat up.

"I said maybe." I closed my eyes, lost in a post-orgasm haze.

"I'm taking it. No maybe about that shit. I earned it," he murmured as he nudged my legs farther apart.

I smirked, closing my legs. "You didn't earn shit. Eating my pussy *was* your reward."

"I'll stick it in your ass, then, but I'm taking something," he said as he flipped me onto my stomach.

I reached back, covering my ass with my hands. "Oh, no you don't!" I yelled. Then I felt a sharp sting on my ass as the sound of the smack he'd just landed filled the air.

"You know you want my sweet cock, Izzy. Don't play hard to get. It's not a good look on you."

I laughed into the blanket as the bed sprang back from the loss of his weight. He opened his bag on the old wooden desk next to the television. The man could wear a pair of blue jeans. He looked in the mirror and caught my eye before turning with a condom in his hand.

"Liking what you see, baby?"

"Eh, it's all right," I mumbled putting an unimpressed look on my face. I did, but no fucking way would I ever tell him and let my foot off his throat.

With a smile, he unbuttoned his jeans and pulled them down before kicking them off. His cock bobbed as he straightened, waving at me in all its hard glory. He tore the wrapper open with his teeth, sheathing his stiff, curved member before walking toward the bed.

"Not even going to take your shirt off?" I asked, staring at his cock. Then I forced myself to look at his face.

"You didn't." He pointed to me with a shitty smirk.

I didn't even care. All I'd wanted was his mouth on my pussy and the orgasm that had been just out of reach during the trip to Daytona. "I'll fix that. You, off the bed and totally naked," I commanded, pulling my tank top over my head.

After grabbing the back of his collar, he pulled it over his head, exposing his washboard abs. Fuck. He was a sight. Then he crawled up the bed, his cock swaying and a shitty-ass grin on his face.

"I know you want it. You need my dick more than you'll ever admit, Izzy. No one makes you come like I do," he whispered in my ear as he rubbed his hard length against me. "You want it?"

"If you think you're man enough to give it," I challenged. I loved when Flash felt like he needed to prove himself. He worked harder at it, fucked me better, and outdid himself each time.

"I'm busting that shit, Izzy. I'll show you how a real man fucks." He stood on top of the bed, pulling me up by the hips. "Ass up, princess," he said as he smacked my other cheek.

I giggled into the comforter. Dipping my stomach toward the bed, I pushed my ass in the air, wiggling it.

"Don't move," he said as he landed another blow to my already stinging flesh.

My laughter became uncontrollable as I buried my face deeper into the blankets, trying not to hurt his pride. Flash was hot. But controlling? Not one bit. I'd let him play the part for the pleasure of feeling his cock in me.

He pushed into me in one quick thrust. His fingers dug into my hips as he pounded me. I moaned each time the head of his cock stroked my G-spot. I fisted the sheets, closing my eyes, and tried to remember to breathe. His body bounced off mine, slamming into me to the hilt before he withdrew. As our bodies collided, my ability to keep my upper body in place began to slip. I reached back, wrapping my hands around his ankles, holding our bodies together.

He rested his palm against my lower back and placed his finger against the one hole I'd never given him. I opened my eyes, looking behind me. He towered over me with a hand on my hip, his abs clenching and relaxing, and a trail of spit falling from his lips. I squeezed my eyes shut, trying to get my body to relax as he rubbed the saliva against my flesh.

7

"Fuck," he muttered as he pulled out his cock and pushed his thumb inside my ass.

I whimpered, wanting the feel of his cock as I dug my fingernails into his ankles. He rammed his cock into me, filling me in both holes. Pleasure shot through my body as he worked one in and the other out. Moving out of sync and in absolute fucking perfection.

"Who's fucking you, Izzy? I want to hear you scream my name." He stilled.

I mumbled, not able to form words.

His thumb dug deeper, pulling upward, hooking me. "What's my name?" he growled, taking out his cock.

"Flash. Fucking Flash," I answered in one quick breath, burying my face in the comforter.

He pummeled me, his balls slapping against my clit, the curved shaft stroking my G-spot, his thumb caressing my ass. The second orgasm tore through me without warning as I chanted his name.

I lay there panting as the world came back into focus. My grip slipped from his ankles as I became putty in his hands. Flash picked up the pace, slamming into me a couple of times before resting his chest against my back and twitching. He gasped behind me, trying to catch his breath. Our bodies were stuck together by sweat-soaked flesh.

"Fuck, darlin'. I've missed ya," he panted in my ear as his cock slipped out.

"I missed your cock, Flash." I chuckled, earning me a swift smack on the ass. I started to crawl off the bed, ready to hit the town and get out of this shithole of a room.

Flash grabbed my foot. "Where are you slithering off to?" he asked as he pulled me against his body.

"I wanna shower and go out. I'm ready for a little fun." I sighed.

"Just lie here for a minute. I'm tired and I want to hold you." He jerked me back, holding me tighter to his chest, and nuzzled his face in my neck.

I relaxed against him. He did feel really good, but I wasn't here to snuggle. Flash and I had never had that type of relationship.

"You want more pussy this weekend? If you do, you'll rest while I shower and take my ass out. Understand what I'm saying?" I looked at him, seeing only his eyes as he bit down on my shoulder.

He released me, pushing me off the bed. "What the fuck ya waiting for? Go shower, wench."

I laughed as I grabbed my bag and flipped him off. Pussy was the great equalizer and always won when you needed to get one over on a guy who thought he was "the man."

\*\*\*

When he'd said that he'd take me out and show me the town, I hadn't thought that included the shittiest biker bar in all of Daytona Beach. The place reeked of cigarettes; the air was hazy from the smoke. A band was playing behind a cage like in that movie 'Roadhouse'. I walked through the door with Flash at my side. The floors were filthy and the men inside didn't look much better.

"None of your mouthy bullshit that I love so much when we talk to these guys, got it?" Flash cocked an eyebrow at me, standing like a statue as he waited for my answer.

"I'm not mouthy," I insisted, crossing my arms over my chest.

"Darlin', ya are, and I fuckin' love it." His smile grew wider, giving me a glimpse of why they called him Flash. He had a perfect smile filled with shiny, pearly-white teeth, one that could charm the pants off any girl. It did funny things to my brain, and I couldn't say no to him. "In this bar, with these guys, it's not the place. Understand? I'm a prospect, and that shit won't fly here."

I slid my arm around his waist, looking up into his baby blues. "I got it. I'm to be seen and not heard?"

He grabbed my shoulders and stared back at me. "That's how these guys are. You don't like something they say, just keep quiet."

9

The last thing I wanted to be was a piece of arm candy that faded away in the background. It was not how I'd been raised. "Let's get one thing straight, Flash. I know you're badass and all, but I don't stand in the shadows for anyone. *Understand*?"

"Fucking hell," he muttered, rubbing his face.

"I'll play the part this once, for you, but hear me now, mister. I'm not a club whore and I sure as hell ain't your old lady. I don't know what in the hell we are exactly, but if you want to be more than whatever the fuck this is"—I waved my hand in the air between us—"I will not stay quiet and be a mindless twat."

"Calm the fuck down, woman," he croaked as he wrapped his fingers around my wrist. "I don't think of you that way. This is for them." He turned his attention to the table full of rough-looking men about twenty feet away. I could handle big and burly. I hadn't grown up a pussy. "Just please do this for me and I'll make sure to make it worth your while," he said, wiggling his eyebrows and giving me a cocky-ass grin.

"I won't make a scene and walk out, but you owe me big time." I tore my wrist from his grip.

"Whatever you want, Izzy. You know that." His eyes softened as he looked down at me.

"I'm going to use my *silent* time to come up with something really *big*." I swiped my fingers across the small hint of chest hair just below his throat.

"I can do big." He laughed and grabbed my hand to pull me toward the table.

"Fucker," I muttered to myself as I followed behind.

He looked over his shoulder and said, "I heard that."

When he stopped suddenly, I ran into his back, and it felt like hitting a brick wall. I used his body as a shield from the men at the table. I didn't know if I had an off switch, but this wasn't really the place for me to test it. I just needed to keep my eyes down and pray their little hello didn't last long.

Flash leaned over the table, shaking their hands as I stood behind him pretending to be invisible—something I'd never done for anyone. Ever.

When he'd said that he wanted to take me to Bike Week in

10

Daytona Beach for the weekend, I hadn't been able to imagine anything better than the feel of the wind in my hair, the sand between my toes, and a shitload of hot bikers. What could be bad about that?

I hadn't expected this, and I didn't like it one bit. Flash would have to pay and pay dearly to make up for this "be seen and not heard" bullshit.

"And who do we have here?" a rough voice asked, pulling me out of my thoughts on how to torture Flash.

Flash shifted and reached around to grab my hand, tugging me to his side. "This is Izzy, my woman." He tightened his grip on my waist.

I glared at him.

What the fuck? I wasn't his woman. We had an agreement, but to call the naughty shit we did a relationship was overstating it just a tad. I gave him the stink eye and saw the corner of his mouth twitch.

"Well aren't you stunning, Izzy. Is that short for Isabella?"

I turned my attention to the genius and smiled the biggest bullshit smile I could muster. "Yes, it is." I swallowed the other words I wanted to say, still smiling like an idiot.

He wasn't a bad-looking man for someone his age. His long, gray hair was pulled back in a low-slung ponytail, making his emerald-green eyes stand out. A small patch of salt-and-pepper facial hair framed his thin lips. He looked a little like Santa Claus on crack. The vest covering his black t-shirt was the same cut as the one Flash was wearing, but it had more patches—including one that stated he was the VP.

"Why don't you sit down with us and have a drink?" He lightly patted the empty chair next to him, never taking his eyes off me.

Flash moved in front of me and started to sit, but the VP grabbed his arm.

"I meant her, you idiot. Not you."

Flash stopped dead, with his ass hovering just above the seat. "Oh, sorry, man."

What type of man would let another one talk to him that

way? The way he'd said "idiot" hadn't been the same as when my brothers called each other "jackass" or "dumbfuck." His dislike for Flash was clearly evident in his tone, but Flash did as he was told, like a good soldier.

I slid into the wooden chair as Flash gripped my shoulder. "Thanks," I whispered, folding my hands in my lap.

"My name's Rebel," he said as he brought my hand to his mouth, running his prickly lips across my skin. "These are the guys." He placed my hand on his leg, patting it, and then grabbed his beer.

Flash's grasp on my shoulder hardened, but I didn't dare look up at him.

Fuck. How had my dumb ass gotten into this situation? Flash was a stupid bastard. I should've listened to Joe and Mike, but then again, I never did.

"Hey," I said, slowly looking around the table. I tried not to linger on any one man too long.

They all said, "Hey," and smiled—except for one man. The long hair hid his face as he picked at the label on the bottle. His reaction to me wasn't friendly or welcoming like the others'. Nope, he was avoiding me.

"So, Isabella," Rebel said, pulling my attention back to him. "Can I call you that? You don't mind, do you?" He leaned into my personal space and squeezed my thigh. The stench of cigarettes and stale beer invaded my nostrils.

Flash gripped my shoulder and Rebel held my thigh. I knew Flash wouldn't do shit. He was the prospect, the one trying to get in the club, and Rebel knew it. I just needed to be agreeable and get the hell out of here for my sake and for Flash's pussy ass.

I bit the corner of my lip before responding. "Sure." The only people in my life who called me Isabella—who I allowed to call me by my full name—were my parents. I didn't think telling Rebel to go fuck himself would be good for anyone.

The tiny hairs on the back of my neck rose, and I felt like someone was watching me. Without looking, I noticed him staring at me out of the corner of my eye as I kept my attention on Rebel. It bugged the fuck out of me. I wanted to get a glimpse of him, just for a second, but Rebel wanted my total attention.

"Flash, go fetch me a beer and get something for the beautiful girl too," Rebel demanded, staring at me, paying no attention to Flash or anyone else.

My eyes flickered to his face as he barked orders to Flash. "I'm fine. I don't need anything to drink." The last thing I wanted was to drink anything that wouldn't allow me to be in control. Being around Flash was one thing, but I didn't trust the men sitting at the table.

Flash didn't move. He kept his hand on my shoulder, squeezing it lightly, and I could almost feel the tension radiating from his body.

"What the fuck are you waiting for? Get the fucking drinks, boy!" Rebel roared, slamming his fist on the table.

I jumped. The anger that oozed out of him put me on edge. My heart stuttered in my chest and I wanted to get out of here. Flash released my shoulder, leaving me alone with Rebel.

Rebel leaned over, twirling my hair with his fingers. "So, darlin' Isabella, tell me about yourself."

I looked down at my hands, trying to stop the urge to bat him away. "Not much to tell," I whispered.

He pushed the hair over my shoulder, running his fingertips down my skin, lingering on my collarbone. "I doubt that, Isabella." As he drew out my name, rolling the last bit off his tongue, his breath tickled my nose.

Small prickles slid down my neck, the hair still standing at attention. I leaned back in my chair, trying to escape his invasion of my personal space, pissed off that Flash had brought me here and then left me like a pansy ass.

"Tell me about you, Rebel." I was deflecting. A man like him had to be full of himself, drunk off power, and I prayed it would take the focus off me.

"Tsk, tsk," he said, shaking his head. "I know all about me. I want to know about you." His eyes bored into me as he started to slide his hand up my leg before settling on my thigh.

I swear to shit I wanted to rip Flash's dick off and shove it down his throat. I didn't care if I ever fucked him again. His cock was not worth this bullshit.

"I'm a tattoo artist," I said with a sigh while looking into his eyes, knowing that I wasn't going to get out of the situation without being cordial. It wasn't one of my better traits, but I knew how to play the game. "It's my life." I plastered a fake smile on my face, trying to maintain eye contact with him. I wouldn't show weakness. I was a Gallo girl, not a shrinking violet.

"I love a girl who does ink. Maybe I should come to you next time I need some work done. I wouldn't mind dropping my drawers for you, beautiful."

I wanted to heave. The mere thought of seeing any of this man's junk or ass made me gag. "I'm between gigs right now," I lied, biting the inside of my cheek.

"The MC has a shop. Job's yours if you want it." Rebel squeezed my thigh, running his hand farther up my legs, stopping mere centimeters from my pussy.

"Just like that, huh?" I couldn't keep my mouth shut. I didn't want to seem too eager to please, or too easy. "Maybe my skills are shitty. Then what?"

He inched his chair closer, squeezing my thigh again. "If your ink skills are shitty, I'm sure we can find *other* ways for you to earn."

"Listen," I said, about to lay into him and give him the nicest "fuck off" he'd ever had, but the sound of Flash slamming the drinks on the table stopped me from finishing the statement.

"Flash, you fucker," Rebel said, releasing my leg and leaning back in his chair. "You spilled my beer," he growled, wiping the glass with his finger. He turned to me, drawing his fingers into his mouth and sucking them as he stared.

Sam, a.k.a. Flash, didn't speak. Cool biker nicknames were reserved for badasses, and Sam had lost that right when he'd pussied out on me. He hadn't stood up for me, and left me high and dry in the hands of Rebel.

As Rebel grabbed the bottle to bring it to his lips, I turned and gave my "I hate you" scowl to Sam. He shrugged, grimacing before giving me a halfhearted smile. I closed my eyes, trying to calm the fuck down, because at this point, I wanted to tell Sam exactly how I felt and get the fuck out of the shitty-ass bar. I counted to five like they'd taught in a college psychology course I'd taken on a whim. I slowly opened my eyes to find Rebel staring at me *again.*

Sam leaned down, resting his hand on my shoulder, and whispered in my ear, "Want to get out of here?"

What a clusterfuck. Would he have balls big enough?

"I'm getting tired," I complained, standing to say goodbye. Before my ass was five inches off the chair, Rebel had his hand on my wrist, pulling me back down.

"I wasn't done talking to you." He smiled, licking his lips.

My eyes flickered to Sam, who now had wide eyes and an "oh fuck" face. I narrowed my eyes at him, wishing he'd man the fuck up, but nope. He must've checked his cock at the door. I turned back to Rebel, looking down at his hand, which was still wrapped around my wrist. *Be diplomatic, Izzy. Do not piss off the MC vice president.*

I turned my wrist, breaking the hold he had on me. "I-I," I stuttered, trying to figure out something other than, "Keep your fucking hands off me."

Just as I opened my mouth, a voice called out to Rebel. "Leave the fucking girl alone, you horny ol' bastard."

I turned to look in the direction of the gravelly voice, where Rebel's attention was now focused. My breath vanished and a dull ache settled in my chest as I sat there wide-eyed and in shock. The blue eyes shooting daggers across the table at me I'd seen before—I knew them. They were mine looking back at me.

The smile I loved so much and the handsome, boyish looks were gone. His features were hard. Small lines had formed around his eyes since the last time I'd seen him. He didn't look like the man who had pushed me on my swing set and taught me how to throw a punch to defend myself. The man's lips were set in a firm line as his glare focused entirely on me. He didn't look anything like the brother I remembered, like the Tommy I loved.

"You want a piece of this ass?" Rebel asked, looking from

15

me to Thomas. "I wouldn't blame you, Blue. It's mighty fine," he said as he turned back toward me, running his finger down my jaw.

I snarled, moving my face away from his fingers. Rebel gripped my hair, yanking my head back and holding me in place.

"Where do you think you're going, Isabella?" He stared into my eyes, a smirk on his face.

My heart started pounding, growing louder by the second as it beat out of control. This was bad, a real fucking nightmare.

"I want her," Tommy said, slamming his hand down on the table. "You got the last piece of ass and this one's mine."

Rebel laughed, releasing my hair. "Want me to get her warmed up for you, brother?"

"I don't want your filthy hands on her. She looks too innocent and pure. I want to take that from her," Tommy replied, laughing with the rest of the guys, his eyes only on me.

"If you don't do it, Blue, I will," Rebel promised.

"Oh, I plan to do all of her, and she's going to like it."

Thank God the words were coming out of Tommy's mouth, because I'd be totally fucked otherwise. Sam released my shoulder. The fucker still hadn't said a word. He'd stood there like a fucking idiot and stayed silent.

"Don't I get a say?" I whispered, grinding my teeth. "I'm not a piece of property."

"Flash brought you here, darlin', and you came out of your own free will. If Blue wants you, he gets you," Rebel said, laughing like a hyena. "You can thank Flash later."

I turned to Sam as his eyes dropped to the floor. "Don't you have anything to say?" I hissed, the venom dripping from my voice.

He shook his head as he kicked an imaginary piece of dirt on the floor.

"Fucking pussy," I muttered before turning back to look at Thomas.

A small smirk played on his lips; he knew I could never hold my tongue.

Rebel slapped Sam, his laughter filling the air and mingling with the other guys'. "Even the girl can see you're a pussy, Flash," he teased, wiping his mouth with the back of his hand.

I would've pissed myself by now if it hadn't been my brother claiming me for the night. I had fucked up, and although Tommy might have smirked, I knew I was in big fucking trouble.

# CHAPTER 3
# CLUELESS

IZZY

"WHAT IN THE fuck were you thinking?" Tommy screeched as he slammed the hotel room door and locked it.

"Clearly, I wasn't," I quipped as I sat on the bed, avoiding his eyes. Fuck. I looked at the ceiling, my stomach flopping around like I was about to be chastised by my dad.

"I know you do some dumb shit, Izzy, but this takes the motherfucking cake." He paced near the door, checking the peephole, as he ran his finger through his hair. "How in the hell do you get mixed up with an MC guy?" He stopped pacing, turned toward me, and tapped his foot.

I shrugged, not really having a good answer for him.

"A shrug. I get a goddamn shrug?" he groaned as he walked toward me. "Izzy, look at me," he barked.

I looked up into his piercing blue eyes and could see a storm behind them. My mouth suddenly felt dry and I was at a loss for words—something totally out of my realm of comfort.

"Thomas," I whined, trying to find the right thing to say.

"You are in over your head, Iz. This is some serious shit. If I hadn't been there tonight or if Rebel had decided that he wanted you for himself, you'd be fucked, and so would I." He rested his hands on either side of me and leaned into my space. "I mean that literally. This is a fucking nightmare."

I blinked slowly, taking in the sight of my very pissed-off

brother, and sighed. "I just wanted to have fun, Thomas. I wasn't expecting all this bullshit." I swallowed and concentrated on breathing through my nose. Pissed-off Thomas was a scary fucking dude.

"All this bullshit?" he whispered. "All this bullshit is what comes with an MC. They make their own goddamn rules." He backed away, grabbing my hand as he sat next to me. "I have to keep you safe and get you the hell away from these guys." He pinched the bridge of his nose and exhaled loudly.

"I'm sorry," I choked out, tears forming in my eyes. "I thought Flash would protect me. He promised a weekend getaway." God, I sounded like a fucking idiot. Mike and Joe had warned me. They'd pleaded with me not to go, but as always, I did whatever the fuck I wanted to.

"Flash is a fucking pussy and a complete moron. I worried he'd recognize me, but he was too young to remember me. Plus, he's an idiot. Nice kid, but dumb as a box of rocks."

"Why are you still here, Tommy?" I inquired. He'd always be Tommy to me—my big brother who had been missing from my life for more years than I'd like to admit. "Why haven't you come home?"

He looked up at me; his shoulders slumped before he spoke. "I'm in deep, sis. I've moved up the ranks. I'm sergeant-at-arms now. I'm in the inner sanctum and doing everything I can to bring this club down. I don't want the shit to be half-assed, either. I need to bring it to its knees. Cut off the head and burn the body. Leave nothing behind."

"It's so dangerous." I knew my statement was obvious, but I didn't have anything else to say. The thought of something happening to him made my heart feel like someone was squeezing it in their fist, and I didn't want to feel it pop.

"It's my job, Izzy. I have to see it through. I promise I'll come home to everyone, and I'll do it soon."

"You better. Ma is beside herself with worry. Joey is going to have a baby. The family is changing and you're not there to see," I grumbled. I wanted to run out the door with Tommy in tow and head home.

"Joey's going to be a dad?" he whispered, his eyes growing wide.

"Yes. You're going to be an uncle soon. You need to come home."

"I will, love. I will." He wrapped his arms around my shoulders, bringing my face against his chest.

I rested my hands on his shoulder blades, gripping them for dear life. I didn't want to let him go. I couldn't remember the last time I'd seen my brother, let alone been able to touch him. How was I going to be able to walk out the door and leave him behind?

"Now what?" I asked, my voice muffled by his t-shirt.

"Well, everyone thinks I'm banging your brains out." He blanched and gagged. "After, I have to bring you back." He sighed, pulling away from me as my hands slipped from his back. "Let me make a call. Do you have your phone? Mine isn't safe."

I grabbed my purse, which I'd dropped on the floor when I'd sat down. I rummaged through the contents, pulled out my phone, and handed it to him.

"Who are ya going to call?" I asked. I did not want any of my other brothers in harm's way. It was bad enough that I'd put Tommy in this fucked-up predicament, let alone the others.

"I only have one person near by I can trust to get you out of this clusterfuck." He tapped the buttons on my phone but didn't look up at me.

"Who?" I asked. "Don't call Mike or Joe either," I pleaded, lying back on the bed.

"Fuck no, woman. I'm calling a law enforcement buddy. Only he can pull this off without it looking like I had anything to do with it." He stood, bringing the phone to his ear.

Well okay, then. He still hadn't answered my question. I looked around the hotel room as he walked away from the bed. This place was an even bigger shithole than the place Sam and I had booked for the weekend. The room hadn't been updated since it had been built in the '70s. The color scheme was straight out of *The Brady Bunch* on meth. Mustard yellow, burnt orange, and avocado green decorated the flowery wallpaper and the bedspread. I didn't want to even think about all the things that had been done on this bed. It had to be crawling with germs.

I stood, walking toward my brother, stopping to look out the peephole. The green shag carpeting did not make me want to kick off my shoes and feel the lushness. It was matted and trashed.

"Hey," Tommy said into the phone. "I need your help."

I turned, studying him as he moved around the room. He would've worn a path in the carpeting if the shag had still been good. I grabbed my purse and sat down on the bed, pulling my lip-gloss from my purse as I listened.

"My sister's here. I need you to help me get her the fuck out," Tommy said, running his fingers through his hair. "I know. She showed up with one of the prospects and Rebel almost claimed her for the night, but he offered her to me—thank fucking God." Tommy stopped and listened before moving again. "Yeah, Izzy," he said, his eyes darting to me.

My eyes grew wide. The person on the other end knew who I was, but I didn't know them.

"She's the only fucking sister I have, James. What the hell kind of question is that?" Tommy glared at me as James spoke on the other end of the phone.

I looked up at him, my mouth dropping open when I heard his name. James Caldo. He was the smug bastard who'd come to the wedding uninvited to drop off a card for Tommy. We'd shared drinks—way too many drinks. I'd woken up the next morning slinking out of his hotel room without saying goodbye. I'd gotten what I'd wanted, gotten the hell out, and never looked back.

James was…how do I say it? Hot as fuck, but a little too bossy for my liking. He reminded me of my brothers, but times ten on the macho bullshit. I'd waited for him to grunt, "Me caveman. You're mine," after he'd fucked me into a coma after the reception.

If I hadn't been plastered by an abundance of Jack and Coke,

I wouldn't have been seduced by him and ended up in his bed…
against the wall…on the floor.

Fuck. Why did he have to call James? My stomach started to
flutter, a wave of nervousness filling my body. My leg began to
shake, a nervous habit I had when I couldn't control a situation,
as I sat there and listened.

Maybe I wouldn't have to see him. *Oh God, please don't let
me have to see him.* Maybe they'd devise a plan to get me out
and that would be that. I closed my eyes, fell back on to the bed,
and stared at the ceiling. I listened while crazy scenarios played
in my mind.

Maybe James wouldn't help because I'd hit it and quit it.
Would he be that cruel?

Maybe he'd want payback with me on my hands and knees
as a thank-you for my rescue. The sound of that wasn't bad, but I
would be subservient to no one, and certainly not James.

"Yeah. I can find a way to get her on my bike after we leave
here," Tommy said, sitting down next to me. He scowled at me,
maybe having heard something from James about what had
happened that night. "Okay. I'll have her text you when we're
leaving the bar, and you handle it from there. I trust you, James.
Only you. She needs to be safe and brought home. She shouldn't
be here. Can you do that for me, brother?" He stood again and
walked into the bathroom, closing the door.

I exhaled, letting go of the breath I had been holding while
thinking about James. I didn't like the sound of this one bit. I
closed my eyes and tried to block out the sound of the outside
world and focus on Tommy's voice, but it was no use. I couldn't
hear a fucking thing over my heart beating like the drummer in
Anthony's band. I wanted to run in the bathroom and throw up,
but I stayed glued to the bed, waited for my brother, and closed
my eyes.

The sound of the bathroom door smacking against the wall
made me jump. I sat up quickly, looking toward the noise to see
Tommy staring at me.

I gave him a fake smile and tilted my head. "Everything

worked out?" I asked, my voice hoarse as I tried to hide my curiosity.

"Fucking perfect," he grumbled as he moved toward the window, peeking through the now yellowed, sheer drapes. "How well do you know James?" he asked, turning to me.

"Um," I said. Fuck. *Lie—do not tell him the truth.* "I met him at Joey's wedding. He brought your card and we had a drink together." I kept the fake smile plastered on my face, speaking quickly so as not to trip over my words.

"Just a drink?"

"Maybe two," I replied, still smiling as my eyebrows shot up. God, I was horrible at the angel act.

"James seemed to be very interested in helping get you out of here. Maybe a little too eager," he complained as he moved to stand in front of me.

I looked up at him. He could be intimidating, but he'd always be just my brother. I didn't have anything to fear from him, but I wouldn't tell him about my night with James. No fucking way.

"He's your friend, Tommy. Naturally, he wants to help out. You called him for a favor, and as any good friend would do, he agreed to help."

Tommy shook his head, a grin slowly spreading across his face. "You've never been a good liar, Izzy. I'll kick his fucking ass if he tries anything with you." One of his eyebrows rose and the muscles in his jaw ticked. "No one touches my sister," he warned, the tiny grin disappearing.

"Thomas, I'm not a child. We had a couple of drinks, and even if I wanted more—which I don't," I insisted as I stood. "But if I did…it wouldn't be any of your business." I poked him in the chest, driving the point home.

His head dropped, his eyes staring at my finger as I held it against his chest. A rumble started underneath my finger and bubbled out through his mouth. He threw his head back, his laughter filling the room before he looked back at me.

"Izzy, love," he said, grabbing my face, his blue eyes shining with tears. "That has to be one of the funniest damn things you've ever said."

"What the fuck? It wasn't funny." I poked him harder and with my nail. "I'm a woman now, if you haven't noticed. I make my own decisions." I tilted my head and glowered at him.

He was still laughing as he wiped his eyes. He shook his head as he spoke. "You'll always be my little sister. Flash is going to get his ass kicked." His laughter died. "He won't know why, but I will. He'll be hurting because I know he dirtied you. He's not worthy of you."

"Flash is just a friend," I said, because it was the truth.

"He's been in your pants, sister. Don't try and bullshit me." He glared at me, studying my every twitch. "He'll pay."

I sighed, blowing out the air I'd stored in my cheeks. "Whatever," I blurted.

"James better not touch you either."

"I don't like James like that. I thought you boys were bad growing up, but he makes you guys look like pussycats."

Tommy's eyebrows drew together. "You got all this over a couple of drinks?" His jaw worked back and forth as he ground his teeth together. The sound sent shivers through my body.

"Yeah." I kept it simple. No need to throw up a flag that alerted his big brother Spidey sense that James had fucked me senseless.

"Swear?"

"Yep."

He sighed and wrapped his arms around me. Then he kissed my temple, and the warmth of his body felt great against me. He was my brother, and I had proof that he was safe and alive.

"We'll leave here in ten minutes. We have to make it believable, Izzy."

I looked up at him. "What do you mean make it believable?" I questioned, scrunching my nose as I thought about what that could mean.

"They have to believe that I had sex with you," he said.

"Fuck," I muttered, gnawing on my thumbnail.

We smudged my lipstick, tore my shirt at the bottom, and

messed up my hair. The bar was dark enough that hopefully it would pass. The most important part would be my attitude.

"Don't pretend to like me, but don't hate me either. You aren't attached to Flash, but you didn't have a choice in coming with me, either."

"I love you, brother. You're cute, so it's not like I would've had to bang Rebel."

"Do not say the words *bang* and *Rebel* in the same sentence." He cringed, opening the door for us to head back to the bar. "When we get there, just stay quiet and let me talk. I want to get us the fuck out of there as soon as possible so James can grab you."

I sighed, wishing the fucking night were over and that I were in my bed...at home and on the other coast. "You know how quiet and I work out, Tommy."

He stopped dead in his tracks and turned. "From here on out, I am not Tommy. Blue is my name. For fuck's sake, Izzy, do quiet for me just this one time," he pleaded before walking away.

"Men suck," I mumbled.

As I approached his bike, Tommy turned and faced me. "I won't see you again for a while, Iz. Although I'm pissed about you being here, I'm happy at the same time. I've missed you, baby girl." His face softened as he held his arms out to me.

I looked around, wondering if someone was lurking in the shadows, unsure if I should hug him.

"It's okay. Come here." He motioned with his finger, beckoning me into his arms.

I wrapped my arms around his waist, holding on to him for dear life. What if I never saw him again? I couldn't think that way. Thomas was the toughest man I knew. If anyone could live through all this bullshit and come out on the other side unscathed, it would be him.

"I'll miss you," I said, choking back the tears. I squeezed him tighter, rubbing my face against his t-shirt. "Come home soon."

He released me, wiping the tear off my cheek with the pad of his thumb. "Don't cry. I got this." He grinned, his beautiful blue eyes twinkling from the streetlight. "Let's get this shit over with so I can know you're safe. You listen to James and do whatever he says, Izzy. He'll keep you safe."

I rolled my eyes, unable to hide my annoyance. My shoulders slumped as I thought about being trapped with James for any amount of time. It would be a total clusterfuck.

"Fine," I sang, grabbing the helmet and putting it on my head. "I don't like it, but I'll try to be good."

"He'll keep you alive. Remember that." He climbed on his Harley and turned the key.

"Got it," I said as I nestled behind him and encased him in my arms.

I rested my cheek against his back as we took off, headed back to the guys. I use that term loosely; they were more like animals that could talk.

If my brother had known the sordid details of my night with James, he wouldn't have asked me to obey his every command. James hadn't contacted me after the wedding, and for that, I was thankful. I hadn't had to avoid his calls or block him from my phone. The man knew how to take a hint, but thrusting the two of us back together without being able to be in control freaked me the fuck out.

Why did I care so much about seeing him again? I closed my eyes, getting lost in the memory of the night that happened four months ago. James had been more of a man than I'd ever been with. He was a true alpha and didn't take bullshit. Bullshit and me were the best of friends. He'd called me on everything, and I'd felt like he could read my thoughts. I didn't want to be the type of woman that people could figure out. He knew when I was full of shit, and I didn't like when anyone could figure me out so easily. I wasn't a girl. I was fierce and no one's pushover. Isabella Gallo was not subservient.

# CHAPTER 4
# THE GREAT ESCAPE

IZZY

WHEN WE WALKED BACK into the bar, no one really seemed to care. Rebel gave me a once-over and quickly patted "Blue" on the back. They exchanged words as I sat down, my unhappiness evident from my tear-stained cheeks. They thought it had been caused by the sex I hadn't wanted, but really, it had been at the thought of saying goodbye to my brother.

After a round of drinks with Thomas's arm draped around my shoulder, protecting and claiming me all at once, the group decided to head out for the night. Parties were happening all over Daytona, and they had club business to attend to before they hit the sack.

"She's riding with me," Tommy declared as we walked outside and were greeted by the thick, humid Florida air that smelled like the ocean.

"Whatever you say, brother," Rebel conceded as he threw a leg over his bike.

"Where's Flash?" I asked, looking around one last time for him.

"Fuck Flash, darlin'," Tommy snarled, holding out the helmet to me.

"But—" I started to speak but saw his lips set in a firm line as he glared at me.

"He's been sent off to do club business with some other

27

members." He shoved the helmet in my hands. "Get the fuck on. We don't have time for your bullshit girl stuff," he barked, turning around and starting the bike.

The roar of the engine made me jump, and I quickly put on the helmet and pulled the straps tight. Climbing on the bike, I realized that this would be the last time I'd touch my brother for months. The guys took off just as I nestled myself behind him.

When the roar of the bikes and the distance between them and us was sufficient, Thomas turned to me and smiled. "Make the call, Izzy. Love ya, kid," he said before turning around and quickly taking off, hot on the tail of the other guys.

I hit dial, ringing James's phone to alert him that we'd left the bar. Thomas had said that James would stop us shortly after leaving the bar, and he'd had me put a baggie of cocaine in my pocket. James would do a search for some bullshit reason and place me under arrest.

Daytona was crawling with cops and DEA during Bike Week. Undercover, I presumed, since I didn't see a crazy amount of police presence, especially not with the amount of bikers that flooded the city during the event.

Rebel led the pack and we pulled up the rear. Tommy had wanted it that way, figuring it would be easier to be pulled over by James. I tried not to think about what was about to happen as I held on to him, taking in all that was my big brother—strong, kind, caring, and protective.

He'd made me laugh as a little girl, holding on to my hands and twirling me in the air like I was a blade of a fan. My mother would scream, but Tommy and I would just laugh and collapse in a heap of giggles. His face had been softer then; the years of undercover work and biker-life wear and tear hadn't yet entered his life. I wondered if he could ever go back to that fun-loving, carefree guy again. I hoped he would, but living this life had to alter you in some form and stick with you for the rest of your days.

My heart stammered in my chest as the sound of police sirens filled the air. I opened my eyes, the red and blue lighting bouncing off of Tommy's jacket. I gave him a squeeze as he slowed the bike and waved off the rest of the guys.

We pulled off to the side of the road as the police cruiser stopped behind us. The lights continued to flash, but the screeching siren noise turned off before I heard a car door slam.

"Sir," the familiar voice said as he approached us.

The sound of his voice alone had my pussy clenching. Fucking cunt had always been a problem. I didn't like James. It needed to cool its fucking jets and not think about his cock. James wasn't the man I wanted...I couldn't top him.

Thomas sat still, peering in his side mirror until James came to a stop at our side. The others were far enough away, leaving us behind to deal with the cop issue.

"Get her the fuck out of here. Blow is in her left jacket pocket."

"Hey, Iz," James slithered out as he slowly looked me up and down.

I lifted my chin, staring him in the eye without a smile. "Jimmy," I replied, the corner of my lip twitching.

God, he looked fucking good. No, good wasn't the right word. He looked fucking amazing dressed in the law enforcement uniform. The brown dress shirt hugged his muscles, looking like a second skin against his tan flesh. The shitty polyester pants the force handed out clung to his muscular thighs, showing off every dip and crevice in his body. The gun sitting around his waist reminded me that he wasn't a man to be crossed, though I liked to push his buttons. He could easily overpower me, and for some reason, the thought turned me on.

His jaw ticked as I spoke his name. He hated when I called him Jimmy, said it reminded him of a child. I'd used it to only piss him off, crawl under his skin like he had mine.

Tommy handed over his license and registration, shoving it in James's hand as he openly gawked at me.

James turned his attention to Thomas and cleared his throat. "What the hell are you going to tell them?" he asked, motioning toward the red taillights off in the distance.

"I'll figure some shit out. She's just another pussy to them. She's not a club whore or an old lady. She's inconsequential."

"Men are such fucking pigs," I bit out. "How can you even be around those douchebags? You don't think that way, do you?" I asked, looking at Tommy.

"Fuck no. I'm just playing the part. Ma did not raise me to think that way."

James laughed, drawing my attention in his direction. Why did he have to be so damn handsome? I mean, Jesus. Why couldn't he be plain and not fantasy inspiring?

"And you?" I asked him, wishing I could wipe that shitty smile off his face.

"Oh no, doll. I love women. Not all of them are just a piece of ass. Not even the ones who slink out of my hotel room before the sun rises." He grinned.

My eyes grew wide as a lump formed in my throat. He wouldn't dare tell my brother. Would he? I mean, the man had cockiness down pat, but he wouldn't be dumb enough to clue my brother the fuck in on our sex Olympics.

Tommy shook his head and turned to look at me. "Can I trust you to listen to him?" he asked, squinting as he peered at me.

"I'll listen," I said, as James began to chuckle. I moved my eyes from Thomas to glare at James. "I can't promise I'll do as he asks, but I'll listen and do what I feel is right."

"Izzy, for fuck's sake. Just fucking listen for once in your life. I know you bow down to no man, but this is your life we're talking about. I have enough shit to worry about and don't need to worry about you getting home safely," Tommy snarled, keeping his eyes focused on me.

"I'll be good to her," James promised as he stopped laughing and cleared his throat. "I won't let her out of my sight and I'll keep her safe. You couldn't put her into more capable hands." James smiled, giving me a quick wink.

I turned to Tommy, unable to take the smug smile on James's face any longer, and spoke the words he wanted to hear: "Yes, I promise to do whatever is necessary to get home safely."

"Off the bike, ma'am. I need to search you. You too, Blue," James barked out, stepping away from the bike.

We climbed off, me with the assistance of my brother, and turned our backs to James. He frisked Tommy first. I straightened my back and watched him as he touched my brother, moving quickly and thoroughly and finding nothing. It was all for show. I knew I wouldn't be so lucky. As he turned his attention to me, I closed my eyes and waited.

I knew he wouldn't be so quick when touching my body. He wouldn't make it obvious to my brother or the eye of an outsider, but I remembered what his hands had felt like on my body. The amount of pleasure the strong hands had given me. The feel of them on me and in me was like nothing else I had ever experienced.

"Back on the bike, sir," he ordered. "Ma'am, hands behind your head and do it now!" he roared, as I was lost in my memories.

As Tommy took his place on the bike, keeping a lookout for any stragglers from the club, I sighed and tangled my fingers together behind my head. Thankfully my back was to him. In this position, my breasts were pushed out farther, leaving myself exposed. He started at my wrists, brushing against my skin with the tip of his rough fingers. Tiny sparks shot down my arms, a direct line to my nipples. I opened my eyes, sucking in a breath before closing them again.

I didn't have to see his face to know that he had a grin dancing across his lips. His giant hands swept down my arms and stopped just above my ribcage. The tips of his fingers grazed my breasts as his hands slipped down the front of my torso before he searched my waistband.

No matter how hard I tried to control a reaction or think of anything other than his hands on me, my body responded. I twitched and silently swore. I rolled my eyes at the feeling of being defeated. He knew in that moment that he had an effect on me. I was fucking doomed.

I could feel his breath against my ear. My body shuddered as my heart skipped a beat, before it was gone and his hands slid down my legs.

*Please don't...*

Fucker.

His thumbs touched the holy land as his hands glided up my legs. As he reached the V of my legs, I swear to shit my heart stopped dead in my chest. I sucked in a breath, trying to calm my insides as my head dropped.

I was happy when his hands left my legs until he caressed my ass, all in the name of a search, but I knew he was enjoying it too much when he gave it a quick, hard squeeze.

"Must you?" I whispered as he moved closer, reaching into my pockets.

"Yes," he whispered back, his mouth coming close to my ear. "Think of all the *fun* we're going to have as I give you a *ride.*"

"You're an asshole," I hissed, turning my face to look at his profile.

"That's one part of you I haven't *yet* explored," he whispered in my ear, low and close enough that Tommy couldn't hear.

I gulped, closing my eyes and using all of my self-control not to turn around and give him a piece of my mind. I couldn't react in front of my brother or the other eyes that could possibly be on us.

"What do we have here, ma'am?" James asked, pulling his hand from my pocket and dangling the small bag in front of my face.

"It's not mine, officer," I pleaded, shaking my head and playing the part.

"Place your hands behind your back. I'm placing you under arrest," he said, grabbing my arm, gingerly moving it away from my head and down to the small of my back.

"Must we do this?" I asked, looking toward Tommy.

Tommy winked, not giving any other physical indication that everything was okay.

"We must, doll. Give me your other hand."

I wrinkled my nose and ground my teeth as I felt the cold steel of the handcuffs slap against my wrist. Great. Not only was

I being placed in his custody, I was starting off bound and in his possession without a means of escape. Being with the men of the MC had felt less scary than what I felt about being a captive for James.

"I'll leave them loose so they won't pinch, but you can't get out. Not yet at least," he said as a low, slow laugh tickled my ear.

I glared at Tommy, not looking at James as he marched me toward the back of the police cruiser. He placed his hand on my head as he helped me into the back seat.

"Stay put," he ordered as I moved my legs inside.

"Where the fuck am I going, genius?" I blurted out, the anger dripping from my voice. My hands were restrained behind my back and I was about to be locked in the police car.

"You better watch that smart mouth of yours, doll." He grinned, leaning against the frame of the car.

"Or what? Are you going to rough me up, Jimmy?" I snuggled back into the seat, adjusting my body and trying to find a comfortable position.

"I'd hate to add resisting arrest to your charges." His grin turned into a smirk as he wiggled his eyebrows and licked his lips.

"Just get this shit over with so we can get the fuck out of here," I hissed, not finding him charming at all.

"As you wish." He slammed the car door, leaving me with my thoughts as he approached Tommy and spoke with him.

I watched through the windshield as they exchanged some heated words—or at least they made it seem like they were. A dull ache settled in my chest as I watched them speak. This would be the last time I'd see my brother for some time. The not knowing was the worst part. Tommy looked over at me a couple of times as they finished their conversation. My nose began to tickle as tears threatened to fall.

When James slid into the front seat, he didn't speak. He turned on the car and started to pull away after Thomas had sped down the road.

"When are you going to let me out of these fucking cuffs?" I asked. My wrists already felt the bite from the metal digging into my skin.

"Tomorrow," he answered calmly, looking at me in the rearview mirror. His eyes changed from the smile I couldn't see but knew was there.

"You can't keep me like this until tomorrow." Anger built inside me. My body was almost vibrating as I stared at him in the mirror.

I knew I was now a pawn in his game. I'd have to play by his rules. I was pissed at Thomas for leaving me with James, and at asshole Flash for being an idiot and not realizing the amount of shit he was bringing me around this weekend.

James looked at the road, the corner of his eye crinkling as he spoke. "Harder for you to run away like that. Plus, you look fucking sexy when you're pissed off, Izzy."

"Jimmy, look, I didn't mean—"

"James." His eyes momentarily flashed in the rearview mirror before leaving me again.

"James," I hissed, holding the end, letting the letter stick between my teeth. "I'm sorry about what happened." I looked down at my knees, chewing the inside of my lip.

"I'm not," he said flatly.

"It wasn't nice of me to leave without saying goodbye. I was a jerk. Can you forgive me?" I wasn't really sorry for anything, but I wanted the damn cuffs off my wrists.

"It won't work, Izzy."

"What?"

"Your fake apology," he said as he pulled up to the red light and his eyes returned to mine. His face had a red sheen from the traffic light. He looked like the devil I figured he really was. He'd torture me as long as I was in his custody.

My mouth dropped open and a scream was crawling up my throat. "It wasn't—"

"Yes, it was."

I closed my mouth, grinding my teeth as the car started to pull away, and his face changed color. "I had fun with you and we both got what we wanted out of that night." I swallowed, remembering the feel of him against my skin. Those sweet-ass lips that were pissing me off right now had brought me so many orgasms that I'd lost count, the amount of alcohol I'd consumed not helping my memory.

"Maybe I'm sensitive and wanted a kiss goodbye?" he said, tilting his head up to look at me. I could see the corner of his mouth as it almost kissed his eyes. He was enjoying himself.

I sighed and pushed my shoulders back. Glaring at him, I said, "That's total bullshit."

"Maybe so," he said, looking away, "but I did want that kiss."

Fuck, his voice was sexy. It matched him entirely…big in all ways. "You're not going to play fair, are you?" I whispered, but I already knew the answer.

"Did you?" he retorted with a clipped tone.

"I'm sure you did the walk of shame many mornings, James."

"Doll, I've never been ashamed of spending the night in the company of a beautiful woman—especially you."

A knot formed in my stomach, and it felt like James had reached inside and was using his giant hands to untie it. He made my belly feel funny, and I didn't like it. I pursed my lips, not taking my eyes off the back of his head.

"It was easier for both of us," I whispered, trying not to give anything away in my voice.

He shook his head. "Can't stop the bullshit from rolling off your tongue, huh?"

"Are we there yet?" I was annoyed and pissed off. James did not get to question me on my truthfulness.

"To the police station, yes, but not the entire trip."

"I can find my way home. I'm an adult woman."

"Why don't you start acting like one, then?" he asked sarcastically.

I felt like he'd punched me in the chest. No one talked to me the way he did—no one with a dick, at least. The only people who could get away with calling me on my shit were my girls, but not a man. Not even my brothers or father.

"I am acting like an adult. I can rent a car and get myself back to Tampa. It's only a couple of hours away."

"Izzy, listen up, because this is how it's going to go." He pulled the cruiser over on the side of the road, rolling to a stop. He turned around, resting his arm on the back of the passenger's seat. "I promised your brother *I* would take you home. I promised him *I* would keep you safe. I will not just release you to fend for yourself." He licked his lips, and my eyes moved to his mouth as he continued speaking. "It's late, after two a.m., and I'm tired. We're going to return the car and then find a hotel for the night and drive back in the morning. That's the plan, and I don't want your brother to worry that I'm not following the plan. He has enough shit on his plate right now. Understand?" He glared at me, waiting for my response.

"Wow. Didn't know you knew so many words." I smirked, watching his jaw as he tried to stop a smile. "Fine, but I want my own room," I requested, knowing that I didn't have a choice in the whole "how to get Izzy home" plan, but I sure as hell wasn't going to share a room with him.

"One room, double beds," he growled, turning around and pulling back on to the road.

"No fucking way. I will not share a room with you."

"It's for your own protection."

"Not happening," I declared, looking out the tinted window, seeing the police station sign in the distance.

"Yes, it is. Don't fight me on this, woman."

"I don't want to spend the night in your room."

"Our room, and you do."

"Jesus, you're infuriating."

"Touché."

"Ooh, he knows French too. Didn't know cavemen were bilingual."

"Must you always be a smartass?" he asked, parking the car in the "reserved" space.

"Nothing good can come out of sharing a room," I said as I sat up, unable to stop the anxious feeling. I had to get the hell out of this car.

"I remember a lot of ear-shattering moans the last time we shared a room. I'd say only good can come from it," he murmured, a low, smooth chuckle escaping his lips before he climbed out of the car.

"Fucker," I muttered as his door slammed.

"Out you go, doll," he said when he opened my door, the hot, humid air hitting my skin. He reached in and grabbed my arm, trying to help me up, and I fought the urge to pull away.

"I hate that term," I said, climbing out with his hands still on me.

"Doll?" He smirked, giving my arm a light squeeze.

"Yes. It's patronizing," I hissed as I turned my back to him.

"As long as you call me Jimmy, I'll call you doll. And what the fuck are you doing?" he asked, grabbing my shoulder.

"The cuffs. I want them off." I glared at him. Why did he have to make everything so fucking difficult?

"I can't take them off yet. You never know who has eyes on the station," he said, and laughed.

"You're a prick."

"You're hitting every word I like to hear—come, prick, fuck. What else do you have to say?" He smiled as he grabbed my upper arm and pulled me toward the station doors.

"Let's just get this over with." I sneered at him as I tried to keep up with his large steps.

"I'm going to enjoy this," he whispered in my ear as he opened the door and waited for me to pass by. "So fucking much."

My body shuddered. This gravelly tone of his voice shorted the wiring in my brain. I'd spent too many years trying to block guys like him out, and I'd been successful. James was an entirely different beast. I didn't know how to deal with him. He always had a reply. It was fucking infuriating.

I closed my eyes, taking the final step into the station and hopefully to freedom—or at least an escape from him.

# CHAPTER 5
# ISABELLA

JAMES

WE ONLY SPENT a few minutes at the police station returning the uniform and equipment they let me borrow to rescue Izzy from the clutches of the MC. She sat on the chair, her eyes never leaving me as I talked with a few of the officers. If looks could kill, I'd be dead and buried.

After we finished at the police station, Izzy and I headed to find a low-key hotel just outside of the county. I wanted to be far enough away that no one would find us, but close enough that, if shit went down, I could get backup. She climbed on the back of my bike after protesting and arguing for a few minutes. She knew it was futile. I wasn't letting her out of my sight.

Feeling her body wrapped around mine—her thighs squeezing me tight, her arms holding on, and her tits against my back—was fucking perfection.

When Thomas had called and asked if I'd help rescue his sister, I'd jumped at the chance to see her again. It wasn't that I loved her—fuck no. I'd only spent a night with her, but there was something about her.

No one had ever sneaked out of my bed the next morning without saying a word. Izzy was the exception to that rule, and for that, I gave her props. She was her own person. I knew she didn't play by anyone's rules but her own. Thomas spoke of her often, and I could feel the love he felt for her with his words.

Thomas and I had met back during training. We'd both joined the DEA right after college. I knew it was where I wanted to be, and had dedicated my life to ridding the world of drugs. I knew it wasn't possible, but I'd do my best to not make it easy for the sleazeball criminals who preyed on the innocent.

I'd joined because I'd lost my little sister to an overdose. She was only seventeen and I was in my sophomore year at Florida State. Getting the news that your one and only sibling has died is indescribable. It crushes your soul and had made me question everything in my life. I'd felt like I'd lost direction in my life, and the only thing I'd wanted was retribution. The only way I knew how to do it legally was to join the one group that had the ability to stop the flow of illicit drugs. The DEA became my home and my new family.

Yes, I still had my parents, but they'd fallen apart after the death of my sister. They weren't the same people anymore. They walked through life as shells of their former selves, the sorrow too much for them to bear.

When we met, we were excited and looking to kick some major ass in the drug world. We spent a lot of time talking about our families—his happy and mine not so much.

We each had sisters, his alive and mine dead. Even though I could never touch my sister again and I couldn't protect her, I still loved her more than anyone else on Earth. We spent our nights drinking too much beer and talking about life. Our conversations always veered off course and would turn to our sisters as the main reasons for us being there.

Thomas said that Izzy wasn't into drugs but he always felt a need to protect her, and others like her who didn't come from such a loving family. I'd wanted to join because the same drugs had reached in and plucked my sister from my life.

I was out for payback. After we graduated training, Thomas and I were partnered with veterans and taught the ropes. Years later, we were paired up, and it felt like coming home. He was the brother I'd never had. I was his go-to person when he was placed undercover. I was his link to the DEA and his call of last resort. I kept tabs on him and picked up information when he found a way to get it out.

His case was solid, but at times, I worried about Thomas. I'd never admit it to him—he'd call me a pansy—but he was in deep. Deeper than I'd ever thought possible. He'd been able to move up the ranks and solidified his position with the club. I made sure to do my best to keep his cover intact and my ears to the ground in case shit went down.

Leaving him for the weekend to drive his sister home was a sacrifice I wasn't sure I could make, but how could I say no to him? I didn't want him to go through the same loss that still squeezed my heart and hung heavy on my soul even after ten years. Loss is loss and it never goes away. We learn to deal with it, but the desperation and longing never fade. I didn't want Thomas to experience what I had.

I found a replacement in the agency, someone I trusted to cover for the weekend while I made the round trip with Izzy. I felt at ease knowing that he was protected and I could do the one favor—the only one, in fact—that Thomas had ever asked of me. His family was his number-one priority.

I'd felt shitty after fucking Izzy when I brought the card on his behalf to his brother's wedding. I felt like I knew Izzy after having heard stories about her ball busting for years. I'd seen pictures of her, but her beauty in person couldn't be conveyed in a photograph.

Her smart mouth, killer body, and bombshell looks had my cock throbbing and my mind reeling as I had a drink with her at the bar. A back-and-forth conversation over Jack Daniel's left me hard as a rock, and I needed to crawl inside that sweet cunt of hers. After too many drinks to make a proper decision, I sure as fuck wasn't thinking of her brother, and invited her to my room.

I wasn't surprised when she accepted, following me to the elevator as the party raged on. As soon as the elevator doors closed, I had her against the wall. I claimed her mouth, her tongue sweet from the Jack and Coke lingering on the surface as

I devoured her. Caging her face in my hands, I stole her breath and replaced it with my own.

When we reached my floor, I broke the kiss. She didn't move as her eyes fluttered open, and her breathing was ragged. I grabbed her hand, pulling her toward my room, a little too eager to feel her skin.

The chemistry was off the charts. We tore at each other's clothes as soon as the door shut while our lips stayed locked. The need I felt to be inside her bordered on animalistic as our heavy breathing and pants filled the room.

I dropped to my knees, looking up at her, and said, "I need to taste you." She was a vision. She had on thigh-highs that connected to a garter belt and cock-hardening stilettos.

She didn't reply, but spread her legs. I cupped her ass, bringing her body forward as I swept my tongue through her hair. I could smell her arousal as I flicked her skin with my tongue. I wanted to worship at her altar.

I lifted her with my hands, placing her legs over my shoulder as I feasted on her. I sucked like a starved man, licking every ridge and bump as she chanted, "Fuck yeah," and "Oh my God." I didn't relent when she came on my face, her legs almost a vise around my head. I dug in deeper, sucking harder as I brushed her asshole with my fingertip. Her body shuddered, the light touch against the sensitive spot sending her quickly over the edge.

It's not that I didn't want to take her in every way, putting my cock in every hole and making her dirty, but I wasn't ready to go there—not yet, at least. I wanted to feel her pussy squeeze my cock and milk me. I needed it.

I don't know what time we both passed out. I'd never had sex so much in one night, but even after it all, I wanted more. She was the one person I couldn't get enough of, and it didn't sit well with me. When I woke up and found her gone, I won't lie, that shit stung. In the end, I knew it was for the best. I didn't need the headache in my life.

I couldn't tell Thomas what had happened—no way in fucking hell. He'd murder me and hide my body. That shit I knew. I hadn't chased her or tried to contact her. Let that shit stay buried in the past.

"Turn around or close your eyes," she said.

Lost in the memory of our first night together, I blinked. "What?" I asked, shaking my head, trying to clear my mind. I took in the surroundings of a very different room. It wasn't the lush accommodations from the night of the wedding, but a crappy, run-down motel.

"I need to undress," she said, tapping her foot as she stared at me. "I don't have my bag of clothes and I can't wear this shit to bed."

"I've seen it all."

Her clothing didn't do much to hide what I already knew lay underneath. The skintight jeans that narrowed around her ankle just above the black high heels had my dick aching. I wanted to feel the bite of them against my skin as I pounded into her.

"I was drunk," she groaned, her eyes growing into little slits.

"Are you saying I took advantage of you?" She couldn't be fucking serious. I didn't do that shit. She'd wanted it as much as I had. I'd known from the moment she'd called me Jimmy that she'd wanted me. I'd known enough about her from Thomas that I'd had her MO down pat.

"I wasn't thinking clearly. You aren't my type." She wrinkled her nose, twirling her finger like I was going to roll over like a dog and face the other way.

"Doll," I teased.

"Fuck you and that 'doll' bullshit. Turn. The. Fuck. Around," she hissed.

Laughing, I kicked back on the bed and covered my eyes with my hand. "Happy now?" I asked, leaving space between two of my fingers to get a clear view of her undressing.

"Very." She turned around, facing the opposite direction as she removed her Harley tank top that framed her breasts but left little to the imagination.

Underneath, she was wearing a black bra that lay just below her shoulder blades. She reached back, unhooking the straps with her fingers. Black nail polish decorated the tips, and I wanted to see them wrapped around my cock and her eyes watering from choking on taking me to the back of her throat.

She bent down, pulling off her jeans, and her breasts fell to the side, giving me a marvelous view. They were full, round, and natural. I licked my lips as my mouth watered, while watching her tits sway as she stepped out of her jeans.

She climbed in the bed opposite mine, lying back, her tits on full display and her tiny black G-string the only thing she'd left on. Yeah, like that would protect her and keep her pussy safe from me.

She pulled the covers up to her chin, closing her eyes for a moment, and then said, "All done. You can look now."

I turned to my side, resting my head on my hand, and smiled at her. "Now close your eyes," I commanded, watching her face contort.

"For what?" she asked, staring at the ceiling, avoiding eye contact.

"I need to get undressed too, and I don't want you to catch a glimpse."

"Please, Jimmy." She laughed. "I've seen it all." She rolled over and smirked.

"Felt it too, but I still want you to turn around or close your eyes."

She rolled her eyes, throwing her hands down and slapping the mattress at her sides. "Really? You worried that I'll jump on you and beg for your dick?" She made a *pfft* noise with her lips, blowing out a quick breath of air, causing her hair to blow away from her face.

"Just do it, doll. I know if you see it you'll be begging for me to crawl in that sweet cunt of yours and fuck you like no man has done before or since me." I twirled my fingers, giving her the same patronizing gesture she did me.

She stuck her tongue out and covered her eyes with her hand. "Just get fucking undressed so I can go to sleep already. I'm exhausted," she said, resting her other hand against her breast.

I could see that she was doing the same as I had—left a

space between her fingers so she could peek. I knew she wanted me.

"I bet I could find a way to wake you up," I taunted as I sat up, pulled my shirt off, and threw it across the room, just catching the back of the chair.

I pushed my shoulders into the mattress, lifted my ass, and contracted my abs, knowing that she was watching and taking in the view. I unbuttoned my jeans and pushed them down at a painfully slow pace just to prolong her show. I wasn't the type of man who wore underwear, either.

As soon as I lowered my jeans below my thighs, my dick sprang free, bobbing as if waving hello and calling her over. I knew it remembered Izzy as much as I did.

Izzy sucked in a breath as soon as my cock entered the room devoid of covering, the piercing shimmering in the light.

"You okay over there?" I asked, smirking because I had further evidence that she wanted me. She wanted me badly.

"Yeah. Just a piece of dirt in my mouth." She swallowed and coughed, playing the lie to the fullest.

I wrapped my hand around my shaft, stroking my length as I spoke. "Want something to wash it down?" I had to bite my cheek to stifle the laughter I felt coming to the surface. The only thing better than fucking her was fucking with her mind.

"No," she breathed.

"You sure? I can find something to help that tickle in your throat. I have something close at hand." Fuck, I felt like a creeper. Only to her would I say such fucked-up, bigheaded shit to, because she was Izzy—ball-buster champion of the world.

"I'm fine. I don't need anything you have." The corner of her mouth twitched.

Damn, her cockiness was such a fucking turn-on. No one had ever made my dick as hard as she did. The torture, too much for even me to bear anymore, made me kick my jeans off the rest of the way and toss them to the floor.

"Shit," I mumbled, remembering that I'd left my gun on the stand next to the television. I never slept without it next to me in bed or on my nightstand.

"What?" she asked in an annoyed tone.

"My gun is by the TV. I need to get it. Keep your eyes closed," I demanded as I placed my feet on the floor and faced her bed. I'd called dibs on the bed closest to the door in case anything happened. I'd be the one to protect her. I'd step in front of a bullet before I'd let anyone hurt her.

"They're still covered, Jimmy." She smiled, thinking she was slick.

"Uh huh," I said as I climbed to my feet and stretched, my front on full display for her peep show.

Her mouth parted and her tongue darted out, sweeping across her bottom lip. I wouldn't call her out on peeking because, fuck, it was just too much fun to watch her suffer in secret.

I stalked toward the television, taking small steps until I stopped and grabbed my gun. I lifted my head, catching a glimpse of her in the mirror that hung on the wall. Her fingers were spread apart for a moment, a smile playing across her lips before she closed the gap. Maybe she knew I'd caught her, but if she did, she didn't confess.

I walked back, my dick swaying and bobbing as it passed close enough to reach out to touch her as I gave her a full show. I wanted her to remember what I had to offer physically. She couldn't fight it forever.

After I pulled the covers just above my waist, I said, "You can look now." I turned off the light and flipped on the television, needing some lighting in the room. I had to keep an eye on Izzy and be able to see if anything were to happen.

She nestled in her pillow, placing her hands above her head, the sheet slipping just enough that I could almost see the pink skin that lay underneath. I silently prayed the sheet would slide an inch lower, exposing her piercings and the hard nipples that were outlined by the thin material.

"Good night," I yawned, trying to be a gentleman. "Sweet dreams."

"Yeah," she whispered as she closed her eyes.

I rolled toward her, resting my hand under my pillow as I watched her. Her face illuminated by the television, shadows playing across her features, she was even more stunning at peace. She looked like a different person as she slept. Her face was softer, but I knew the bite those sexy, full lips held when she was awake.

I didn't feel guilty for staring at her, watching her chest move up and down as her breathing slowed and grew shallow.

Would she sneak out again? The woman was more pigheaded than any other person I'd ever met. She wouldn't risk her life…would she?

I couldn't take the chance. I had to find a way to keep her in the room, and I knew just how I'd do it.

I waited, watching the clock and her body as she slept. I needed her to be in a deep enough sleep that small noises wouldn't wake her. When I felt she was ready, with small snores falling from her lips, I gingerly climbed out of bed, trying to avoid the box spring creaking with my weight.

I walked quietly to the bag I had set near the end of the bed and unzipped it, listening to it snag on each tooth as I pulled it open. I grabbed my cuffs, holding them together in my palm. I stood and approached her bed, trying not to wake her.

I'd never been so thankful for a shitty, old, '70s-style bed frame. It was perfect to attach the handcuffs to in order to keep her exactly where I wanted her. I opened the cuffs, connecting them to the bed, wincing as I closed it around the wood slat.

Her hand rested just below and in the perfect spot to quickly put them on before she'd have a chance to react. As I reached out to grab her hand, she moved and her face turned away from me. I held my breath and prayed she didn't wake up as I stood next to her. My balls and dick were too close and at eye level. I wanted to keep them and have them intact and functioning. I didn't need her attacking me.

I pushed down on the pillow with the metal as I slid it under her wrist. As soon as they were closed, her eyes flew open and she yanked her arm, but it stopped, held by the handcuff.

"What the fuck?" she screamed, pulling against the cuff that trapped her. "Get this shit off of me, James."

I laughed, moving out of the way of her kicking feet. "Calm down, Izzy."

"How the fuck can I be calm when you did this shit?" she fumed, holding up her arm and shaking her wrist.

"I wanted to make sure you didn't sneak out again." I shrugged and smirked. "I used the only way I knew. Thomas said to 'use any means necessary,'" I said, making air quotes.

"I don't think he meant naked and handcuffed."

"Details," I muttered.

She grabbed the wooden slat with her free hand and began jostling it back and forth, trying to break it free from the frame.

"Stop," I warned. "You're going to hurt yourself."

"Is this really necessary?" she complained, lying still and glaring at me.

"Yep," I crooned as I crawled back in bed.

Minutes passed as I heard her moving in bed, tossing and turning the best she could with one arm suspended above her head.

Finally, she stopped moving, the sheets crinkling as she turned to me. "James," she whispered.

"Yes?" I answered, closing my eyes. Hearing her whisper my name with that sugary-sweet tone had made the bottom of my stomach drop like I was on a rollercoaster ride and had just plummeted from the first hill.

"I'm scared."

Now that I *knew* was a load of shit. From what I knew of and had experienced with Izzy, she was never scared—or at least she wouldn't admit to it. She was hatching a plan, but I'd play along.

I glanced over at her, taking in her beauty and feeling slightly guilty, but not enough to make me undo her cuffs. Izzy restrained was priceless. She was like MasterCard—everywhere I wanted to be.

"I got ya. I won't let anything happen to you."

She had let the sheet drop down a bit when she'd turned. Her nipple was almost showing, and my hands and mouth itched to feel her.

"Will you lie with me?" She pouted with sad eyes, trying to pull me in and break me down.

Obviously she didn't give me much credit in the intelligence department. Did men always fall for her bullshit? I imagined that, with having four brothers, she was well practiced in getting her way and using her femininity to her advantage.

"That I can do, Izzy." I didn't bother to tell her to cover her eyes. I threw back the blanket and climbed to my feet. Fuck it. I could play too.

Her eyes grew wide as they traveled up my thighs and became fixated on my cock. "You could've warned a girl."

"I don't see a girl here, and you're well acquainted with what I have." I smirked, rounding the bed, not looking over my shoulder. I didn't have to see her to know that she was staring at my ass, taking in my bare skin. "Like what you see?" I teased.

"Yes," she whispered.

There were two things I knew with her words. The first thing I knew was that her answer wasn't a lie. She was affected no matter how much she wanted to deny it. The second was that the niceness that had oozed out of her mouth was bullshit. There were no weapons near her, and I assumed she hoped to charm me with her nakedness to gain her freedom.

"You sure about this?" I asked as I stood on the opposite side of her bed, stark naked and unashamed.

She nodded and pulled back the blankets for me to climb in next to her.

I slid across the stiff sheets that sounded more like paper than cotton as my body moved closer to her. I punched the pillow a couple of times, trying to find comfort in my limited amount of space, but it was useless with Izzy this close to me. My semi-hard dick had grown rock solid with her proximity.

"James, will you hold me?" she asked, turning to me with those same doe eyes.

"Always," I said as I faced her, placing my front to her side. I rested my hard length against her thigh and saw her eyes grow wide before a small smile played on her lips.

I couldn't hide how attracted I was to her. I'd never had the capacity to turn off a hard-on. There was only one way to tame the beast, and she was currently at my mercy.

Turning her face toward me, she stared in my eyes, and I could see emotion behind her wild sapphire eyes. As part of the agency, I'd been trained in reading emotion and knowing when someone lied during an interrogation. Izzy wasn't hard to read, since I knew her personality from firsthand experience and Thomas's stories.

"Kiss me," she blurted out, and bit her lip.

"I thought you'd never ask."

There was nothing more I wanted in this world than to taste her again, but I wouldn't get to taste all of her like I wanted. It would be an appetizer. Just enough to drive me mad and remind her of our night together.

I leaned over, hovering just above her lips as I looked into her eyes. "Last chance," I warned, waiting for her to respond.

"I want you, James," she whispered against my lips before moving her mouth to meet mine.

Her mouth felt soft, and I craved to feel her lips wrapped around my dick, sucking me off and choking on my hardness. What started as a gentle kiss turned hot and heavy as my need for her intensified. Leaning over, I held her face in my hand, resting my thumb against our mouths.

She didn't smell the same. The stench from the biker bar had almost washed out her perfume. I hadn't been able to be near a woman who wore the same scent without growing hard.

Her mouth was unforgettable. The way it moved across my skin, devouring my lips, and took all of me was something I could never wipe from my mind.

She moaned as I swept my tongue against hers. I nipped her lips, drawing them into my mouth and sucking with enough pressure to cause them to be swollen tomorrow. I wanted her to remember where I'd been.

Moving my hand away from her face, I let it fall to her neck, feeling her pulse race under my palm. What started as a plan had turned into something more, something that could swallow us whole and suck us in so deep we wouldn't be able to turn back.

She dug her nails into my back, scraping down, and rested her hand just above my ass.

As she whimpered in my mouth, pushing her leg against my dick, I pulled back and looked at her. "You want me? " I asked, resting my forehead against hers.

Breathing raggedly, she swallowed and answered, "Yes," as she slid her hand down to my ass and squeezed.

I smirked, moving myself on top of her before taking her lips again. I captured her moans and tiny whimpers in my mouth as I pushed my cock against her G-string, driving her closer to the edge.

"James, my hand," she whispered, grinding her pussy against me. "Please. I want to touch you."

I was tempted to free her hand. I wanted to feel her fingers roam my skin and her fingernails scratch down my back, but I hadn't been born yesterday.

Sliding my tongue down her neck, I latched on to the sensitive spot near her collarbone. She cried out, flinching from the pressure of the bite. I fisted the thin scrap of lace she thought was underwear, ripped it from her skin, and tossed it on my floor.

She sucked in a quick breath, pushing her hips into me. "Hand," she whimpered.

Hearing her beg made my dick harder than it had been before. I could feel her wetness against my length as I feasted on her skin. She was right where I wanted her—horny and ready to take all of me.

Placing my hands on either side of her, I captured her lips, moving my hips to glide against her heat. I backed away, stared in her eyes, and pushed myself off her.

As I stood, her eyes grew wide and she pulled at the restraints. "What the fuck?" she thundered.

"I know your game, Izzy," I replied as I walked toward my bed.

She kicked the mattress and grunted. "I don't know what the hell you're talking about. Get your ass over here and finish what you started."

I smiled, sitting on the edge of the bed, my cock standing at attention, and looked at her. "You started it. You only want me to take off the handcuffs, and that shit ain't happening."

"I wanted you, James." She stilled in the bed and stared at the ceiling.

"You'll get me when you're not trying to play me for a fool."

"I wasn't," she pleaded, closing her eyes and exhaling.

"The next time you have me, you'll be begging for it, and maybe, just maybe, I'll give it to you."

"I won't beg."

I smiled, fisting my shaft as I stroked the length. "I won't fuck you again until you're begging for me to fuck you. Fuck you like I did months ago."

She turned toward me, her eyes staring at my dick. "I won't beg."

I continued to move my hands up and down, teasing myself just as much. "You. Will. Beg."

"You're an asshole. I've never begged a man for cock," she said through gritted teeth with her body uncovered and on full display.

"Those were boys, Izzy. I'm a man. I remember how hard you came with me, how many times you came on my cock and in my mouth. You fuckin' loved it."

"I was drunk," she protested, stroking the space between her breasts with her fingertips as she moved them up to her neck and traced the same path down toward her belly button.

Sweet fucking Jesus, watching her touch herself made me want to throw my brilliant plan out the window and fuck her senseless.

Her olive skin was highlighted with tattoos. Most of her tattoos were hidden from public view. They were for her personal enjoyment. She had a dragon down her left ribcage with the word "Gallo" underneath. Near her left breast, she had an intricate hibiscus flower in vibrant reds and oranges. The leaves and vines wrapped around her breast, almost cradling it. For a tattoo artist, she hadn't overdone the artwork yet.

Her piercings captured my attention the most. Her nipples

and the hood just above her clit were pierced. I wanted to yank on it with my teeth and scrape against her clit, causing her to chant my name. The small piercings hanging from her nipples had me fantasizing about the ways I could put them to use. I imagined restraining her using those alone. Fuck, I needed to stop thinking about fucking her.

"Not an excuse. I didn't take advantage of you," I said, pulling on the tip, running my fingers over the apadravya. "And I know you loved feeling this," I declared as I gave the piercing a tug, "stroking you from the inside."

"I'll admit, the happydravya is a nice touch," she conceded, pursing her lips.

"Happydravya?" I asked, tightening my grip around the shaft.

"It's a nickname for that type of piercing."

I released my cock, too close to coming, and placed my legs in the bed as I swiveled around. "Go to bed."

"That's it?"

"Yep. That's it, doll. You won't get my cock until you're on your hands and knees, begging for me to fuck you. It won't be as a ploy to untie your hands."

"Asshole."

"I'll fuck you there too. I'm taking all of you the next time I sink my dick in you balls deep." I punched the pillow, resting my head against the lumpy mess.

"You're so full of yourself," she whispered as she lay on her back and pulled the covers over her breasts.

I smiled, knowing that she was right. I was an asshole and full of myself, but she was right there with me. The girl had confidence and bullshit down pat. She was a master and could get her way with any man—anyone but me. I was impervious to her charms.

"You'll be full of me again someday soon."

"Fuck off," she hissed.

"Good night, Isabella," I crooned as I switched off the lamp and closed my eyes.

She didn't reply. I could hear her breathing, jagged at first,

52

begin to slow. Once she was asleep, I allowed myself to think of making her mine as I drifted off.

Isabella Gallo wasn't an easy target, but nothing worth having ever is.

She didn't know it yet, but I had my sights set on her, and I always got what I wanted.

# CHAPTER 6
# LYING TO MYSELF

IZZY

MY BODY WAS COVERED with sweat as I kicked off
the sheets. James had invaded my goddamn dreams. Motherfucker had gotten into my head last night with his smug bullshit.

The brown '70s alarm clock on the nightstand read eight.
The drapes were closed and blocking out the sunlight, but the
illumination of the television made James glow like an angel.
Not an angel sent by God, but a fallen one put on Earth to torture
me. The numbness in my arm had woken me from the wet dream
I'd been having. Once again, I'd been denied the orgasm I
needed and wanted.

The blankets had shifted as he slept. One leg rested on top,
the other still underneath and hiding. I sat up, placing my back
against the headboard, and took in his wicked beauty.

He was exactly how I liked him best—silent.

I'd never had the chance to really look at him. I couldn't
bring myself to give him the satisfaction of drinking him in. He
towered over me. He was wide too, more than twice my width,
and he easily overshadowed me. Not only was he bigger than I
was, he was cockier too.

He looked like a giant in the tiny-ass bed. The man needed a
California king to look like a normal-sized person. His feet
touched the end and almost hung off as his head rested just
below the headboard. Even when he was sleeping, when his

muscles should be the most relaxed, everything was taut and hard.

His washboard abs looked like a product of Photoshop, and flexed with his breathing. His black hair was longer than the last time I'd seen him. It lay across his forehead in a wild mess, touching his eyebrows. His lips twitched slightly, and I ached to touch them. They were full and made to be kissed. It was a shame they usually spouted such smug shit.

I admired his tattoos, which flowed down his shoulder and ran up his ribcage. He must've spent hours in the chair. It wasn't colorful artwork—all of it was black with gray shading. Waves stretched across his side, reaching from his hip to just under his armpits. Riding the waves were koi fish and Japanese-inspired flowers. His shoulder piece was as unique as the other. The claws of the dragon touched his pec, ran down his shoulder, and ended a couple of inches above his elbow.

Each one of my brothers had a dragon tattoo, and even I had one on my ribcage. It was a family thing—a symbol of our togetherness and all that bullshit. I'd just thought it was a kick-ass tattoo.

The fact that James had a dragon tattoo could enter him into the Gallo brotherhood without needing extra ink. I hoped he never discovered that simple fact. He'd probably go off about how we had been made for each other. Yada, yada. The man probably thought he was God's gift to women.

"Like what you see?" his deep-sleep voice asked.

I closed my eyes, knowing that I'd been caught, and sighed. "Just looking at your ink and nothing more."

"Sleep well?" He rubbed his eyes and yawned.

I jiggled the cuffs in the air. "How do you think I slept?" I growled.

"Stiff?" he asked, a playful smile spreading across his lips.

"Sounds like your problem, not mine." I laughed, but inside, I was secretly dying.

We had been so close to having sex last night. What had started out as a plan to get him to let me go had turned into something more. The memories from Joey's wedding night came flooding back, and I wanted more. I'd rather him think it had all been just an act. That was preferable to admitting that I wanted him.

"Can you take these off now? I have to pee."

James stood, stretching his muscles and showing off his body. The man had no shame. I didn't either. He grabbed the key off the desk near the door and sat on the bed, staring at me.

"What?" I snapped, annoyed and over the entire situation.

"I like you like this." He smiled, rubbing his chin as he ran his finger across his lips.

"Well, you better memorize it, because you'll never see me like this again," I muttered, chewing the inside of my cheek.

"I bet I will, Izzy. You can't resist me forever."

"I didn't know you were trying, Jimmy."

Starting at my wrist, he lightly ran his fingers down my arm and traced a path to my chin. He stroked my cheek and stared into my eyes. "I'm telling you now. I love a good chase and a worthy adversary. You. Will. Be. Mine," he said calmly, swiping his thumb across my bottom lip.

I swallowed hard, trying to get the lump that had formed in my throat to disappear. "I don't go for the caveman shit," I insisted, trying not to let him hear the delight his words had caused me.

"You do. You just won't admit it." He leaned forward, kissing the corner of my mouth.

I closed my eyes, savoring the scent of him. He smelled amazing. The light hint of musk and leftover cologne invaded my senses.

I turned my face and said, "I have to pee or I'll do it right here."

"You always have an excuse. Keep running, but I'll get you in the end."

What a cocky-ass motherfucker. I'd grown up with cocky. I knew it well. My ability to sniff it out had been honed since I was a child. I'd spent years trying to avoid it. It wasn't that I wanted a pussy; I just didn't want someone who felt like they owned me. No one told me what to do. I was Izzy Gallo. Slave to no one and master of my destiny.

I glared at him, about ready to start shifting in the bed from having to go and the effect James was having on me. "Please let me up," I said, playing the sweet card.

"Do your business and then let's hit it. I want to get you home as soon as possible so I can get back to Thomas," he replied as he reached for the cuff. Holding my wrist, he worked the key in the lock, freeing me.

After pulling my wrist down, I rubbed it, soothing the spot the metal had rubbed against all night. "Thomas should be your priority right now," I said as I rolled off the other side of the bed and away from him. "Not me."

"I'm a multi-tasker." He laughed. "Plus, your sweet ass is the one in front of me, so you take the top spot."

As I walked by the bed, he reached out quickly and swatted my ass. I jumped, turning to face him, and glared. "What the fuck was that for?"

"I couldn't help smacking that beautiful ass. Next time I do it, I'm going to be buried inside you and you'll be begging me for more."

I grabbed my clothes off the floor near his feet and stood, leaning into his space. "You'll be the one begging, Jimmy. You bet your tight, hard ass on that one."

The corner of his mouth turned up and his emerald-green eyes sparkled. They were an amazing shade of green. A picture would never capture their beauty and the depth of color. I needed to stop thinking of how beautiful he was and stick to my guns. James would not get what he wanted from this girl.

"Doll, I'm flattered you noticed my tight, hard ass." He laughed, grabbing my face quickly and planting a kiss on my lips.

I felt the spark, just like the one I'd felt the first night he kissed me in the elevator. We had electricity—enough that we could probably light up a small town for a year—but no spark was worth dealing with his smug ass every day.

Pushing him away, I smacked him. "Don't ever do that unless I want it."

"Oh, you did," he said, shaking his head and breaking out into laughter.

I placed my open palm against his head, pushing him backward. "Clearly we need to go over when no means no."

I could hear his laughter as I walked toward the tiny bathroom. After closing the door, I tossed my clothes to the floor and leaned against the cool wooden surface. Sealing my eyes shut, I rested my hands on the door, and breathed.

James had my number. I was so totally fucked. I didn't know if I should be happy or totally pissed off. I liked the idea of the chase. Fuck, it could be fun as hell, but knowing what it meant if I were to be captured did not make me overly excited. I loved a good sparring partner as much as the next person, but James was an entirely different animal. He wasn't a pushover, an easy victim. No, he was the worst kind of all—a clear-cut victor and an opponent I couldn't beat.

I had to channel my inner Tyson. The man had known that Holyfield would kick his ass and he wouldn't win with his fists alone. He'd resorted to biting the dude's ear off to not show his weakness. I'd be like Mike. Play dirty or lose it all.

A small knock made me jump. "What?" I yelled as I slowly peeled myself off the door.

"Just wanted to make sure you didn't slip out on me. I didn't hear any activity."

Where the hell would I have gone? There wasn't even a window in this craptastic bathroom. "I'm almost done," I sang, hovering over the toilet.

I heard his footsteps as he walked away, giving me privacy. It had never felt so good to go to the bathroom. Shivers racked my body from having held it so long. Afterward, I threw on my clothes and washed my face. What I wouldn't have done for some makeup and a toothbrush. The motel had been kind enough to supply not only soap, but also a small bottle of mouthwash. I cracked open the top, taking a mouthful and swishing it around. Using my finger, I scrubbed my gums and teeth before spitting it out. I wasn't high maintenance, but this was a little beyond my comfort zone.

As I opened the door, my eyes took in James—fully naked and leaning against the wall.

"Have you no shame, man?" I asked as my eyes traveled up his body and stopped on his face.

My face felt flushed and my belly dropped. I wanted to jump on him, wrap my legs around his hard body, and rub my pussy against him. I hated him. His devilish grin, his sparkling eyes, and his beautiful face pissed me off. The man played games and played them well.

"What's to be ashamed of? I saw you staring last night. I thought I'd give you one last look before I got dressed."

"You're obviously delusional." I glared at him and started to walk past him.

He grabbed my wrist, pulling me back. "Stay right here."

"Why?" I asked, looking down at his grip on me.

"I don't trust you not to bolt. You stay right outside this door or I can handcuff you again. I prefer the second option, but I leave it entirely in your hands."

"I'm not going anywhere. Just do what you need to do so I can get the hell away from you." I tore my wrist from his hand and sneered.

"You're never getting away from me, Izzy. Right here." He pointed to the spot outside the bathroom, close enough that he could keep his eye on me while he was inside.

I saluted him, feeling the need to be a smartass, as he stalked into the bathroom and left the door ajar. "Where's my phone?" I asked. It wasn't in my pants pocket where I'd left it.

"Nightstand."

"Can I grab it, master?" I asked.

I heard him suck in a breath, pausing a moment before answering. "You don't know what those words do to me, and yes, you may."

I rolled my eyes just for the sheer satisfaction, because there was no one else to see me do it, and walked toward the night-stand. As I grabbed my phone, something on the floor caught my eye. Sticking out from under the bed skirt was my black lace G-string. Unable to help myself, I picked it up and stuffed it in his bag next to the door.

"Where are you?" he yelled from the bathroom.

"I'm coming!" I yelled back as I headed toward my assigned spot.

Jesus, the man was a control freak.

"Mmm, I like the sound of that," he said as he walked out with a smile.

"Get dressed already." I sat on the bed, crossing my legs, and enjoyed the increased pressure on my core. Why couldn't he have dressed while I'd been in the bathroom? "Or I'll leave without you." I wouldn't, but he didn't need to know. I didn't even know where the fuck we were to have someone to pick me up.

"Keep your panties on. I'll be ready in two seconds." He grabbed his clothes, pulling on his jeans first, tucking his dick inside, and then zipping them. His t-shirt he slowly pulled over his head, thinking he was torturing me.

I didn't stare at him, but I watched him out of the corner of my eye as I pretended to check my phone. The only messages I'd received overnight were from Flash. He seemed to be in a panic.

"Who ya texting?" James asked as he looked over my shoulder, catching me off guard.

"Flash is worried."

"Fuck Flash. Put that phone down." He grabbed my hand, plucking the phone from my grip.

"He's my friend," I said, glaring at him.

"He sold you out and left you at the hands of the MC. That's no friend I ever want."

"You don't know him."

"I know enough about him. Do not respond to him. If you never listen to me again, Izzy, please do on this one thing." He ran his fingers through his hair, taming the strands that had wandered when he had put on his shirt.

"I know he's a pussy. Trust me. I'm pissed the fuck off at him, but I want to tell him that I'm fine."

"You wait to do that shit when I have you on the other coast and in the protection of your family."

"You worry too much," I argued, grabbing the phone and pushing it in my back pocket.

"You don't worry enough." He lifted his bag, touching the small of my back as he opened the door. "Let's go."

I squinted when the bright Florida sun hit my face as we walked out of the dark motel room. I hooded my eyes and looked around. We were in the middle of nowhere and far from home.

"This is going to be a long-ass ride."

"You make it sound like a bad thing," he said as he walked to his bike, grabbed the helmet, and held it out to me.

I approached, ripping it from his grasp. "Three hours on the back of your bike doesn't sound like a joyride."

"You say the word and I'll pull over and give you something to smile about," he murmured as he touched my cheek.

With my free hand, I batted his hand away from my face and put the helmet on, cinching the straps tight. "In your dreams," I huffed out, standing next to the sleek Harley V-Rod Muscle bike. I'd spent enough time around boys with their toys to know my Harleys. It wasn't traditional, but it matched his personality perfectly—strong, sexy, and loud.

"It'll be my reality. Just you wait, beautiful." He climbed on, twisting his body before patting the back seat.

I stared at the sky, closing my eyes and making a silent plea to put distance between us. Why had I fucked his brains out the night we met?

Holding his shoulder, I adjusted myself. Wrapping my arms around his torso, I smashed my tits against his back and smiled. I'd make the ride just as uncomfortable for him as he always made me. I'd invented games.

# CHAPTER 7
# UNFORGETTABLE

JAMES

THE GIRL HAD game and mad fucking skills. I'd never met a female who was as full of shit as I was. Izzy was everything I'd ever wanted in a woman—fierce, strong, driven, and full of attitude.

Riding with her on the back of my bike for over three hours should've been boring and tedious. I was finding out that nothing we did together could be described with those words.

She'd taken every chance to brush against my dick when we were stopped at a light. Running her hand down my thigh, all in the name of stretching her back. She hadn't just held me to stay on the bike. She'd felt me up and I fucking knew it.

As I pulled into her drive, I could feel my semi-hard dick I'd been sporting for the last twenty miles start to stiffen. It wouldn't happen today. I had shit to do, including a long ride back to Daytona.

I parked the bike, securing it in place before turning off the engine. Izzy pushed off using my shoulder and plucked the helmet from her head. Leaning over, she shook out her hair, flipping it like a wet dream. She was a fucking tease.

"Thanks for the ride." She smirked, holding out the helmet.

"Can I use the bathroom before I head back?" I asked. I figured I could have a little more fun with her before I walked out of her life for a short time. I knew I'd be back. No one could keep me away from Izzy Gallo.

She rubbed her face and stared at the ground. "If you must," she mumbled, bringing her eyes to meet mine.

In the sunlight, her eyes matched the color of the Gulf on a sunny day. Turquoise with hints of sky blue. They were lush and big for her face. I didn't speak as I hopped off the bike and stretched.

She walked away, heading for the door, and I followed behind, admiring her ass. Looking over her shoulder, she glared at me before stopping in front of her door and unlocking it.

The house sat on a canal, the Gulf of Mexico not far away from the multistory dwelling. The façade was white with muted orange trim, and it stood three stories tall. Following her inside, I took in the beauty of the living room. It was like Izzy—loud and unforgiving and alive with vibrant color. Large windows lined the back of the house as the sun cascaded through the room and shone on the dark wooden floors.

"Restroom?" I asked, looking around, taking in the layout of her home.

"Over there," she replied, motioning to the left with her head.

I walked away, finding a hallway where she had pointed. I stopped when I passed an open door that held a bedroom. I didn't think it was hers. It was all white and too plain for her tastes. I continued to the next room and found the Holy Grail.

*This* was Izzy's bedroom. The walls were painted a deep red with black trim. Black curtains hung from the floor-to-ceiling windows. Along the opposite wall was a king-sized bed with black satin bedding. It wasn't feminine, but totally her.

"Find it?" Her voice carried down the hallway, forcing me back into the hall.

"Yeah!" I yelled, and moved toward the last door on the right.

After I was done, I didn't bother looking around before I headed back to find Izzy. She was standing in the kitchen, moving with ease, a coffee pot in hand.

"Want a cup before you head out?"

*Look at Betty fuckin' Crocker.* "Sure," I said, my voice uncertain.

"It's the least I can do. I need you to make it back to my brother safely."

"Well, I'm kind of hungry too." I smiled, taking a seat at her breakfast bar.

"I don't cook, and you're pushing it."

"I'll grab something at the gas station down the street," I responded, propping my chin on my hand and staring at her.

She blanched. "I have some leftovers from my mom's place." She opened the fridge and bent over to look through the contents.

It was a perfect ass shot. I grinned, watching her move.

"How about some pasta?" she asked with her head still stuck inside.

"Perfect." I leaned back, looking away before she turned around. I wouldn't fuck with pasta from Mrs. Gallo. Thomas always raved about it.

She pulled off the plastic wrap and splashed a bit of water on the plate before sticking it in the microwave. "Is my brother really okay, James?" she asked with her back to me.

I sighed, wishing I could fuck with her mind, but I wanted to put her at ease. "He's doing okay, Izzy. He's smart and tough. He's made it deeper than any other agent." I tapped my foot on the floor, feeling uncomfortable while trying to shovel a load of bullshit at her.

No one in the life was safe. It could all end without notice, in the blink of an eye.

"That doesn't sound so promising." The microwave beeped, and she grabbed the plate from inside. "Will he be done soon?" she asked as she placed the pasta in front of me.

"Hopefully. We're trying to get him out ASAP, but you know your brother. He wants more. He's never content."

She grabbed a fork from the dish strainer and held it out to me. "That's how all the Gallos are. We always want more." She smiled.

"I'm counting on it, doll." I snatched the fork from her hands before she could throw it at me. I knew she hated it, but I wanted to change the subject from Thomas to something that made me happy.

"Just eat and shut up." She took the dishrag from the sink and wiped down the counters.

Shoving the first forkful in my mouth was sheer happiness. Even a couple of days old and dry, the taste exploded in my mouth. I hadn't had homemade sauce this damn good since my grandmother passed years ago.

"Mmm," I mumbled, taking another forkful. "I never pictured the domestic side of you." I laughed, placing the noodles on my tongue.

"Someone has to clean. I do it all myself, except cook. That is my weakness. Never had the patience for that shit."

Swallowing my food, I offered, "I could teach you."

Her hand stilled as she looked at me with big eyes. "You cook?"

"I've been known to, yes. I'd love to get your mom's recipe for this sauce."

She shook her head and stared. "That is for Gallo family members only. It's a closely guarded secret. So, what do you cook?" She leaned over the counter and gawked at me as I attacked the pasta.

"Anything you want. I had to learn to cook, being single. I couldn't maintain this body and eat shit food all the time."

"Interesting," she mumbled, watching me shove the fork in my mouth. "Never took you as a Paula Deen."

I laughed, almost choking on my food. "I think of myself as a better-looking version of Emeril."

"His food is so damn good. I'll never believe you can cook like that."

"Someday you'll find out." I wiped my face after I inhaled the pasta.

She pulled my plate from the counter, setting it in the sink. "I won't, but I'll take you at your word."

I smiled but didn't respond to her remark. She turned me

65

down at every opportunity, but I was fine with the chase. Fuck, I loved a good game of cat and mouse. It was one of the reasons I'd joined law enforcement.

"It's quite a place you have here," I said, swiveling around on my stool.

"Want to see the upstairs? It's my favorite part of the house."

"Sure. And I'd love that cup of coffee."

"You can bring it up with you," she said as she grabbed two cups. "Black?"

"Yes, please."

She filled the cup, adding sugar to hers before turning around with her hands full. "Here," she said, placing it in front of me. "Let's go."

Once I took my cup, I followed her closely up the stairs I hadn't noticed before. I had been lost in my thoughts of her and all the dirty things I wanted to do to her.

"This is why I bought the place," she said when we reached the top.

As I made my way behind her, the stunning landscape came into view. She had a view of the Gulf of Mexico in the distance. The sun shimmering across the water made it look like a sheet of glass covered in glitter.

"Stunning," I muttered, sipping the coffee.

"Come outside on the deck and have your coffee before you go." She pulled open the sliding glass doors.

"I'm not used to the nice-girl act," I said as I followed her.

"I'm not always a twat." She laughed, sitting down on the swing, facing away from me. "Close the door, please."

"I'd never call you a twat, Izzy. You have such a mouth."

"You love my mouth, from what I remember, James."

"I so fucking do." I sighed as I closed the door and made my way toward her. As I sat, I said, "This is a little slice of heaven."

"It's my serenity. When shit gets bad or my life feels over-whelming, this is where I come to center myself."

Listening to her talk while we sat together, I felt like I was seeing the real Izzy for the first time. She had her guard down and was speaking to me differently. There was no sarcasm in her voice, no smartass comment—just Izzy. I liked this side of her, but the other one made me wild and drove me crazy.

A comfortable silence settled between us as we sipped our coffee and gently rocked back and forth. The last thing I wanted to do was get back on my bike and leave her, but I had to. Duty called. If I didn't go back and something happened to her brother, I'd never be able to make her mine. All hope for the future would be killed.

"I better go," I said. "Thank you for the perfect ending to the last twenty-four hours." I didn't look at her as I spoke. I stared off into the distance, taking in the beauty of the Gulf and longing for this life.

I loved my job, but some nights, I wished for someone to be mine, someone to spend my life with. I didn't want to lead a senior-citizen lifestyle. I wanted a partner, someone I could spar with and make love to at the drop of a dime. Izzy was what I wanted; she just hadn't accepted her fate. She couldn't resist me for long.

"This has been nice. The rest, not so much. I could've done without the cuffs, James." She turned to me and smiled.

I laughed. "You'll learn to love them." I winked at her, and her cheeks grew flushed.

"In your fucking dreams," she shot back, rolling her eyes.

I reached up, stroking her cheeks, and leaned into her space. "I know many uses for handcuffs besides arrest. Imagine your body at my mercy. I could feast on your flesh for hours, Isabella," I murmured against her lips.

She blinked slowly and stared into my eyes. "You say such pretty shit, but I'll pass on the offer."

Running my hand to the back of her neck, I gripped her roughly, holding her in place. "I could have you right now if I wanted. Don't kid yourself. I don't buy your bullshit. You want me as much as I want you. You haven't forgotten how good my cock feels inside you."

Her eyes flashed and her tongue darted out, swiping against my top lip. "You'll never—"

I captured her words in my mouth, crushing my lips to hers

to quiet her. The smart-mouthed woman I fucking craved was back, and I couldn't control myself. I didn't want to listen to her lies. I knew I'd have her again.

As my tongue slid across hers, mingling her taste with mine, the sweetness of the sugar from her coffee made my mouth water. She tasted so fucking good. I'd leave her with a reminder of what I felt like and how I tasted.

The tiny hairs on the back of her neck rose, brushing against my fingers as we kissed. She panted into my mouth, kissing me back with her hand resting on my forearm. Her body spoke the words she was too afraid to say.

I backed away, breaking the kiss, and stared at her face. We were both breathless and didn't release our grip on each other.

"What were you going to say?" I asked, trying to calm my breathing.

"I don't know," she said, her voice breathy and her face flushed.

"I can show myself out." I stood and grabbed my coffee cup off the small table next to the swing.

Izzy sat there looking like a deer in headlights as I reached to open the door to the house. "Wait!" she yelled, standing on shaky legs.

"Yes?" I asked, turning to her.

"I can at least show you out," she said.

I smiled and released the door handle.

"It's more for self-preservation, really." She opened the door, trotting down the steps in front of me. "I want to make sure you don't leave a reason to come back."

"I don't need to leave something behind," I said as I reached the last step, following her into the kitchen and toward the front door. "I'm all the reason you need." I walked up to her as she stopped by the door and pressed her against the flat surface, brushing my lips against hers. "My cock is a good reason. I remember you mumbling something about God when I was finger-fucking you. And then...then there's my mouth; you almost suffocated me to death. Do I need more reasons?"

She glared at me and exhaled loudly, her breath hitting me in the face. "James, I think it's you who can't forget my pussy. It was so damn good you keep coming back for more. We'll see who's begging." She ducked, weaving out of my grasp, and laughed as she stood behind me.

I hung my head and smiled. The girl had smartass perfected. "Maybe we both have a problem." I straightened my back and turned toward her. "We'll find out soon enough. Thanks for the meal and coffee, doll."

A flash of anger clouded her eyes before a small smile spread across her lips. "You're welcome. Keep my brother safe, ya hear me?"

I opened the door and waved, leaving her behind. "I will. That I promise you, Isabella."

I climbed on my bike, smiling as I pulled away, and caught a glimpse of her standing in the door watching me head away from her home. No one did that if they hated the person. The girl had it just as bad as I did. Now I had to figure out how to get her to admit it.

# CHAPTER 8
# GALLO FAMILY CLUSTERFUCK

IZZY

I SPENT the rest of Saturday at home relaxing. No one expected me at work, so I didn't bother. I answered a few text messages and lay around. Even Flash got a short response. I told him that I was fine but too pissed to talk to his sorry ass. He took the hint and left me alone. I mean, what the fuck could he say anyway? "Sorry I left you at the mercy of an MC guy so he could rape you"? He was a total dumbass.

I didn't feel like hearing bullshit from my brothers if I went into the shop. I'd have enough explaining to do showing up at Sunday dinner, but I had to go. I needed to tell everyone that I had seen Tommy. They'd be relieved that he was well, but totally pissed off at me.

I rubbed my face as I stood outside my parents' front door. I could hear everyone inside laughing and carrying on. We were never a quiet bunch.

"Here goes nothing," I whispered to myself, trying to put on a happy face and come up with a bullshit excuse.

I opened the door, walked into the foyer, and dropped my purse next to the stairs. "I'm here!" I yelled, heading toward the great room.

The smell of pasta sauce filled the home and made me think of James. He'd looked so damn hot sitting in my kitchen, scarfing down pasta like it was the best fucking thing he'd ever eaten. I wanted to plop my pussy on the plate and let him attack it like it was his last fucking meal.

I shook my head, clearing James from my mind. The man had me all crazy and losing focus.

"What the fuck are you doing here?" Anthony hollered, standing from the couch and stalking toward me.

"Nice to see you too, brother." I smiled, wrapping him in my arms and patting him on the back.

"You weren't supposed to be back until tonight. What happened?" he asked, backing away and looking me up and down. "Are you okay?"

"I'm fine, Anth. Really. Bike Week just wasn't for me."

Out of the corner of my eye, I saw Joey and Mike striding toward us. *Here we go. Let the inquisition begin.*

"Hey, guys," I said, turning toward them and holding out my arms.

"Don't give us that bullshit, Izzy. What happened?" Mike growled, coming to halt and glaring at me.

"I just wanted to come home. I'm not built for that life." I looked at Joey, trying to wrap him in a hug.

"I call bullshit, little sister. You better spill and spill quick before I track Flash's ass down and beat him to a bloody pulp," Joey snarled.

I pinched my nose between my fingers, trying to massage away the stress. "Honestly, I'm fine, guys. I made it home in one piece. I just missed you, is all."

"Bullshit," Anthony coughed, and looked at the floor.

Glaring at him, I sighed. "Listen, I'll tell you all about it, but I want to say hi to Ma and Pop first."

"You will spill, Izzy." Joey crossed his arms over his chest and did his best to look intimidating. He wasn't to me; I'd known him my entire life. I knew the man underneath the big, hard exterior.

"I know, I know." I threw my hands up, walking away to find Ma, who was in the kitchen, pouring the sauce over the angel hair pasta.

"Hey, Ma," I said as I wrapped my arms around her from

71

behind. I loved her more than life itself. She was everything to me, even though she thought I favored my pop over her. I did at times, only because he was a pushover and I loved him for it.

"I'm so happy you're here, baby girl. I thought I heard you walk in."

"Probably heard the three stooges out there."

She laughed, her body shaking in my grip. "They can be a pain in the ass, can't they?" She giggled, turning in my arms.

"Ma, I haven't heard you use that language in a long time." I kissed her cheek, a small laugh escaping.

"Sorry. I'm just stressed. Dinner!" she yelled over my head and toward the four men, who were now sitting in the living room along with the other two females in my life, ones I adored like they were my sisters.

I flinched, covering my ears as she yelled. Years of raising five children had given her the lung capacity to not need a megaphone to be heard over the loud, obnoxious cackles of their voices.

"Jesus, Ma. Warn a girl before you yell in her ear. Will ya?"

She chuckled and grabbed the giant bowl of pasta from the counter. "I want to hear all about your weekend. Was it exciting?" she asked as I followed her to the dining room.

Everyone was already seated. They must've run when they'd heard her voice. No one kept her waiting—at least not if they liked their life too much. She wasn't to be fucked with.

"It wasn't what I'd expected." I sighed.

I sat down in my usual chair next to Joey, who sat at the head opposite my father. My mother always took the seat to his right; often, I'd catch them holding hands while they ate. Suzy sat next to Joey in the same manner my parents sat. Mia and Michael were across the table next to my mother, and Anthony sat on the other side of me. We all had our places, but there was always a void at the table—Thomas's spot.

All eyes were on me. I felt them. They were waiting to hear why I'd returned early. The only ones not paying attention were my parents. My ma was speaking with my father and dishing him out a heaping helping of pasta.

"So, dear, tell us about your trip," Pop said after Ma filled his plate.

Smiling, I began to speak. "Well, it was a train wreck of sorts." I looked down at the table, grabbing my napkin and placing it across my lap. I rested my elbows on the table and caught Joey's watchful eye. "Don't say it," I warned him, holding up my hand.

"Are you okay?" Ma asked, continuing to work her way around the table.

"I'm fine, Ma. I wasn't hurt."

"What the hell did Flash do?" Michael asked, cracking his knuckles as he glared at me. I knew that suspicious look; he'd used it on me many times as a child when pulling information out of me.

"He didn't do a thing. That's the problem." I laughed, preferring to freak everyone out for a moment.

"Izzy," Pop warned.

"Not like that, Pop. I saw James," I croaked out for some unknown reason, hoping to take the heat off Flash.

"Oh my God," Suzy screeched, with a giant smile.

"Who the hell is James?" Anthony asked, looking at me with knitted brows.

I opened my mouth to speak, but Suzy, in her excitement, answered for me. "He's Thomas's friend. He brought the card from Thomas to the wedding. Izzy met him there."

I nodded to Suzy, not worried about anything else she'd say about James. No one, not even Suzy, knew that I'd slept with James the night of the wedding. That information I hadn't shared with a soul. I knew when to keep a secret, and that was one I'd hold close to the vest.

"Isabella, did he have anything to say about your brother?" Ma asked, and I couldn't hold out any longer.

"Well, that's the thing." I swallowed, readying myself for the barrage of questions and some pissed-off brothers. "Flash took me to a biker bar and we ran into his club."

"I told you to stay the fuck away from that MC," Joey interrupted.

"Language, son," Pop said, and then returned his eyes to me. "Go on."

I shifted in my seat, worried that the dinner would turn into a free-for-all, but I knew the information about James would both be a relief and a worry. "When I got there, one of the men at the table wouldn't look at me. He was acting funny." No one was eating, and everyone was staring at me. "When he finally made eye contact with me, I knew it was Tommy," I said, leaning back in my chair.

A collective gasp sounded around the table as my words seeped in.

"Is he okay?" Ma asked, dabbing at her eyes.

"Yeah, he's good, Ma." It wasn't an outright lie. He was okay, relatively speaking.

"Did you get to talk to him?" Pop asked, resting his fork next to his dinner plate.

"I did. We spent an hour alone together." I nodded and smiled. The last thing I wanted to do was add more worry to their lives. "He promised me he'd be home soon and he asked me to send his love. He misses us all."

"How did he look?" Joey inquired, leaning forward with his hands clasped over his plate.

"He looked tired, but otherwise good," I answered.

"How *exactly* did you get time alone with him?" Anthony asked, the perpetual scowl on his face intensified.

"That's not important," I snapped, glaring back at him and biting my lip.

"Like hell it isn't. Spill it, sister," Joey growled with snarled lips.

"Jesus," I muttered. "He kinda called dibs on me for the night." I smiled, pretending like it was no big deal.

"I'll kill Flash!" Joey yelled, slamming the bottom of his fist on the table.

"Fuck," Anthony groaned.

"Dead man walking," Mike growled.

"Calm the shit down!" I yelled over their ramblings.

"What's that mean?" Ma asked, confusion written all over her face.

Pop shook his head, patting my mother's hand. "I'll explain it later, love," he said to her.

"No matter how it happened, I was able to spend time with Tommy," I said, looking around the table. "I wouldn't trade my time with him for anything—not even the nonsense I had to go through to be with him."

"Tell me more about what he said," Ma said, ignoring the others at the table.

I spent the entire dinner talking about Tommy and answering questions. Knowing that he was alive and breathing was something we didn't know on a day-to-day basis. Not being able to hear his voice over the phone or get a text message were the hardest parts to deal with.

He'd been missing from Sunday dinner for so long that it had become the norm. His seat was never filled; it sat open, waiting for his return.

I ate my last forkful of pasta, placing my napkin on my plate, and sighed. I felt relieved to get the information off my chest and be done with the questioning by my family.

"Thanks for the great dinner, Ma."

She patted my shoulder as she walked by me on the way to the kitchen. "Thank you, Isabella."

I smiled at her, nodding. As she left the room I looked over at my brothers, who were still wearing scowls. They were like little girls who couldn't let shit go easily.

"We're not done here," Joey barked, standing from his seat and carrying his plate in the kitchen.

"Oh boy," I whispered, breaking out into a fit of giggles.

Pop winked at me. He always knew when shit was going down. He had my back. That I knew. He'd make sure the boys didn't get too crazy.

As I stood, plate in hand, Suzy stood too, following behind me.

"James, huh?" she teased, elbowing me as we entered the kitchen.

"Yeah." I rolled my eyes, placing my plate on the counter next to Ma. "Want help?" I asked her as she rinsed the pans.

"Nah, baby. Go sit with everyone. You've had a long weekend. I'll be fine."

I sighed, turning and running into Suzy. She smiled and winked at me. She wanted to know only about James, and it made me uncomfortable. I walked by her and made my way toward the family room and my usual spot on the floor.

"Did you talk to him?" she asked before my ass hit the carpet. She settled down next to me instead of next to Joey.

"Who?" I asked, playing stupid.

"James," she groaned. "Come on. I know there's more there than you're saying." She grinned, tilting her head and studying me.

"We spent some time together."

"Ooooh," she whispered, positioning herself next to me as she sat Indian style.

Suzy was now five months pregnant, and showing. I couldn't imagine having a lump sticking out of the front of me. I always lay on my stomach and would be uncomfortable during the entire pregnancy. I winced thinking about childbirth and babies. I loved them, but fuck. I was nowhere near ready to become a mom.

"Don't you have a man to sit next to?" I hinted, motioning toward Joey.

"Nah. He's okay for now. They're talking sports." She rolled her eyes and put her finger in her open mouth and stuck out her tongue, making a gagging sound.

"What else is new?" I turned toward the television, hoping she'd drop the topic.

"I know there's more to you and James than you're saying, Izzy." She nudged me with her side, almost knocking me over.

"What are you talking about?" I asked, shaking my head and looking into her eyes. "There's nothing between us."

She giggled, covering her mouth with her hand. "I saw you two sneak out of the wedding reception."

I looked at her, my mouth gaping open, shocked by her words. "You never said anything to me before."

"I forgot with the honeymoon and then the baby." She rubbed her belly in a circular motion as she spoke. "You mentioned his name and it all came back to me."

"Lucky me," I whispered, resting my head in my hands.

"Did you sleep with him?" she asked, wiggling her eyebrows.

"No. Wait. When?"

"I knew it!" she roared, breaking into a fit of laughter. "Tell me all about it." She fluttered her eyelashes, moving closer to my face. "I won't tell a soul." She crossed her fingers.

"He got me out of Daytona, but no, I didn't sleep with him this weekend."

"Tell me you did on my wedding night. I want all the juicy details."

"It was such a huge mistake," I whispered.

"Why?" she asked, her eyebrows shooting up and her smile vanishing.

"I knew it the moment I woke up in his hotel room. I got my shit and got the hell out of there."

"Oh, no. You hit it and quit it?"

"Where in the hell did you hear that phrase?" I asked as I started to laugh.

"I've been hanging around you for too long." She laughed, biting her lip.

Talking to Suzy always made me feel better. I knew what I told her never made its way to Joey. He never questioned me on anything I confided in her, and I knew without a doubt he'd ask if it had. My brother couldn't keep a secret. No one in my damn family could, except my girls.

"What are you two talking about?" Mia asked as she stretched out on the other side of me.

I was now in the middle of a Mia and Suzy sandwich, and I couldn't be happier. These were my girls. The sisters I hadn't had growing up, but I was thankful for them now.

"James," Suzy blurted, drawing her lips into her mouth.

"Me likey," Mia said, and laughed.

"How do you know him?" I asked, turning to her, confused.

"Suzy told me about him at the reception. We watched you slink out with him and not return." She cocked her eyebrow and stared at me.

"Fuck," I muttered. "Did anyone else see?"

Mia shook her head, pursing her lips. "I don't think so, and if they did, no one has said anything."

I looked toward the ceiling and sighed. "Thank Christ for small miracles."

"Is he the one?" Mia asked, a giant smile on her face.

"What? I've seen him twice in my entire life. That's quite a leap, Mia."

"I knew about Michael after only a couple of dates."

"When the hell are you two going to get married, then?" I asked. "If you're so sure, why wait?"

She shrugged and picked at her nail. "I'm waiting for him to pop the question."

"Fuck that old-school thinking. Ask him to marry you," I insisted, shaking my head.

"No way in hell would I do that. Michael's too old school and he'd have a coronary."

"Have you two talked about marriage?" Suzy asked.

"Yeah. Neither of us is ready to take that plunge."

"He'll ask when the time is right. It took Joey's accident before he popped the question," Suzy said.

"I'm not worried, ladies. I love Michael and we're in a really good place. The clinic is doing so well right now, and living together is enough for me."

"Makes shit less complicated," I said, cracking my knuckles.

"When you're in love, everything is complicated," Suzy said, smiling and rubbing her belly. "Joey has made my life complicated since the moment I met him."

"You didn't fall in love with him right away." I remembered how he'd had to chase Suzy and make her admit her feelings.

"I don't remember not loving him. Sometimes you can only lie to yourself for so long."

"I don't believe in love at first sight," I lied, but didn't even convince myself with that statement.

"Girl, sometimes there's a spark you can't ignore." Suzy rubbed my shoulder. She was always so touchy-feely.

I hung my head, as the girls seemed too ecstatic about my time with James. "Ladies"—I cleared my throat—"I don't do relationships, and certainly not with a man like James. I fucked him once and that's it."

"What do you mean a man like James?" Mia asked with raised eyebrows.

"Mia, you keep wiggling those things up and down and you're going to get a cramp." I laughed, slapping the floor.

She scowled. "Shut the fuck up and spill it, woman. Your deflection doesn't work on me."

"Fine. You two are nosy bitches."

"That's the pot calling the kettle black." Suzy giggled.

"You both know how Mike and Joey are, right?" I whispered.

They looked at each other with dopy smiles, and nodded.

"I don't *like* how they are, and James makes them seem like kittens compared to him."

Mia's mouth opened into an O shape, and Suzy's smiled grew wider. Half of my sisterhood understood my dilemma.

"What's wrong with how your brothers are?" Suzy asked, looking over her shoulder at Joey.

"Um, hello. Bachelorette party ring a bell?" I asked, shaking my head. "They're bossy, demanding, and cocky as hell."

"Yeah," Suzy whispered, turning back to me with that lovesick-puppy look. "I've grown to love it."

"I can't believe I'm going to say this, Suzy, but that man has seriously scrambled your brains." I rested my face in my hands, hiding my eyes and wondering what happened to my girls.

"I get it," Mia said, touching my shoulder. "I get it more than anyone here. Mike made me crazy at first. I had been on my own too long to put up with his bossy bullshit, Izzy."

"Add Joey and Mike together and they don't equal James."

"Fuck me," Mia whispered.

"Exactly." I sighed. "He's too much for me, ladies."

"I felt the sizzle and pop between you two, Izzy," Suzy said.

"Suzy, it was electric, but that doesn't mean I want the man as a part of my life."

"You're scared 'cause he has you nailed," Suzy replied.

"He nailed me all right," I said, trying to hold back a laugh. "And it was fucking amazing."

"I don't see you with someone like Flash. You need someone who won't put up with your brother's bullshit. James is that man. Don't you think so, Mia?" Suzy asked, looking toward Mia.

"That's hard to say, but she definitely needs someone who will tell these boys to go to hell. No wimpy guy will survive in this family. No way in hell."

"He drove me home Saturday." I don't know why I felt the need to share that fact with them, but maybe they needed to understand the caliber of man I was dealing with here.

"And?" Suzy asked, moving closer to me.

"Let's go outside or for a walk. I can't tell you where the others will hear." I sat up, quickly moving to my feet. I held out my arms, helping Suzy and her growing belly off the floor. "We're going to sit outside and enjoy the fresh air," I told the guys, not caring if they were okay with it or not.

They grunted and waved goodbye as the three of us wandered onto the lanai and sat around the table. I faced the living room so I could keep an eye out for anyone heading our way.

"Mia, reach back and close the door all the way," I said, motioning toward the glass siding door with my chin.

"This must be juicy," Suzy shrieked, rubbing her hands together.

I loved her. She was sweet and pure, and she always wanted to think the best of everybody. Usually, she was misguided, but thankfully, she was my biggest cheerleader. Someone like her needed a man like Joey to protect her. It wasn't that she was weak; Suzy was just naïve and way too kind for her own good.

"First off, I did *not* have sex with James this weekend."

"Darn it," Suzy whispered, snapping her fingers as Mia laughed.

"Tommy called James and had him bring me home."

"Sounds like no big deal to me," Mia said, leaning back in the chair, twirling a piece of her long brown hair in her fingers.

"It is a big deal. When I slept with him on your wedding night"—I looked at Suzy before I continued—"I didn't stick around for a goodbye. I grabbed my things and left before he woke up."

"Oh, you're a bad girl," Mia crowed, laughing. "That takes balls."

"Hey, I am who I am. Well, Friday night he didn't want me to 'run away' again."

"Oh boy," Suzy said.

"Anyway"—I turned back to Mia—"he waited for me to fall asleep and he handcuffed me to the bed." I put my head on the table, banging it lightly against the glass surface.

"I like him already," Mia whooped.

"He didn't?" Suzy asked with her mouth hanging open and her eyes as large as saucers.

Lifting my head, I answered her: "He did." I nodded, a small smile playing on my lips. "I tried to convince him to free me, but my charms didn't work."

"Did you try to seduce him?" Mia asked, covering her mouth and laughing.

"Fuck yeah, I did, but he didn't fall for it."

"He left you like that?" Suzy asked. "All night?"

"All night."

"Hold up. How did you try and seduce him?" Mia inquired, leaning forward, clasping her hands together in front of her.

"Well…" I sighed. "I told him I was afraid. He crawled in bed with me and we started to make out."

"Ooooh," Suzy cooed, resting her hands on top of her blossoming belly.

I laughed at her response. It was sexy looking back at it, but when it had happened…well, fuck, it had been sexy then too.

"I asked him to free my hands because I wanted to touch him."

"What did he do?" Mia asked, her right eyebrow shooting up toward her hairline.

"He ripped my panties off and left me in the dust and hand-cuffed to the bed."

"He plays dirty." Mia laughed. "Yep, I like this James guy."

"Oh fuck off, Mia," I hissed, but couldn't hold on to the fake anger. "He's so fucking bossy."

"He knows your game, sister, and that's why you're scared." Mia smiled, her eyes teary from her laughter.

I blew out a breath through puffy cheeks. I knew she was right. My schemes didn't work and he seemed to know my next move.

"I don't like him," I whined, crossing my arms over my chest.

"Yes, you do," Suzy argued, nodding as she smiled.

"No, I don't."

"You so do. You're fucked." Mia cackled, leaning in her chair and throwing her head back.

"I'm totally fucked," I whispered, closing my eyes as I tried to come to terms with this knowledge.

I didn't want to like James. Men like that always rubbed me the wrong way, but when James did it...well, it sent sparks through my body.

It was a traitor.

# CHAPTER 9
## THE CHASE

JAMES

BIKE WEEK ENDED, and this year had been relatively quiet compared to previous ones. The Sun Devils MC, along with Thomas, headed back to Leesburg—a town north of Tampa, and their home base.

It had almost been a week since I'd walked out of Izzy's house and headed back to Daytona. I couldn't get her out of my mind. She was like a wet dream I couldn't shake. Her smile, her taste, her smell—everything about her had stayed with me, and I wanted more.

It didn't help when I found her G-string shoved in with my shit. I'd walked out of her house with a hard-on, wanting to slam her against the door and take her. The throbbing in my dick and aching in my balls needed some attention, and I'd do what I needed to do to make it happen.

I twirled my phone in my hand, wondering if I should pull the trigger. Send her a text and find my way in. I couldn't wait any longer. It was fucking killing me. Either I'd die of blue balls or boredom. Izzy Gallo was the only thing that held my attention. It was ten p.m., but I figured she had to be awake. She didn't strike me as the type of girl who turned in early. Plus, she might still be at work.

**Me: Hey, beautiful. Thinking of me?**

Within seconds, my phone beeped with a reply.

*Sexy Fugitive: Who the fuck is this?*

I smiled as I thought about how I'd added my number to her phone while she'd slept. I woke up in the middle of the night to check on her and saw the screen light up. It captured my attention, and I couldn't stop myself from sending a message to steal her number. I saved it and added mine to her contact list. I didn't use my name. No, that would have been too boring. I put myself in as…Man of My Dreams.

I laughed, picturing her pissed-off sneer as she looked at her phone and read my message.

*Me: I can't stop thinking about you.*

*Sexy Fugitive: Creep.*

I typed with a dopy-ass grin on my face.

*Me: Only for you, doll.*

I didn't have to add in the nickname she claimed to hate, but I thought I'd clue her the fuck in if she didn't already know it was me.

*Sexy Fugitive: What do you want, James?*

*Me: You.*

What more could I say?

*Sexy Fugitive: Well…you know where to find me.*

I stared at the screen with my eyebrows knitted together, rubbing my chin. Was this an open invitation or was she busting my balls?

*Me: You can't resist me forever.*

*Sexy Fugitive: Catch me if you can.*

*Me: Catching isn't the hard part… It's keeping you that's the challenge.*

*Sexy Fugitive: You seem to be the type of man who doesn't take no for an answer.*

*Me: I always get what I want, Izzy…always.*

*Sexy Fugitive: Smug bastard.*

I laughed. No matter what she called me, I knew she liked me. Even when her words were venomous, I still knew. She tried like fuck to deny the connection we had, the electricity that flowed through our bodies when we touched, but I felt it.

*Me: You know you want me…*

No quick response came from Izzy. With an aching dick so hard it was ready to break off my body, I crawled out of bed. I put on some clothes and set my sights on her. I had the weekend off, and the last thing I wanted to do was spend it in this sleepy Florida town. I wanted her and I couldn't stay away any longer.

Izzy Gallo would be mine tonight.

As I locked my front door and headed for my bike, my phone beeped in my pocket.

***Sexy Fugitive: I can't talk now. I'm working.***

I wasn't surprised by her text. She never wanted to admit her attraction to me. The entire time I spent with her last weekend had been a barrage of bullshit denying what her body betrayed.

***Me: When do you get off?***

***Sexy Fugitive: As often as I want.***

Fuck. My dick hardened, straining against the denim, as I thought about the sounds she made as she came.

***Me: On my way...***

Just as I was about to shove my phone in my pocket and climb on the bike, she replied.

***Sexy Fugitive: Now?!?!***

***Me: On my way, and I won't take no for an answer this time. I'm bringing my handcuffs too.***

***Sexy Fugitive: Fuck.***

***Me: Two hours, Izzy, and you're mine.***

I didn't wait for her reply. I put the phone on vibrate, placing it in my back pocket. Throttling the engine, I thought about her screaming my name, and took off toward the only woman who felt right in my arms.

She'd be mine tonight.

Her days of running were over.

***

I pulled into Izzy's drive just after midnight. Her sleek black Infiniti sat in the driveway, and the front porch light illuminated my pathway to her pussy.

I almost expected her not to be home. That would be something she'd do. She'd avoid me and play hard to get, denying herself the one thing she was too stubborn to admit.

I turned off my bike, stretching as I climbed off, and then secured it for the night. I didn't plan on leaving until the next morning at the earliest, but I hoped to stay the whole weekend.

It was rare for me to have this kind of time off in my line of work, but since returning from Bike Week, the club had been lying low and things had been calm. I'd been told by my supervisor to take some R&R for the weekend and be ready to hit it hard when I returned on Monday. His ideas of R&R were different than mine—mine did include hitting it hard. I planned to fuck Izzy until she couldn't even remember her name, let alone her smartass attitude.

I knocked gently, trying not to startle her even though she knew I was on my way. I heard voices and rustling inside, and I leaned in, trying to hear their words.

"You better get the hell out of here," Izzy said, her voice muffled by the thick wooden door, but I could still make them out.

My heart started to pound so hard I felt like I'd just run a forty. My mind started to race with thoughts that someone was inside and it wasn't me.

"Izzy!" I yelled as I banged on the door. "Open up!"

"Go, Flash. I won't ask again!" Izzy yelled, quieter this time, but loud enough that I heard with my ear pressed up against the door.

Hearing his name made my blood run cold. I knew exactly who the little prick was. Flash was a prospect in the MC Thomas had been working undercover in for over two years. Flash was also the cocksucker who'd brought Izzy to Daytona and thrown her to the wolves.

"Fuck no," he replied. "I'm staying right here. We're going to have a little chat."

I'd had enough. I was getting in the house if I had to bust down the motherfucking door. Leaning back, I shouted, "Izzy, I'm going to bust this door down if you don't open the fuck up!" I pounded on the wood, the door jumping under my fist.

"Coming!" Izzy sang, her shoes clicking against the wood floors as she moved closer.

I needed to calm myself. Murder wouldn't be the best way to start the weekend.

As soon as she opened the door, I took quick stock of her appearance. She looked unharmed and calm, but maybe a little frustrated.

"Izzy, what the fuck is going on?" I barked, looking over her head to see a pair of boots resting on her coffee table. "What the hell is he doing here?" I touched her cheek, caressing her skin with the pad of my thumb.

"He's harmless, James." She looked at my face but didn't make eye contact.

"Izzy." I gripped the back of her neck, forcing her eyes to mine. "He's not harmless. I know exactly who he is, and he's leaving your house with or without my help."

"No," she pleaded, placing her hand on my chest.

"Yes, doll, he is." I released her, grabbing her shoulders and picking her up as I moved her out of the way.

The door closed behind me, her heels clattering as she followed me. I rounded the corner, getting a full view of Flash leaning back on the couch, his arms outstretched and his feet up. "I think the lady asked you to leave," I growled as I fisted my hands at my sides.

I didn't want to spill blood and break shit in Izzy's home. Breaking shit from hot fucking, I enjoyed. Doing it to beat some punk's ass? Not so much.

"I came here to speak to you," he answered as he rose to his feet and looked at Izzy before turning to me with a smile. "Man to man."

I stepped closer to him, breaking his line of sight with Izzy. "I have nothing to say to a piece of shit like you." My voice echoed in the house, the wood floors carrying it throughout the open space.

"There are things I need to explain," he said.

"James," Izzy begged, grabbing my arm from behind. "Just talk to him." Her face was soft, all smartass gone. This was Izzy

87

asking me to do something I didn't want to do. Not one fucking bit.

I looked over my shoulder, staring in her eyes, and nodded. I turned back toward Flash. "You got five minutes and then I'm showing you the fucking door."

"Outside." He started to walk toward the French doors that led to a staircase to the backyard.

"Wait for me in your room," I ordered, holding her by the arms. "If shit gets bad, I don't want to worry about where you are."

"James, really. I'm a big girl." She smiled, crossing her arms over her chest.

"I never said you weren't. This is for my sanity. I'll let him speak his piece and I'll fill you in when I come up."

"I don't like being told what to do," she hissed, pulling away from my grip.

I rubbed my face. The woman could be trying at times. "I'm asking you to please do this for me."

She nodded, glaring at me as she walked down the hallway, and disappeared in her bedroom. I made a beeline to the backyard, ready to get Flash the fuck gone.

"Make it quick and get the hell out," I grunted as I descended the stairs and stopped in front of Flash. "You have two minutes to convince me why I shouldn't beat the fuck out of you."

"You don't know who I am," he growled, moving a step closer to me.

"I know exactly who you are."

He shook his head and reached into his back pocket. "You don't."

"I know all I need to." I kept my eyes trained on his hand, ready to fight back if he pulled a weapon.

"I know you're law enforcement, James. DEA to be exact," he replied as he pulled a black wallet from his pocket.

My stomach sank as he spoke. That information was a closely guarded secret. I wondered if he knew about Thomas.

"How do you know that?" I asked, stepping closer to him.

He flipped open the wallet, flashing an ID and badge at me.

"I'm FBI," he whispered. "Not many people know that about me. Not even Izzy. I live the life and I'm totally immersed."

"Fuck," I grumbled, raking my hands through my hair.

"I'm prospecting, trying to make a name for myself within the club. I'm not supposed to take a dominant position inside. I'm their ears and eyes on the inside."

"How the fuck didn't I know this?" I asked as my nostrils flared and my anger turned toward the law enforcement branch of the US government.

"My boss thought it would be better if I was treated like everyone else." He swallowed, turning his back to me. "I only found out about you and Thomas"—he paused—"when Blue took Izzy out of the bar."

"How could you be so reckless?"

"I know, I know. I didn't think shit would go down like that." He shook his head as his shoulders rose and fell.

"Reckless as hell, Flash."

"Sheer stupidity. I have no other excuse." He sighed.

"How did you find out about us?" I didn't understand how he knew about us but we had no fucking clue about him.

"When she left with him, I freaked the fuck out and went to my contact. Immediately, my supervisor was informed and they called me in. I was told about the two of you and reassured that Izzy was safe."

"That's all it took, huh?"

"Listen," he said, turning back to face me. "That girl in there?" He pointed toward the house and continued. "I love her. There's no one like her. I know she'll never be mine, but fuck, I'd kill for her." He closed his eyes, regaining his composure. "They were worried I'd blow my cover and start ripping shit up to find her."

"You love her?" I repeated, glaring at him as my heart started to pick up speed, the sound of blood gushing through my ears.

"I do," Flash responded, rubbing the bridge of his nose.

"Fuck me," I muttered.

"James, she doesn't want me. She never has. We've been friends since we were kids. We'll never be anything more."

I felt bad for Flash. To love a woman and not have the feeling returned had to be fucking gut wrenching, but there was something he wasn't saying.

"You've fucked her?" I inquired, trying to contain my rage.

"That's not important. We're only friends," he answered quickly, holding his hands up. "I'm not a threat, James."

"All men are threats," I growled.

"Not me. I'm too busy building my career and focusing on my work right now. Plus, I know when I'm not wanted. She's all yours."

"All mine?" I laughed. "You must not know her as well as you think you do, bud."

He shook his head, kicking at the dirt. "She told me tonight when I came by that she wouldn't see me anymore. She dropped your name and I tuned out. Izzy has never spoken of another man. Don't listen to her bullshit. She acts tough as nails, but she's a powder puff."

His words shocked me. Izzy had talked about me... mentioned me when breaking off contact with Flash. One of us was being bullshitted, and I hoped it was me. I knew she wanted me physically, but maybe, just maybe, there was more to us. Either way, I'd do whatever I could to convince her to give us a shot.

What could go wrong?

The connection we had, the lust I felt, and the current that surged between us couldn't be ignored any longer. I'd make sure of it.

# CHAPTER 10
# HARD TO SWALLOW

IZZY

AS I WATCHED from the window, Flash and James talked, and it didn't seem to be a pissing match. My heart raced as they'd stood toe to toe in my backyard. I'd expected it to go down very differently. I had figured one of them would end up bloodied before it was said and done. Who the fuck was I kidding? Flash would've been the one a heaping pile of broken bones after James had beaten him. Instead, they'd acted like grown men. They'd spoken low enough that I hadn't been able to make out the words, even after cracking my window to be able to hear better, and the handshake at the end had sure as fuck thrown me for a loop.

No fists were thrown, Flash disappeared between the houses, and James made his way up the stairs and back into the house. I walked down the hallway toward the kitchen as I heard the back door close. "Everything okay?" I asked as I turned the corner and almost ran right into James.

He was grinning with his head tilted and the corner of his mouth curved. He looked proud with his chest puffed out. Any moment, he might have broken out with "Me Tarzan" by the way he carried himself. His eyes were fiery yet playful.

"Perfect," he whispered, grabbing my chin.

My belly sank—but in the most wonderful way—as he held my face in his hands. I felt his hot, sweet breath against my skin, and the small hairs on the back of my neck stood up. Just like when you're waiting for something that you know will scare the holy fuck out of you to happen—James was my holy fuck. He scared the piss out of me.

"Izzy," he growled.

"Yes?" I responded, my voice weak.

"You want me?" His eyes pierced me, held me in place even though my mind was screaming for me to run.

I looked down, unable to maintain eye contact, or maybe I just didn't want to look into the eyes of the boogeyman. "Yes," I whispered, placing my hand on his muscular forearm. I needed the extra support when saying those words. Letting James in was the biggest leap of faith I'd ever taken in my life. I just hoped there wasn't a rocky bottom I'd dive into headfirst.

"Just give me tonight," he breathed, moving his lips closer as he kept his eyes locked on mine.

"One night," I said with wide eyes as I swallowed hard. I felt like my airway was closing and I couldn't breathe.

"Just feel me, Izzy. Feel us and how our bodies respond to each other."

He didn't wait for me to respond as he crushed his lips to mine. He gave me the air I hadn't been able to find moments before. Wrapping his arms around me, he pulled me close and held the back of my head.

"James," I moaned into his mouth as his hand grabbed my ass, squeezing it roughly.

He pulled away, grinding his rock-hard dick into me. "I'm not taking no for an answer tonight. I barely survived last week-end, having you so close and not sinking my dick into you. It's heaven, and I won't let you deny me again."

Well fuck. How could I say no to that? Shit, I didn't want to say no. The man did me better than anyone ever had. The entire week, all I'd thought about was him. The asshole had even invaded my dreams. I tried to put him out of my mind when I was awake, but once I closed my eyes, my subconscious took over, and it, along with my extremely wet pussy, both wanted James.

Pushing me against the wall, he placed his lips against my neck and nibbled just below my ear. Goose bumps broke out across my flesh as tingles cascaded across my skin like water drops finding their path to my feet and rooting me in place. I clawed at his t-shirt, wanting to feel his skin. When I pulled it up, my knuckles skimmed his ribs.

As he sucked in a breath, he stole the air in my lungs. Releasing me, he pulled the shirt off his body, revealing his mouth-watering chest. I placed my palms against his hard pecs, kneading the muscles with my fingers as he kissed a path down the opening of my tank top. His hands found my thighs, looping underneath. As my feet left the floor, I wrapped my legs around his torso, grinding my pussy against him. He carried me down the hall, his lips back on mine, as he held me tight against his body.

His grip lessened just over the threshold of my bedroom doorway, causing me to slide down him. I grinned, looking into his eyes and seeing the desire on his face.

He took a step back, crossing his arms and cocking his head. "Strip," he commanded.

My body swayed as his words hit me like a ton of bricks. "What?" I blurted, shocked by the forcefulness in his voice.

"Strip, and make it good." He didn't move or change expression.

"Excuse me? Is that any way to talk to a lady?" I barked, kind of turned on but not willing to share that little nugget of information.

I glared at him, my eyes raking over his body and stopping dead on his crotch. I could clearly see the outline of his long, thick cock straining against the material. I knew how it felt to have that monster inside me, and it made my mind mush. I started to slowly take down the straps of my tank top without waiting for his response.

"Don't I get music or something?" I quipped, cockiness in my voice as I removed the material from my arms. I turned as I gathered the tank in my hands. Bending at the waist, I stuck my ass in the air as I shimmed out of my shirt and then tossed it

93

across the room. Shaking my hips, I started to hum as my ass bounced, and I peeked at him between the gap in my legs.

He leaned against the wall with his arms crossed, and studied me. He seemed pleased with what I was doing. Turning around, I held my hands over my breasts, covering my hard nipples as I shook them in my hands. Bouncing them in my hands, I licked the top of my breast. The skin feeling like velvet against my tongue.

"Fuck," he hissed, his lips turning up into a snarl as his nostrils flared.

My body warmed from his reaction, and I felt a sense of confidence in my movements. Stripping for someone when it's your idea is entirely different than doing it when being told to. James's reaction made it fun, and I figured why the fuck not tease him in the process?

"You like when I cocktease you?" I asked, opening my fingers, letting my nipples show. A black lace bra covered my breasts, leaving little to the imagination. I rolled my nipples in between my fingers as I licked a path to my other breast, peeking up at him through hooded lashes.

"Lose the clothes, Isabella."

He dropped my formal name, once again causing the bottom of my stomach to flutter.

"Yes, master," I responded, curtseying to him and unable to hold my smartass comments.

His face changed as he squinted at me. "Those words make me so fucking hard," he whispered.

Was James one of *those* men? Was he the type of guy who got off on being in total control and wanting a sex slave in the bedroom?

After I peeled off my pants, leaving nothing between him and me except my lace black panties and bra, I stood still, my tongue sticking out as it hovered just above my breast. I wanted to be touched, and if he wouldn't do it, then I sure as fuck would be the one to take up the task.

"Crawl to me," he demanded.

I shrugged, thinking, *What the hell? Why not?* and dropped

to my knees. Moving slowly across the wooden floor, I crawled to him like a cat stalking its prey. Sticking my ass up in the air, I raised my shoulders as I approached him.

Funny that I didn't feel weird or humiliated crawling to him as he'd asked. It turned me on, and from what I could see from being eye to eye with his dick, he was hard as a rock.

"Unzip me," he said, his voice softer.

I looked up at him, taking a moment to drink him in. Yeah, I was totally fucked. Perching up on my knees, I pulled his zipper down, releasing his cock.

It was bigger than I remembered, especially up close. Then again, I might have had half a bottle of Jack by the time we'd ripped each other's clothes off in the hotel room.

Palming his thickness, I stuck my tongue out, capturing the small drop of liquid off the tip. Divine saltiness spread across my tongue as I leaned in to take him in my mouth.

"Wait," he said, grabbing my face with his hands.

"James," I groaned, leaning back on my heels to look up at him. "Make up your mind."

"No hands. I want only your mouth on me," he growled. This was a side of James I hadn't expected, but I liked it.

I nodded, gripping his thighs with my hands before I slid his jeans down his legs to give me better access to his hardness. The hair lying across my back moved as he wrapped his hand around it, fisting it tightly. Small tingles started at my neck before shooting down my spine and straight to my core. I ached to be filled by him, and would do whatever it took to have him thrust me over a cliff of ecstasy.

I gripped his firm, muscular thighs, placing my fingers just below his ass. I dug my nails into his flesh. He hissed, sucking in air as I swirled my tongue around his piercing. The metal felt soft compared to his throbbing cock as I slid the length of him across my tongue until it touched the back of my throat. I gagged slightly, pulling him out to relieve my body's reflex to repel the contents.

"Take all of me. You can do it." He thrust his hips forward, jamming his cock to the back of my throat.

My eyes watered as my ability to breathe was cut off from the foreign object filling my mouth. He gripped my hair roughly, pulling his cock from my lips before sliding it in over and over again. His grunts and moans spurred me on and kept me focused.

Drool pooled at the corners of my mouth, slowly oozing from the sides as he pummeled my throat with his rock-hard dick. Tears streamed down my cheeks, my fingers digging into my skin as I took the torture, wishing it were my pussy on the receiving end of the blunt force trauma.

Just as I felt his cock grow bigger, filling my mouth further, he moaned, "Fuck." Then he pulled my hair back, releasing his dick from my mouth. "Not yet. Not like this," he moaned on a shaky breath. His fingers slipped from my hair and slid across my face, capturing the moisture from my chin. "You're so fucking sexy right now."

I blinked, wondered how I possibly looked sexy. I had drool on my face, blurry eyes, and tear-stained cheeks. That didn't fit my idea of fuckable, but then again, I didn't have a cock.

A thought occurred to me as I kneeled before James. I thought women who acted like I just had—following sexual commands without question—were weak, but that's not what I'd felt. I'd felt empowered and in control. Even though James barked out the orders, I was the one to carry them out, and I held his world in my hands—or in this case, my mouth.

A small smile spread across my face as I used my tongue to grab the moisture from the corners of my mouth. His eyes zoned in on my tongue as his cock bobbed. "Fuck, Izzy," he hissed, holding his hand out to me. "Off your knees before I lose control staring at that fuckable mouth."

I grabbed his hand, letting him pull me from the floor, and slid up his body. My tits rubbed against his skin. Feeling the hardness against my throbbing nipples sent a shiver through my body. Having him in my mouth and remembering our first night together had driven my body so close to the edge that I knew it wouldn't take much for me to come.

I stared in his eyes as he held my face in his palm and my neck in his grip. Just as I was about to start rubbing my pussy against his leg, unable to bear waiting any longer, his free hand glided down my body toward the promised land. I silently thanked the gods for taking pity on me. As his fingers slid through my wetness and his palm massaged my clit, my head fell back and my body moved forward on its own.

"James," I moaned as I slid my hands up his arms and dug my nails into his shoulders.

"You're so fucking wet," he murmured.

His finger rubbed my G-spot, driving me closer to the thing I wanted most—an orgasm. A second finger joined the first, stretching me and making me feel full as the others stroked my outer parts. Shivers racked my body as he worked my pussy to the point where, at times, he stole my breath. The pressure was so intense that I could barely form a thought. Wetness and warmth filled my senses as he licked a path up my neck, stopping at the spot where I could feel my pulse beating rapidly under his tongue.

"James." It was the only thing I could say. My mind had become muddled. Everything in my body was tight and ready. I pushed up on my tiptoes, trying to get more leverage and work his fingers deeper inside me.

His hand stilled. "You want my cock?" he whispered against my neck.

I nodded my response. I wanted to come, but I wouldn't mince words with him putting me so close to an orgasm that I felt like I would explode.

"You just want to come," he grunted, pushing my neck forward and forcing my eyes to his.

Heat crept across my face as I looked into his eyes. It pissed me off that he could read me so well. I'd prided myself on being unreadable my entire life, but James had an ability that unnerved me.

"I want you," I pleaded, nipping at his lips.

His fingers began to move at a torturous pace. Slowly, he rubbed my insides as he pulled out and pushed back in with force, but kept his palm clear of my clit.

"Tell me what you want," he insisted, digging his fingers in my neck.

"I want you to fuck me." I could feel the buildup again as my pussy clenched down on his fingers, trying to keep him inside.

"Ask me nicely." He smirked against my lips as his cheeks rose, almost touching his eyes as his hand stilled again.

I sighed, knowing that there was only one way to get what I wanted. I could fuck around and play a game with his mind. I knew he wanted me as much as I wanted him. The proof of that was pressed against my hip.

"James, will you fuck me?" I asked, not breaking eye contact.

"Please," he said before nipping at my jaw and massaging my insides without the in-and-out motion I fucking craved.

He wanted me to beg—something I'd never done for anyone in my life. People begged me. I'd never wanted anything enough to beg. If I couldn't get it for myself, then it wasn't worth having or lusting after.

James was different. He was something I couldn't get without groveling and giving more of myself than I wanted to. I was too close to coming to turn back now and tell him to get the fuck out of my house. A small part of me wanted to tell him to take his junk and leave, but the part I wanted to punch in the face later said, "Please fuck me, James. I want you." Fucking traitorous words. Later, I'd kick my own ass.

His smirk turned into a smile as his fingers slipped out of me. He placed the fingers that had just been inside me into his mouth, and swirled his tongue around them. "Mmm," he murmured as he licked my juices off. "You taste fucking fantastic. Just how I remember."

"You're an asshole. If you're getting your rocks off by making me beg and then you're just going to—" I didn't get to finish the sentence, as he moved my face to his and swallowed my words with his lips.

When he backed away, I was breathless and wanton. I would've professed my love and a horde of children to this man for a single orgasm. He'd driven me so close and then pulled away so many times that I no longer was Izzy Gallo, kick-ass chick—I was Izzy Gallo, cock slave to James. I only mildly hated myself for it.

I swayed as he removed his pants, dug in his pocket, and then discarded his jeans to the side. James stood before me, naked and magnificent, with a giant, cocky-ass smile on his face. As he slipped on the condom, I took in his hotness. He had the entire goddamn package—piercings, tattoos, rock-hard muscles, and a beautiful fucking cock. The only downside to James that I could think of was his mouth, but even though I wanted to smack it sometimes, it did crazy fucking things to me. Things I didn't like to admit.

Before I could move, he lifted me with one arm under my ass and impaled me on his cock with a grunt.

"Fuckin' heaven," he moaned, pushing farther inside.

All negative thoughts about the smug bastard standing gloriously naked in front of me vanished as his piercing stroked me from the inside. Turning us, he pounded into me as he pushed my back against the wall.

Using his arm and the solid surface behind me, he battered my body. Drawing my nipple into his mouth, he drove my body higher, granting him deeper access to my pussy and bringing my tits closer to his face.

As he bit down, I hissed, "Fuck." The pain was soon forgotten as his strokes increased and the mounting pressure returned, more intense than before.

I clawed at his flesh, scraping his skin, as he pounded me into the wall with each blow. He grunted, moaning against my nipples as he sucked and bit on the tender skin.

My eyes found the mirror across the room. There was just enough light for me to clearly see his body as he thrust inside me. His ass cheeks clenched and released as he pushed himself deep, driving me closer to the edge. My arms were wrapped around his torso as I stared at our reflection. The pink streaks caused by my fingernails were visible clear across the room.

Watching him fuck me, and the feeling of his dick slamming into me, made it impossible to stave off the impending orgasm.

"Fuck yes!" I screamed, hitting my head against the wall. "Harder!" I demanded.

My toes curled as his fingers gripped my ass and his cock pulverized my pussy in long, thick strokes.

He released my nipples, pulling my body down harder on his cock. He moved his mouth next to my ear and said, "Come for me, Izzy. I want to feel you squeeze the life out of my dick."

All the muscles in my body grew rigid as he moved his hands to my waist, forcefully pulling me down against his cock. I bounced off his body like a rag doll. Everything around me ceased to exist except James and his dick.

My nails slid against his skin, tearing the flesh as I screamed through the best fucking orgasm of my life. I mumbled and chanted like a person in a trance as one orgasm passed and another started to build.

"Don't you dare come again," he growled, pulling me from the wall and walking toward the bed.

My eyes flew open as I stared at him. "What?" I asked, swallowing hard and trying to catch my breath.

"Not yet, doll. Not like this," he groaned as he stilled inside me.

As we approached the bed and he started to lay me back, I wrapped my legs tighter around him. My pussy ached from the devastation he'd just inflicted upon it, but I wanted more.

"Let go," he ordered as he released me and pulled at my legs.

"No," I cried, pulling him in deeper and increasing my vise-like grip.

He looked down at me and smiled. "Such a selfish girl," he whispered as he ran his fingers over my lips, tracing a path down my body.

His fingers stopped at my breasts, circling around each one, as his fingernail scraped against my nipple.

"I'm not selfish, James, I'm horny." The first orgasm, even in its intensity, hadn't done enough to quell the ache and throb I felt when I was around him. His fingers, mouth, and dick made me want more. That was exactly why I'd done the walk of shame out of his hotel room months ago. He scared me.

"Izzy," he barked, bringing my attention back to him as he pried my legs apart. "Flip over, beautiful. I'm not done with you yet."

My pussy convulsed with his words. That divine clenching of both happiness and anticipation. I shifted, and he slipped from my body. A dull ache was left by the emptiness inside me as he walked away.

"How do you want me?" Why I asked this question, I had no fucking clue. Did it matter?

He bent down next to his pants, and the sound of metal clinking filled the room. My heart stopped in my chest as I closed my eyes and knew what he grabbed. I looked over my shoulder, finding him approaching the bed as he twirled them around his finger.

"I brought these just for you." He leaned over, touching my skin with the cold metal, and dragged it down my spine.

I sucked in a breath, the sensation intense against my hot damn skin. I closed my eyes, enjoying the feel of the icy hardware, and when I opened them, James had a very smug grin on his face.

"Hands behind your back, Isabella." He smirked—as he probably assumed I'd do just about anything right now.

"What are you going to do?" I asked, more concerned with him leaving than anything he'd do to me physically.

"I'm going to get mine now," he said, holding the handcuffs in the air with one hand as he stroked his condom-covered cock in the other. "You want this?" he asked, fisting it rapidly and looking down at his dick. "Then you'll get these." He shook the cuffs, causing them to make a loud clatter.

"Promise you won't leave?" I pleaded, needing to be sure before I handed over total control. Before, when I'd crawled to him and let him fuck my face, that hadn't been giving him free rein, but being restrained and naked left me vulnerable and at his mercy.

"I'd never do that. I want to bury myself inside you until I can't fuck you anymore. Hands," he commanded.

I swallowed, placing my hands behind my back and burying

my face in the comforter. He moved quickly, grabbing my body and pushing me up the bed. Before I could respond, a cuff was around my left wrist and attached to the headboard. The bed dipped and rose as he climbed off and back to his feet.

My stomach sank. The nasty feeling of being duped entered my bones. "Where the fuck are you going?" I snarled, panicking as a lump formed in my throat as he bent down.

As he stood, he said, "To get these," and jiggled another set of handcuffs in his hand.

"Thank shit for small miracles," I whispered low enough so he wouldn't hear. I turned forward, feeling the bed dip as he returned and hovered over my body.

"Give me your hand," he said, holding out his with the handcuff in his grip.

I sighed, reaching out and willingly giving my hand to him. Butterflies filled my stomach as he restrained my right arm to the headboard. I lay there splayed out before him, for his enjoyment and use.

He pushed my hair to the side, biting down on my neck as he slid down my body. His hard shaft left a trail of tingles as he glided across my skin. I looked over my shoulder to see him kneeling between my legs.

"Mmm, so fucking beautiful," he groaned as he squeezed my ass roughly, kneading it in his grip. "I want this."

Closing my eyes tight, I said, "James."

There was no fucking way his dick would go in my ass. No goddamn way. He was too fucking big for that to happen. I started to thrash as he spread apart my ass cheeks, rubbing his thumb over my opening. My body locked up, my ass clenching to stop the assault. I'd let him restrain me. I'd given up complete control.

"You'll love it," he replied as wetness filled my crack.

"Where did you—" I started to ask, but as his fingertip pushed inside, my mouth quickly shut.

Pain sliced through me for a moment and was replaced by a fullness I hadn't anticipated. James had huge hands and, in turn, thick, long fingers.

"I'll make it feel good," he whispered, working his finger inside me as he began to stroke my pussy opening with his other hand.

I'd had anal sex before. I even enjoyed it, but something about James and his size scared the shit out of me. My palms began to sweat; the thought of the pain as he filled me made me nervous.

My eyes rolled back in my head, the pleasure making it impossible to keep a watchful eye on him. I pushed against his hand, needing the pleasure of his fingers pounding into my pussy to forget the burn in my ass. More wetness fell against me before he added a second finger in my ass, driving me over the pain-pleasure threshold. Too many feelings were mixed in my body as my mind turned off from all thought or ability to yell stop.

They worked out of unison from each other. As he moved one hand in my pussy and the other out of my ass, I found myself spiraling dangerously close to an orgasm I thought would stop my heart. The pleasure building up from deep inside had my heart pounding uncontrollably. This could be the destroyer of all men who might grace my future. James was wrecking me and doing it on fucking purpose.

My hands moved, trying to grip on to something to ground myself, but it was futile. I couldn't reach a fucking thing, and I didn't have the strength to shimmy up the bed as he worked my body perfectly.

A moan fell from my lips even as I tried to bite back the words. "Oh, yes. Fuck me, James."

Just then, his fingers left my ass. I buried my face into the bed, both happy and relieved at the loss of fullness. I mumbled something incoherent even to myself as he still thrust his fingers inside my cunt.

Scooping more wetness from my pussy, he rubbed my juices against my ass before jamming his cock into my pussy.

"Still so fucking wet," he said, moving his face close to my ear. "I want your ass, Izzy."

I sucked in a breath, fear gripping me because of his size.

"James," I moaned. I wanted to say no, but everything the man did to me felt fanfuckingtastic.

A few thrusts later, he removed himself from my core and rubbed against my asshole. As he pushed the tip inside, I whispered, "You're too big," and bit down on the comforter.

"It'll fit. You're so fucking ready for me."

Problem was, he was fucking right. I didn't like when James was always right.

"Push out. It'll make it slide in easier," he grunted, placing his hand underneath me and stroking my clit.

"Fuck," I moaned, pushing down with all my strength as he circled my clit with his fingertips. "Yes," I wailed.

I pulled at the handcuffs, wrapping my fingers around the cold metal chain connecting the two parts, and took what he gave me.

"Fuck," he moaned, seating himself fully inside of me.

I moved, grinding my pussy against his hand and hoping it would urge him to move. The only thing worse than being fucked in the ass was someone stopping with their dick inside you. I needed the movement and the friction against my pussy. I needed to come. My body was wound so fucking tight I thought my heart would burst.

"Selfish," he whispered, his hot breath licking my ear as he began to rock in and out of me.

"Just fuck me and shut the fuck up," I hissed, pushing back against him.

His palm came down fast on my hip as he slapped it hard enough to cause me to focus on another point of pain. "You're not the boss anymore, Izzy. I am." His words surprised me more than his palm, and the funny thing was...I liked it.

"Yes, sir," I spouted back, feeling the need to be a smartass.

"Always have to be such a tough-ass," he grunted, gripping my hip and thrusting inside me. He pinched my clit and rolled it between his fingers.

I cried out. The orgasm that had built broke loose. I screamed until my throat was sore and my voice hoarse. I grew limp, my body and mind both sated and in post-orgasmic bliss, as his thrusts grew more punishing.

I squeezed my eyes shut, praying for his release and my freedom. My body couldn't take much more of James and come back unscathed. His movements became sporadic as he hissed, "Fuck," and collapsed against my back.

Our bodies were slick with sweat as he lay on top of me, crushing me against the mattress.

"Jesus," he murmured between labored breaths.

I moved, his dick feeling like an unwelcome guest.

He shifted, pulling his cock from my body as he rolled off me. "Sorry," he said as he stroked my ass with his fingertips.

"James, let me go," I whispered, and yanked at the handcuffs.

"I may keep you like this all night." He traced a path up my ass cheeks to my spine. "I like you so willing and ready."

I glared at him, turning my head in his direction. "My arms are getting numb," I bit out, trying to not yell.

"I'll never believe your bullshit." He laughed, climbing off the bed.

"Where the fuck are you going?" I roared, worried he'd leave me like this all night.

"Getting the fucking key," he responded, bending down and retrieving it from his jeans pocket.

"Oh," I mumbled, feeling like a fool.

As he climbed on the bed, the mattress dipped, much like my stomach from his nearness. As he released my arms, he rubbed my muscles and eased the tension inside. The feeling of his strong hands massaging my limbs felt amazing.

"Mmm, so fucking good," I muttered as he continued the same treatment on my other arm.

"Stay here. I'll be right back."

I watched as his beautiful, tight ass walked to the bathroom until he closed the door. Hearing water running, I closed my eyes and thought about James. I was currently in the love phase of the love-hate relationship I had with him, but I was certain that, soon enough, the orgasmic haze I was in would wear off and I'd slide on the other side of that thin line.

I cracked open an eye as the door opened. He was approaching the bed with a washcloth. "Let me clean you," he whispered, crawling next to me in bed.

Without speaking, I opened my legs and relaxed. The warmth of the towel against my pussy and ass relived the throbbing I'd felt a moment ago. His cock had been brutal, but his kindness and the fucking orgasm made it all worth the abuse.

"Ouch," I hissed as he pressed it against my asshole.

"It'll help. Just lie still," he whispered, working the soft cloth against my skin.

I did as he'd said without a fight. I didn't have the energy to argue with James tonight.

Leaving the washcloth against me, he stood and pulled back a corner of the sheets. "Up you go," he said, cradling me.

I wrapped my arms around him, rubbing my nose against his neck, and inhaled. He smelled like musk, sweat, and sex.

He placed my head on the pillow, climbed over top of me, and settled in the bed. After covering us, he cocooned me in his arms.

With my back to his torso, I closed my eyes and exhaled. My eyes were heavy as I blinked, straining to keep them open.

"Sleep, sweet Izzy," he whispered, increasing his grip around my body.

I drifted off, listening to his breathing in my ear, blissfully sated and exhausted.

James would be the death of me.

# CHAPTER 11
# FINDING AN INROAD

JAMES

I WOKE the next morning to Izzy's light snores in my ear. During the night, she'd shifted, turning her face toward me and wrapping her body around mine. Now, we were in the same position with her face buried in my chest.

I didn't want to move. Izzy looked sweet and almost angelic lying in my arms, curled around me. I knew that, the moment her eyes opened, her wicked tongue and smartass words would be nonstop. The girl needed to stop running—or at least pretending to.

I never believed in love at first sight. Lust, yes, but not love. The problem was that I did love Izzy Gallo. She wasn't like other women who'd spent time in my bed; she was in a class all her own.

I didn't have to peel back the layers to find out who the real Izzy was. Her brother had already told me almost everything I needed to know about her. He had shared pictures with me, told me stories about his wild sister, and sung her praises for years. I had seen the fire in her eyes when I stared at her picture and listened to him talk about her. Meeting her in person had brought it all to life.

I loved her spirit. She grabbed life by the balls and played by no one's rules but her own. I wanted a woman who would challenge me. Ladies caved too easily and gave no chase, but not Isabella. She was my prime target.

I eased her body away from mine, sliding out of bed to make a pot of coffee and some breakfast. I wanted to start the morning off on the right foot. If she hadn't been so exhausted last night, I was sure she would've had a few choice words to hurl in my direction.

Sliding on my jeans, I looked at the bed and Izzy sprawled out amongst the dark sheets. The material hung just below her belly button and her breasts were uncovered, a tangle of brown locks framing her body. I wanted to crawl back in bed and wake her with my dick, but I knew she had to be sore from the pummeling I'd given her last night. I wanted her to remember where I'd been and how I felt filling her from the inside. Izzy Gallo wouldn't be forgetting my territory for days.

I checked the coffee maker, the grounds and water already inside, and pushed the "on" button before heading outside to my bike. I grabbed the bag I'd packed, hoping I'd be spending a couple of days here, and stopped to look around the neighborhood.

A light fog covered the houses in the distance and hadn't broken up yet from the sun. The birds chirped as a few people milled around the neighborhood walking their dogs and hurrying off to God knows where at this time of day.

The aroma of freshly brewed coffee hit me as soon as I walked back into the house. I needed to clean up before the princess woke from her slumber.

After washing my face and brushing my teeth, I grabbed two cups of coffee and headed to the bedroom. Izzy hadn't moved while I was gone. I set the cups on the nightstand and kicked off my jeans, setting my phone on the nightstand. Once I'd crawled back in bed, I stretched out next to her and stared for a few minutes before I stroked her skin.

It was as smooth as silk and free from imperfections. Her long, dark lashes rested against her cheeks while she slept. I traced her lips with my fingers, restraining myself from devouring her whole. I kissed her softly, enjoying the velvety feel of them against mine until she began to stir. Her eyes fluttered open as her lips turned up into a small smile.

"Good morning," I whispered against her lips.

"Good morning," she said after turning her face away from mine and yawning.

"Sleep well?" I moved the hair away from her neck and planted a light kiss against her pulse.

"I'm so tired," she mumbled, curling against my body and drifting back to sleep.

"Izzy," I whispered, kissing her cheek.

"No," she moaned without opening her eyes.

"I brought you coffee." I ran my fingertips over her skin, tracing tiny circles and watching a line of goose bumps break out across her skin.

"What time is it?" she groaned, rubbing her eyes.

"A little after eight."

"Why are you up so early?"

"I don't need much sleep."

Her blinks were slow as she stared up at me. "Did I hear you say coffee?" she asked with a groggy voice.

"I brought you a cup just how you like it."

"I don't want to move," she said, closing her eyes.

I pulled her body against me and stroked her hair. "Just sleep. We have all day," I whispered.

"Wait. What?" she asked as her body stiffened in my arms.

"I have all weekend off. I'm all yours for forty-eight blissful hours." I smiled, biting my lip as I waited for her to freak out.

To my shock, her body relaxed and melted into mine. "Good. I can go back to sleep," she said, closing her eyes and making noises of pleasure as I caressed her back.

Her breathing slowed as she drifted back to sleep. I held her, stroking her body as she snored softly. I'd expected her to throw me out or have a fit when I said that I'd be here for the entire weekend, but to my surprise, she'd fallen back to sleep.

That was the thing about Izzy. She was a woman full of surprises. I couldn't nail down what her reaction to anything would be. She kept me on my toes, and for that, I'd be more than happy to keep her on the edge of her seat.

Just as I was about to drift off to sleep myself, my phone beeped and startled me. Izzy didn't move when I jumped or when I rolled backward to grab my phone.

Tapping the screen, I saw a message in my inbox.

**Thomas: Checking in. Quiet week. Hope you're doing something more fun than I am.**

Fuck. A wave of guilt rolled over me, settling deep in my stomach. Thomas was risking his life while I was busy fucking his sister. I couldn't admit it to him, at least not yet.

**Me: Good. Took the weekend off.**

No reply came, as was usually the case. One message a week was what we were allowed before he'd wipe his phone clean of any remnants of our communication.

Izzy stirred in my arms, touching my face. "Everything okay?" she asked.

"Never better." I turned off the screen and tossed the phone toward the end of the bed.

"Did you say something before about the entire weekend?" she yawned.

"Yep. I'm all yours," I replied, kissing her forehead.

"Um, I have to work today." Her body shook in my arms as she stretched.

"I'd love to see the shop."

"Wouldn't you rather do something else?" She pulled from my grip.

"I'll find something to do today after I drop you off. We can go out later when you're done."

"I work late, though."

"Don't you own the joint?"

"Well, yeah."

"Maybe you can get off early."

"I was hoping to get off now," she said, and laughed, covering her mouth with her hand.

I inched closer, bringing my body to hers. "That I can do," I growled in her ear.

"James," she said, pushing against my chest.

"Hmm mmm." I nibbled on her ear before nipping a path down her neck.

She moaned as I bit down on the tender flesh above her collarbone. Using my tongue, I tasted her skin as I captured her nipple in my mouth and sucked hard, flicking it.

"Keep going." She laughed and dug her fingers in my hair.

Izzy and I stayed in bed for a couple of hours, feasting on each other and drifting back to sleep. Finally, after showering, we were ready to head to the tattoo parlor a little after noon.

As she locked the door, she turned to me and said, "James, I've never brought anyone to the shop." She kicked at the ground with her right foot and looked down.

"Izzy, I met everyone at the wedding. I'll tell them I was in the area and you let me crash on your couch."

Looking up, she rolled her eyes at me. "Yeah, 'cause that's believable."

"Listen, little mama. We can play it however you want to. I can say I fucked you mindless last night or that I just crashed at your place. I'll let you explain it. I thought it would be nice to see the shop Thomas has told me so much about." I climbed on my bike, lifting the stand as I straddled the machine.

"Skip the mindless fucking part," she said, walking toward my bike.

"I'll be your secret." I winked at her, patting the back seat of my bike, and hoped she'd let me give her a lift.

"It's not that I want you a secret. I just haven't figured *us* out yet. I don't know what I want." She squeezed in behind me, gripping me with her thighs. She felt so fucking good wrapped around my body.

"You want me," I replied, laughing as I turned on the engine and revved it. I took off before she could respond, and headed toward her business.

She yelled in my ear when I needed to turn. I didn't tell her that I already knew where it was because of Thomas. Our jobs were dangerous and we had to share everything in our lives with our supervisors. Our families were monitored for their safety, and files were built about them. Thomas knew my life just like I did his. There were no secrets—until now, at least.

She climbed down, shaking out her hair as I turned off the bike. "I can't believe I agreed to this shit," she said loud enough for me to hear.

As I got off the bike and stretched, I said, "They'll be more concerned about Thomas than what I'm doing here with you." I twirled my keys in my hand as I followed her toward the front door.

"Let's hope. This shit could blow up in my face."

"What could go wrong?" I grabbed the door, opening it for her.

"Hey!" she yelled as she walked inside.

The reception area was empty, but there were voices and movement coming from the back.

"Yo! Back here," a male voice called out from the tattoo area.

"Come on," she whispered to me, motioning for me to follow.

I took a moment to look around the shop. It was stunning. Totally unlike some of the seedy shithole tattoo parlors I'd been in. This joint was classy, with colorful walls and beautiful decoration. It had Izzy written all over it.

"Hey, I brought someone," she said as we walked into the back.

Mike, Joe, and Anthony stopped, looking up in unison. One by one, smiles crept across their faces as they recognized me.

"James," Mike said, standing to shake my hand.

"Hey, Mike. Good to see you again." I shook his hand, squeezing it firmly.

I didn't feel out of place seeing the Gallo guys again. I'd met them all at the wedding. I'd spoken with each one of them, sharing the information about Thomas that I was able to without putting him at risk.

"Yo, James," Anthony said, nodding to me without standing up.

I smiled, giving him a nod back.

"James, I'm surprised to see you here," Joe said as he stood and held out his hand to me.

I smiled, taking his hand in mine and shaking it roughly. "I just wanted to see how Izzy was doing."

"Ah." He looked at me with squinted eyes and the corner of his mouth twitching. "I heard all about last weekend." He released my hand, a dull throb in my joints where Joe had squeezed back as I hard as I had him. We were that type of man. We never showed weakness.

"Oh, did you?" I asked, a giant smile playing across my lips.

"Izzy never listens to us. We told her to stay the hell out of Daytona and stay the fuck away from Flash." He sat back in his chair, looking at his sister. "She has to learn everything the hard way. Thank Christ she had four brothers to watch over her."

I laughed as I looked at Izzy and practically saw steam coming out of her ears. No woman liked being talked about in this way, especially Izzy. She wasn't weak and didn't always need to be under the watchful eye of her brothers.

"Yeah, Daytona was rough. She's home safe now and Flash is of no worry. I took care of him."

"Good man," Joe said, opening the drawers to his station and placing tiny cups for the ink on the perfectly laid-out paper sheet to keep the area clean.

"How's Thomas?" Mike asked, leaning back in his chair.

"He's well. It's pretty quiet in the MC right now, but he's kicking ass."

"When the fuck will he be home, man?" Anthony asked.

I felt every eye in the place on me, waiting for the answer to a question I couldn't give a simple answer to. "Soon. He's so close he can taste it. You know Thomas. He won't stop until he gets the job done."

"Izzy said she saw him last weekend," Joe said.

"Yeah. We both did." I didn't feel the need to expand upon the information. The details of which I was sure Izzy hadn't given to them fully.

"She said he looked okay but a bit worn," Joe prompted.

"The life he's leading wears on a person, especially someone like Thomas."

"I just want him home and safe," Izzy commented as she walked up beside me and stopped.

I reached out, wrapping my arm around her, and drew her close. "He'll be home soon, doll," I promised, kissing her temple.

She stiffened in my arm. I looked down at her and followed her eyes to see three very curious faces.

"Want to share something?" Anthony inquired with one eyebrow reaching for the sky.

"Nope," Izzy responded, quickly moving out of my grasp.

I grinned, happy with what had been done but knowing I'd probably catch shit for it.

"I'll let you guys get to work. I'm going to head out for the day." I nodded at them and turned to Izzy. "What time should I pick you up?"

"We don't close until late," she responded, looking up at me.

"Iz, you don't have any appointments after six. You can take off after that," Mike chimed in.

"Perfect," I said, turning to him and winking.

She glared at him. "Thanks," she hissed.

"I'll be back at seven. Walk me out?" I asked, pulling her against my body.

"Fine," she bit out.

"Oh hey, James," Joe called out as we started to walk away.

"Yeah?" I asked, turning around to face him.

"My parents would love to talk with you. Mind going over there tomorrow for Sunday dinner?"

I smiled. The entire weekend was turning out perfect. I couldn't have planned it any better if I'd tried. "I'd be more than happy to see them. I've heard amazing things about your ma's cooking."

"For the love of all that is holy," Izzy muttered, rolling her eyes as she fisted her hands at her sides.

I laughed when her glare was now trained on me. "You okay

114

with this?" I asked her, putting her on the spot with her brothers there for the show.

"Yep," she barked. "Peachy."

She was pissed off, and I loved it. When Izzy was angry, she looked even more beautiful.

"Good," I said to her, and turned toward Joe. "I'll be there."

I grabbed her by the shoulders and ushered her toward the front of the shop and away from the watchful eyes of her brothers.

"Pissed off?" I asked as I stopped near the door.

"Not with you. Not entirely, at least." She looked down and bounced on her heels.

"With them?" I motioned with my thumb over my shoulder.

"Yes." She sighed. "They're nosy bastards. And you." She poked me in the chest. "What the fuck are you doing being all touchy-feely with me in front of them?"

"Just letting them know how it is," I growled, drawing her against me.

She didn't relax or melt into me like she had done when we were alone. "Only I let them know how it is."

Moving my head back, I looked down at her and grinned. She was a pussycat. "I'll behave from here on out."

She rolled her eyes and pursed her lips. "I don't believe a word that comes out of that sexy-ass mouth."

"Probably smart." I laughed, squeezing her tighter as I kissed her lips. Backing away, I stared at her. Her lips were parted and her breathing a bit uneven. She fucking wanted me and she couldn't hide it any longer. "I'll be back at seven."

"Okay," she whispered as I released her.

As she walked away, I reached out and smacked her ass. "Be ready, doll. There's no rest for the wicked."

"Jesus," she whined. "Will you ever get enough? I ache all over."

"When it comes to you, the answer is no. I want that body destroyed by the time I head home. I want you to remember who owns that pussy."

"Caveman asshole."

"Speaking of which, I want more of that too."

"Get the fuck out of here," she demanded, shoving me toward the door.

"Until later, doll," I grunted as I touched her face, letting my fingers slide from her cheek.

I climbed on my bike, heading out to chill on the beach for the day and catch some rays. I'd be back for Izzy well rested and ready to ravage her body all night long. I didn't want to miss a moment together. I'd have her ass loving me and wanting no one else but me before I walked out the door tomorrow.

# CHAPTER 12
# SUNDAY FUCKIN' FUNDAY

IZZY

AFTER TWO NIGHTS WITH JAMES, my body ached like I'd done the Tough Mudder obstacle course. Just peeing was a major issue. Everything hurt—even my face from smiling too much. James had entered my life like a hurricane, slowly building over time and then creating total and utter devastation in his path.

I'd always lived my life like a free spirit. I never gave a fuck what anyone thought of me and I was never apologetic for my actions. The words "slut" and "whore" left a bad taste in my mouth and made me want to rip the nuts off any man who'd muttered them. I acted like many men did; I used people for the physical aspect but never promised them anything more. I wasn't into relationships or being tied down. Having a man tell me what to do and how to act was my biggest fear, and something I'd run from at every opportunity.

Men seemed okay with how I behaved for the most part. Only a few had hurled insults because they'd wanted more. Those boys had ended up on the floor, gripping their balls and crying like babies. Each one of them had thought they could get me, capture my attention long enough for me to fall in love, and be the one. They hadn't been man enough to be worthy of my time, let alone a lifetime of sacrifice.

After having spent thirty-six hours with James, I knew I

needed to end it. Not because he wasn't worthy of my time, but because he was too much of what I wanted. There was a problem. I wasn't ready for someone like James to come crashing into my life and turn shit upside down.

When I opened my eyes this morning and watched him sleep, I knew what I had to do. I needed to gracefully bow out of whatever the fuck this was. James was a big boy and I was sure he'd understand. Maybe I could be his hookup when we both had an itch that needed to be scratched.

I knew I was scared, but fear was enough to make me lash out and run away. James had a way about him that altered the axis on which I teetered. I knew how I liked my life—uncomplicated and simple. He was a complication of epic proportions.

No one bossed me around—not even my four very demanding brothers. When James bossed me around, I bowed and said, "Yes, master," giving more of myself than I ever had with anyone.

"You ready, Izzy?" James asked, walking out of the bathroom as I sipped my coffee.

Setting it down on the counter, I turned to face him. God, he looked amazing. He wore a plain black t-shirt that clung to every inch of his torso and arms, and dark blue jeans that hugged his thighs. His feet were bare. The fucked-up part of it all was that I even loved his motherfucking feet.

"Yeah," I said, watching him approach.

"You look beautiful." He kissed my temple, wrapping me in his arms.

I closed my eyes, letting myself enjoy the feel of him against me. "James, we can't do this at my parents'," I whispered against his chest.

"Do what?" he asked, rubbing my back with his palm.

"Touch like this," I responded, pushing him away. The feel of him had become too much with what I knew I had to do.

"I'm not fucking you, Izzy. It's only a goddamn hug." He crossed his arms, looking down at me.

"My parents are old-fashioned," I lied. My parents were used to my touchy-feely brothers and their girls. Hell, even my parents were prone to public displays of affection. It was one loving and nauseating family.

"Okay, Izzy. I'll keep my hands to myself if it makes you happy." He smiled weakly, his shoulders falling as he exhaled.

"Good. That makes me happy."

"That's all I want. Your happiness is my highest priority."

Fucker. Why did he have to be nice? I'd rather him be an asshole and tell me to get down on my knees and suck his dick. That would make tonight so much easier.

"Ready to go?" I asked as I grabbed my coffee cup and set it in the sink.

"Yep. I'm starving."

I smiled, knowing that he'd enjoy the food my mother had prepared. I was sure word had spread like wildfire about his appearance at Sunday dinner. She'd probably spent all night preparing a feast for the guest of honor. I prayed my brothers hadn't spilled their guts about what they'd seen in the shop yesterday, but they all had loose lips.

"We're taking my car," I told him as I locked my front door.

"Whatever you want, Izzy." James headed toward the passenger's side door of my Infiniti as I unlocked the doors.

We didn't speak on the trip, as I turned the radio volume up high enough to make it impossible. James toyed with my fingers and stroked my arms as I drove. I fought everything in me to not close my eyes and get lost in the feel of him against me. His simple, loving touches were almost enough to push me over the edge and pull the fucking car over and beg for his cock.

I dragged my hand away from his as I parked the car on the street in front of my parents' home. Turning the radio down, I said. "We're here."

"Finally," he replied as I shut off the car. We climbed out at the same time, making our way to the front door. "Wait," he growled, grabbing me around the waist. "I want to kiss you before we go inside. It's a long time not to be able to touch you."

I nodded, biting my lip as I stared up at him. His eyes matched the color of the leaves that had just bloomed on the tree behind his face. His dark olive complexion made his eyes seem brighter than they were. Before I could reply, he kissed me, wrapping his arms around my back as he drew me in.

I melted into him, moaning slightly at his taste. James's kiss was like a hit of a crack pipe for an addict. "Stop," I mumbled against his lips. "Someone will catch us."

"Shh," he whispered before delving deeper inside my mouth.

Just then, the door popped open and I heard, "Oh heavens."

*Fuck.*

My mother had caught us red-handed. I pulled back, heat creeping across my face as I looked at my ma.

"Sorry, Ma."

"Oh no, child. Nothing to be sorry about." She laughed, looking between James and me. "James," she crooned, smiling at him and holding out her arms.

"Mrs. Gallo. It's nice to see you again," he replied, hugging her.

"It's very *nice* to see you again, and with my Izzy too." She winked at me over his shoulder, still tightly holding on to him.

"Ma, we're not together."

"Looks like it to me, dear." Her smile grew wider as she watched me and released him. "Let me get a good look at you, James." She snickered as she held his arms and drank him in.

"Ma, you're embarrassing him." I crossed my arms over my chest, watching my mother rape him with her eyes.

James laughed, leaning forward and kissing her on the cheek. "It's always a pleasure, Mrs. Gallo."

"Oh, sweetie. The pleasure is all mine," she whispered, looking over her shoulder at me. She linked her arms with his and ushered him into the house. "James is here!" she yelled as I closed the door.

I'd already known this was going to be a long-ass day, but having my mother catching us in a lip lock made it that much worse.

"Me too!" I screeched, feeling a little left out.

Suzy and Mia both rounded the corner from the family room with giant smiles on their faces as they looked at James.

"James," Suzy cooed, holding out her arms to him. "I'm so happy you're with Izzy."

"We're not together," I said.

"Uh huh. Sure, hon." Mia laughed, drinking in James at such a close proximity. "I've heard a lot about you, James."

He turned to me, winking with a grin on his face. "You have? That's interesting," he replied, looking back to Mia. "I hope they've all been nice things."

She nodded as her smile widened. "Yep. Izzy's told us all about you," she said as she looked down at his crotch and wiggled her eyebrows.

"Oh," James said, and laughed.

"For the love of all that is holy, shut the hell up, Mia." I pinched the bridge of my nose. A sense of doom seeped into my body.

My ma leaned over and whispered not so quietly to Mia, "They were kissing outside."

"You were not," Suzy said, smacking me on the shoulder. "I knew you liked him," she whispered—also not so quietly.

"Would everyone just shut it, please?" I begged, ready to run out of the house like a little girl throwing a temper tantrum.

"What's all the commotion in here?" Pop asked as he entered the foyer with his eyebrows knitted together. As soon as he saw James, his face lit up like a fucking Christmas tree. "James, my boy," he said, holding out his hand to him before pulling him close. "How the hell are ya, and my boy Tommy?"

"Fine, Mr. Gallo. I'm just fine, and so is your son." James shook his hand, gripping his forearm.

I glared at my girls as they stood there with dopey-ass grins on their faces, staring at James. "Traitors," I mouthed, snarling my lips.

Suzy stuck out her tongue while Mia shrugged and laughed. My ma, on the other hand, was watching James and my pop very closely.

"Come on and sit with the men. Dinner will be ready soon," Pop offered, motioning toward the family room with his head.

"Hello?" I whined, wondering where my greeting was.

"Sorry, baby girl," he said, stopping and walking in my direction. "I got caught up in the moment." He wrapped his arms around me and kissed my cheek.

"Seems to be a problem in this house," I groaned.

"Let's go, son. They'll call us when it's time to eat," Pop said to James.

*Son? Really? What the fuck just happened?*

James gave me a wink before he disappeared with my pop to lounge in front of the television and bullshit. Ma smiled at me and quickly excused herself to check on dinner.

I turned my attention to Mia and Suzy. "What the fuck just happened?" I asked.

They laughed and shrugged. They were no fucking help.

"Just nice to have someone new here for a change," Suzy responded.

"A fucking homeless guy wouldn't get that kind of reception," I bit out.

"Maybe if he was as sexy and locking lips with you he would." Mia laughed.

"Fucking lying bitches," I muttered, walking away from them.

I did love those girls. They were lying through their teeth, but they knew what had gone down between James and me. They were looking for some juicy gossip and they'd get it, but not today.

"Need help, Ma?" I asked as I walked in the kitchen to find my mother straining the pasta.

"You talk and I'll cook," she replied, keeping her back to me.

"I'd rather cook." I leaned against the counter and watched her.

She looked at me with a smile on her face as she tossed the pasta, washing away the last bits of water. "I'm sure you would, but I want to know how James just showed up this weekend."

"The boys invited him to dinner, Ma. I didn't have anything to do with it. I'm sorry." I crossed my arms, watching her.

"Baby girl, I know that. I mean how did he end up locking

lips with you at my front door?" She laughed, knowing that I hated talking about this shit.

"I saw him last weekend and he dropped in to check on me."

"Isabella, I wasn't born yesterday." She snickered as she poured the pounds of perfectly cooked pasta in the serving bowl.

She always had her ears to the ground. She knew everything that went on in this family.

"It's a long story, Ma."

"Do you like him?" She stopped, turning to face me with a grin.

"He's okay," I lied, feeling my cheeks warm.

"Just okay? Looks like he's more than okay, dear." She scooped sauce over the pasta, tossing it to keep it moist.

"Eh. He's not my type." I shrugged, hoping she'd drop it.

But in true Mama Gallo style, she replied, "You doth protest too much."

"Ma, he's bossy," I whined, grabbing the bowl of pasta off the counter.

"Bossy or doesn't put up with your bullshit?" she asked, following me into the dining room.

"We'll talk about it later." I sighed as I placed the pasta in the middle of the table.

"Fine, but I won't forget." She turned on her heels and walked back into the kitchen.

"Dinner!" I yelled toward the family room, and joined my mother in the kitchen.

We filled our arms with her chicken parmigiana, an enormous salad, homemade garlic bread, and a dish piled high with meatballs and sausage.

"You cooked for an army," I said, trying to balance the dishes in my arms.

"I wanted to make sure no one left here hungry." Her feet clattered behind me into the dining room.

Everyone had found their seat around the table, James sitting in the chair next to mine. He rose to his feet, moving toward me quickly, and grabbed two dishes from my arms.

"Thanks," I whispered, placing the other bowl on the table.

"Everyone have everything before I sit down?" Ma asked, standing near her chair.

"We're good, darling," Pop said as he patted her hand.

"Guests first," she said, passing the bowl of pasta to James.

A collective groan filled the room as James had first dibs on each dish. My father went next before the rest of us were able to fill our plates.

"James here said Thomas is doing great and hopes to be home soon," Pop said as he filled half of his plate with pasta.

James nodded, grabbing my leg under the table as he waited for the next dish to be passed his way. "He's an amazing agent."

"How about our Izzy? She's pretty special, isn't she?" Ma remarked as I tried to swallow a sip of water but ended up choking on it.

James patted me on the back as I tried to catch my breath while coughing up the water that had gone down wrong. "There's no one like her," he replied, smiling at me.

I held up my hand, trying to set shit straight, but I couldn't stop choking. God was playing a wicked trick on me. Everyone was in James's corner and no one had my back. *What the fuck?*

"You okay?" Mike asked with a grin on his face.

I glared at him as I tried to clear my throat and rid it of the invasion. "I'm ooo—" I croaked out before choking again.

"So are you two seeing each other?" Suzy asked, biting her lip as she stared at James and tried to ignore me.

"I guess you could say that," he replied, squeezing my knee.

"Wait," I whispered, my throat finally clear enough to speak. "We are not."

"You have a habit of kissing just anyone, baby girl?" Pop asked with his fork in midair.

Goddamn it. I closed my eyes, wiping away a tear that had formed while I'd been choking. "No, Daddy. I just don't want anyone to get the wrong idea, is all." I smiled halfheartedly, hoping that it was enough to stop his line of questioning.

"No one is thinking anything. That's why Suzy asked. We're curious. You've never brought anyone to Sunday dinner before." He stuffed the pasta in his mouth and began to chew.

I shook my head and sighed. "I didn't invite James. The guys did." I motioned toward my three jerkoff brothers around the table.

James leaned in to my ear and whispered, "Way to make me feel welcome, doll."

I glared at him before turning my venom toward my brothers. "You know I feel this is family time."

"James is the closest thing we have to Thomas right now, and for that, I'm grateful that he's here. He's welcome any Sunday he'd like to join us for a nice home-cooked meal," Ma insisted.

"Thank you, Mrs. Gallo. Your cooking is superb. Better than any Italian restaurant I've ever been to, and the closest to my grandmother's cooking I've ever found." He smiled, turning toward me and winking.

I was in a losing battle. I was sinking fast, making a total asshole out of myself, and no one would throw me a fucking life vest. James had turned into the golden boy, and I felt like a major cunt for saying that I hadn't invited him, because in all honesty, I liked having him around and I knew my family did too.

"We mean it, son. You're welcome here any time," Pop reiterated between forkfuls of pasta.

I hung my head, playing with the food on my plate as I wallowed in my asshole behavior. James pushed the hair away from my face and moved into my personal space.

"You and I will work this out later. Eat," he whispered, reaching down and stroking my leg. "You're going to need your energy."

The man was sex crazed. Every part of my body hurt, and there was no way in hell I could have sex with him again. I wouldn't be able to walk right if we did it one more time. He couldn't honestly be serious…could he?

I turned, looking into his emerald eyes, and saw the seriousness behind his words. I ate the rest of my dinner in silence, letting the family talk to James and monopolize the conversation. I'd never sat silent for so long at the dinner table before today. I'd let them ask their questions and hear about Thomas's

125

work within the MC. I knew it was helping dampen the fears each one of them had about his work.

After dinner, we all fell into our usual spots—me on the floor with Anthony and the others on the couches and chairs around the room. James stretched out next to me, facing the television as he twirled a piece of my hair out of view of my parents. They wouldn't have cared, in all honesty. I knew that about my parents, but I worried they'd see how I responded to him. They already didn't believe that he meant nothing to me. I'd have a lot of explaining to do the next time the girls cornered me alone.

James Caldo was like a parasite, although a fucking sexy one.

# CHAPTER 13
# THROWN FOR LOOP

JAMES

I COLLAPSED NEXT TO HER, completely winded from an orgasm to end all fucking orgasms. Izzy Gallo was a beast in the sack. She fucked like a porn star and took everything I had to give. Every moment I spent with her and her family, I fell a little bit farther into the rabbit hole, and I knew I'd never be the same after this fucking weekend.

"Jesus," I murmured through labored breaths.

"I don't know if I can even walk," she whispered, rolling over and resting on her back.

"I can't remember a better weekend in forever, Izzy." My words were true. It had been the most relaxing forty-eight hours I'd had in years.

It wasn't just that it had been relaxing—that I could do with a cold beer and a weekend of football. This was different. She made every minute enjoyable. Just watching her squirm at her parents' had been enjoyment enough.

"I don't think we should see each other again," she said, putting her back to me.

*What the fuck?* "Excuse me?" I asked, turning toward her. "You can't be fucking serious."

"Dead fuckin' serious, James."

"Izzy," I whispered, grabbing at her shoulder as I tried to roll her back toward me. "Look at me."

127

"No," she barked, pulling her body from my grip. "I don't want to see you again."

"Not this shit again," I muttered as I ran my hands through my hair. "Can't even let me enjoy the goddamn afterglow before you start spouting your bullshit. I don't believe a word of it."

"Believe what you want, James. This isn't working out for me."

"Seemed to be working out just fine when you were grinding your pussy on my face and chanting my name." I stared at the ceiling, thinking about what my next play should be to stop the train of destruction that was heading straight toward me.

"That was fucking, nothing more."

"It was more than that and you know it." I curled toward her, trying to hold her body against me.

She went rigid in my arms. "You should go before it gets dark," she whispered.

"That's it, huh? Fuck my brains out and toss me out like a piece of trash?" I asked, mystified at her thought process.

"Yeah," she replied, her body flattening against the mattress.

I knew she was scared, but I was too pissed off to try and calm her fears. I bit back like a wounded animal.

I climbed off the bed, grabbing my jeans off the floor and sliding them on. "We're not done, Izzy. I won't stick around for us to say things we'll regret. Shit we can't take back."

"The only thing I regret is spending the weekend with you."

"You're a fucking liar!" I roared, so pissed off I could barely see straight.

"Think what you want, but you're not my type."

"You just want a pussy you can boss around. I have a dick, babe. One you seemed to love this weekend. You get your head on fucking straight and give me a call when you're ready."

"Not happening, James," she replied as she turned to face me.

I'd already raised my voice, but I couldn't fucking help it. The woman was maddening. "I'm exactly what you need and want. You're too fucking scared to admit it."

She shook her head as she crawled out of bed and started to dress. "You're not all that."

"When you grow the fuck up, call me," I said as I stalked toward her.

"You're a total dick," she hissed, moving to slap me.

I grabbed her wrist, pulling her to my body. Gripping her hair in my fist, I gave it a slight tug as I hovered over her lips. She gasped, holding my shoulders.

"You know you want me," I growled, my lips a breath away from hers. "I wrecked you for any other man. I own your ass, Izzy. I'll let you run, but you can't resist me forever."

I crushed my lips against her, holding her by the hair. She moaned into my mouth as her body betrayed her every word. Backing away, I released her and left her standing in her room half naked and speechless.

The ride back to Leesburg gave me plenty of time to think of my next move. I'd give her space—for a little while—before I came crashing back into her life. We had that spark, that something special that couldn't be denied. Come hell or high water, Izzy Gallo would admit that she wanted to be with me.

\*\*\*

"Who pissed in your damn Cheerios?" Bobby teased as I walked in the office on Wednesday morning.

Bobby was my regional supervisor, but I often told him to go fuck himself. We had one of those relationships. He didn't hold back when pointing out the obvious.

"No one. Just a shitty-ass week," I snapped, throwing my bag on the floor and collapsing in my chair.

"Ah. Pussy problems." He laughed, kicking his feet up on the desk.

"Shut the fuck up," I snarled through gritted teeth.

"You better sort that shit out and get your head in the game," he said, riffling through a file. "There's movement on the coast within a rival MC. We need to keep an eye on Thomas and make sure he's safe."

"I got his back," I grunted, pulling myself toward the desk.

"Not when you have pussy on your mind."

"I got this shit, Bobby."

He stood and walked toward my desk. Leaning over, he placed his fists against the surface. "Sort your shit out. Got me?"

"Yes, sir." I knew he was fucking right.

One thing I'd gathered about Izzy through conversations with Thomas was that she was the most stubborn person he'd ever known. Izzy wouldn't be the one to make the first step or reach out to me. I knew I had to be the bigger person in this nonexistent relationship.

I needed to at least contact her and hope she had changed her mind. If she hadn't, I needed to find a way to help her do that. I needed to break down her walls. Finding the crack was the problem. Once I did, victory would be mine.

**Me: Thinking of me?**

Hopefully she hadn't blocked my number. The girl was feisty enough that she'd do something like that. Try and remove all temptation from her life. I knew that if she responded, I had her.

I threw the phone down on my desk, grabbing a cup of coffee before going through some surveillance footage that had been gathered the night before. When I returned to my desk, I had a message waiting. I smiled to myself as I read her words, feeling victorious.

**Sexy Fugitive: Hey.**

It wasn't much, but it was a reply. The name I'd put in my phone when saving her number fit our situation perfectly. I tapped my pencil against the desk, debating on how to respond.

**Sexy Fugitive: I'm sorry.**

I almost fell off my chair as I read her message. Izzy didn't seem like the type of girl who used those words often. Her stubbornness did not allow her to admit when she was wrong or regretted something. My heart started to pound as I saw a glimmer of hope for us.

Rubbing my chin, I wondered if I should ask about which part. It could be about a myriad of things, including fucking me or kicking me out of bed afterward.

*Me: For?*

I'd let her be the one to explain her need to apologize. No way was I going to fuck up the one inroad I had. No fucking way in hell. Once that shit vanished, it would be gone for good.

I set my phone down, starting the video on my laptop of the MC in action last night. We had surveillance cameras everywhere outside their compound, and in areas Thomas had told us were usual spots where club business took place. When we were finally able to bring them down, we'd have video proof to back up the allegations.

Letting it continue to play, I picked up my phone to read her reply.

*Sexy Fugitive: For being a bitch.*

Her message was still vague and cagey, but perfectly Izzy. She wasn't a fucking fool. No one likes to admit they were wrong, especially not someone as stubborn as she is.

*Me: I wouldn't use that term.*

*Sexy Fugitive: I didn't mean to be a cunt.*

I cringed at her colorful wording. *Cunt* wasn't a word I threw around when describing a woman. That shit would be immediately met with a punch to the face or a kick to the balls.

*Me: I hate that word, especially when thinking about you, unless...*

*Sexy Fugitive: Unless what?*

*Me: Unless we're talking about your beautiful, selfish pussy and how it milks my cock.*

I waited a moment, but there was no quick response. I turned my attention back toward the screen, watching as the prospects, including Flash, exchanged a duffel bag with an unknown man for a package. I didn't know what was inside, but the group was heavy in the drug trade in the central Florida region. Most likely it was heroin or meth.

*Sexy Fugitive: You scare me, James.*

I knew I'd come on strong, but fuck. I didn't want to waste time playing a bullshit game. I'd laid my feelings out for her, made my intentions known. Izzy wasn't just another easy fuck to me.

*Me: Nothing to be scared of, doll. I'm not the boogeyman.*

*Sexy Fugitive: You're scarier.*

I paused the video, Izzy taking precedence over the grainy images on my laptop.

*Me: Why?*

*Sexy Fugitive: I don't want to like you.*

I deconstructed her words. She didn't want to, but she did. I smiled, rubbing my lips as I chose my next words carefully.

*Me: What scares you most?*

I needed to cut off the head of the beast. Face her fear head on and alter her perception. The last thing in the world I wanted was a scared Izzy Gallo. She needed to know that I wasn't the enemy.

*Sexy Fugitive: I swore off men like you.*

Men like me? What the fuck did that mean? I knew I could be demanding in the bedroom, but besides that, I was like every other red-blooded American man. She wanted easy, someone she could control. That shit I was not down for. Just like her, no one told me what to do.

*Me: Men like me?*

I wanted her thoughts. She needed to voice her fears to me. Maybe it wasn't my demanding ways in the bedroom. I didn't want to expand until I knew her reasoning. I always believed in not giving too much information without knowing the enemy you faced. My enemy in this battle was Izzy's fear.

*Sexy Fugitive: You're demanding and bossy.*

I laughed when I read her message. Izzy wasn't a fucking cream puff. Those exact words could be used to describe her.

*Me: The only time I'm bossy and demanding is when we're fucking, doll. I like things done my way in the bedroom.*

I had particular tastes. Most people do. I didn't do missionary style with rose petals spread across the bed. I liked shit raw and rough, and I wanted to be in total control. That's not to say I wouldn't hand over the reins from time to time, but I was a man, after all, and the bedroom was my domain.

*Sexy Fugitive: You want shit done your way all the time.*

*Me: That's bullshit. I like you because you're the most*

*aggressive and strongest woman I've ever met. I don't want a*
*pushover who's going to do everything I ask.*

*Sexy Fugitive: You want me to fight back?*

*Me: Outside of the bedroom, yes. I love that fucking smar-*
*tass mouth of yours. When you get mouthy, it makes me rock*
*fucking hard.*

*Sexy Fugitive: And inside the bedroom?*

Would Izzy understand the difference? Would she be able to
give herself willingly during sex? She'd seemed to enjoy herself
this weekend when I'd told her to strip. She'd had me by the
balls during her striptease.

*Me: I'm the boss in the bedroom.*

*Sexy Fugitive: I don't know if I can deal with that.*

*Me: Did you like when I told you to strip?*

*Sexy Fugitive: Not at first.*

*Me: And then?*

*Sexy Fugitive: I liked teasing you as I danced.*

Sitting there, I thought of her naked, shaking her ass and hips
as she took off her clothes. Her dark olive skin and brown hair
had made me hard in the dim lighting of the room. It had taken
everything in me not to throw her to the ground immediately and
fuck her brains out.

*Me: Did you like when I fucked you?*

*Sexy Fugitive: Yes…*

The *dot dot dot* told me that she wasn't happy with admitting
it, but she had nonetheless.

*Me: Was there anything I did that you didn't like?*

I wanted to know where her head was with what I did to her.
Maybe I moved too fast, but I wouldn't apologize for who or
what I was.

I started the video again, needing to get my head in the
game. I wanted to nail these motherfuckers as soon as possible
so I could get the fuck out of this town. Five minutes later, there
still wasn't a reply from Izzy, but I knew we weren't over.

# CHAPTER 14
# OPINIONS ARE LIKE ASSHOLES

IZZY

"HEY, TERRI," I said as he walked through the door, interrupting my conversation with James. I knew it was shitty spot to leave him hanging, but I didn't have a choice. It would be hours until I could answer the question.

"Hey, babe. I'm ready," he said, cracking his neck.

I winced and patted the chair in front of me. The piece was a monster—an entire back design. I had done the outline previously, and today, we'd finish it. The dude, although not a pussy, didn't like to talk while he got inked. He put on his headphones and blocked out the world while I worked.

My workstation was set with everything I needed, so I was ready to go when he arrived. After a few kind words, I got down to business. I shaded the massive design while he faced the opposite direction.

Since I'd kicked James out on Sunday, I hadn't given myself much time to reflect on what had happened. I'd kept myself busy with work, friends, and family. The last thing I'd wanted to do was linger on my epic fuck-up. I hadn't meant to be such a bitch to him, but I hadn't known how else to handle the situation.

I hadn't been able to even face him when I told him to leave. I hadn't wanted to see his face—I couldn't see it. I would've taken the words back if I'd seen the hurt I'd inflicted. The rub of the entire situation was that I did like James—maybe more than I was willing to admit.

Even when he was a bossy asshole, I liked having him around. The banter between us was wicked fast, and his ability to call me on bullshit was matched by no one outside my own family. Maybe it was his ability to read me that unnerved me the most.

No one in my family, especially my brothers, had ever liked any man I spent time with. James was the exception. He had been welcomed with open arms, treated as family, and invited back.

Would I be willing to let him in my life? Would I still be me after he invaded my world?

I didn't like weak women. They drove me fucking insane. The girls who changed and made themselves the perfect woman for their man. I wanted to be me, and would do everything in my power not to lose myself. I saw it happen all the time with my friends as they settled down, and although I loved them dearly, it pissed me the fuck off.

Would James try and change me? Did he want a meek woman who would agree to everything he wanted? He said that he loved my smartass mouth, but would he feel that way later? Was he just saying the words I wanted to hear to get back into my bed?

I took a page out of Suzy's playbook as I worked on Terri's back. I needed to figure shit out about James. I needed to go through the pros and cons and see which side won. I mean, that's a rational way to make a decision, right?

James had a lot of pros. He was funny, smart, kind, and respectful to my family. He loved my brother, and he was handsome and sexy as hell. He had a dirty-ass mouth, and he was an amazing lover, Plus he made me feel good about myself.

His cons were a mixed bag. He pissed me off...a lot. He was bossy (although that could be a pro in the bedroom—fuck, I did like it). He was too smart for his own good, knew my game before I could play my hand, and didn't put up with my bullshit.

He was a arrogant prick, he knew how sexy he was, and I liked him too much.

The list of reasons not to be with James was longer than why I should give him another shot. In all fairness, the list of bad qualities weren't truly bad. I remembered him saying that I wanted a man I could control, and based off the cons, I'd say his words were true.

Flash was an example of a man who didn't know how to handle me, and for that, I let him hang around and come back for seconds. I didn't have to worry about him overtaking my life and losing myself. Flash didn't ask for much, just a fuck every once in a while and nothing more. He'd tried once and I'd shut that shit down quick. He'd accepted it and we'd continued as friends with benefits.

I'd tried to steer clear of men like my brothers my entire life. Suzy had changed since she'd met Joe, but she hadn't lost herself. It was the opposite, actually. She was stronger than she had been the first time I met her. She spoke her mind, slung profanity like a true Gallo, and seemed more confident. A strong man like Joe helped the real Suzy shine.

Mia was just Mia. Mike hadn't changed her at all. She had still been the same sassy, no-nonsense chick since the day I met her. She didn't put up with his bullshit. She called his ass on the carpet and met him head on in every situation.

Mike and Joe had enough testosterone and bossiness in them that they could rule the fucking world if they put their minds together. The fact that I'd never thought about their inability to change the women in their lives was surprising. I'd thought it happened in every relationship, but maybe I'd just focused on the people I knew who had lost themselves instead of those who had become stronger with the love of a good man by their side.

"I need a piss break," Terri uttered, pulling off his headphones.

I almost didn't hear him, lost so deep in my thoughts as I dissected everything I knew about love and all of my fucked-up theories.

Moving my hand away, I set down the ink gun. "Sure, Ter.

Take as long as you need." I leaned back, stretching my muscles. I felt stiff after sitting for a couple of hours hunched over his back.

I felt like a doormat—totally used and exhausted after not having slept well for three nights. I hadn't felt like I'd slept when I woke in the morning. It was like I had lain there in a trance as the night had passed, haunted by the words that had been thrown around before James left. I felt guilty, and it wasn't an emotion I knew how to deal with.

"What's wrong, Iz?" Joe asked as I stood to stretch.

"I just haven't been sleeping well." I rolled my neck on my shoulders, trying to relieve a headache I felt building.

"Is this about James?" Mike piped in, leaning back in his chair and watching me.

"I don't know. I'm just a fucking mess."

"Izzy, you know I hate any man who is with you or wants to be with you. Yes?" Joe asked, placing dollops of Vaseline on the plastic wrap laid out on his station. "I mean every fucking one of them." He set the small, round inkwells on top, prepping his workstation for his next client.

"I know, Joe. I remember you threatening the lives of more than a few." I laughed, bending over to stretch my lower back.

"I like James," he said, causing me to stand up and look at him.

"You've got to be shitting me," I said, completely in shock.

"He's not a shithead. He's a solid guy. Works hard, likes your brothers, and seems to adore you. Fuck, he fit right in with the family too."

"He adores me?" I shook my head. "Clearly you saw something else than I did."

"I saw the way he looks at you, Iz," Mike agreed, getting up from his chair and coming over to my workstation.

"Like a piece of meat he can control." I knew my brothers didn't want to hear about my sex life, and I sure as fuck didn't want to tell them, but I thought my words could be taken many ways.

"I'm going to talk to you as a friend and not my sister," Mike said, looking down at me with a smile. "Shit's going to be hard to swallow, but I'm going to say my piece."

"Here we go," I whispered, sitting back down and waiting to hear his pearls of wisdom.

"He looks at you like I look at Mia and Joe looks at Suzy. He looks at you like he worships the very ground you walk on, Iz. Men are bossy creatures—it's in our nature. If you find one who isn't, then they don't have a set of balls," Mike explained, shaking his head. "Every boy you liked was a total pussy and not worthy of your time. They wanted in your pants and that's why we ran them off. James is an entirely different animal."

I sighed, knowing that my brother was right. I knew the look on his face when he stared at me. I was sure it was a reflection of how I looked at him, but it didn't mean I liked it.

"He's bossy, Mike. I don't think I can deal with that caveman bullshit."

"You deal with ours just fine." Anthony laughed across the room as he walked toward his seat.

"You guys are different. You're my brothers and you do things to protect me and make me happy."

"Who's to say James isn't the same?" Joe asked, swiveling his chair around to face me.

"I have to love you because we're blood," I said, avoiding his question.

"I try to stay the fuck out of your business, sister, but for once, you're wrong," Anthony interrupted.

"When you guys need help, I'm the first person you run to, and now you think you know what's best for me?"

"We come to you for help because you're the toughest chick we know. You're always one step ahead of everyone and everything. You're a force to be reckoned with, Isabella," Joe said.

I hated when they dropped my full name. It showed that they were serious. Where the fuck was Terri? I wanted him to get the fuck back in here so this conversation would be put on the back burner.

"Listen, boys, I don't need a man in my life to complete me. I'm not weak." Fuck it. I was the fiercest bitch I knew. People didn't fuck with me unless I let them. Many men had been brought to their knees by a swift kick to the balls by me. The only people in the world I let talk to me this way were in this room.

"Weakness is walking away," Mike muttered, grabbing his chair and pushing it close to my station. "It takes strength to face the unknown and do it in the name of love."

"You've been listening to too much Barry Manilow or Lionel Richie or some bullshit. Who's filling your head with this nonsense?" Where had my tough-ass brother gone? I mean, a year ago he wouldn't have been telling me that it took strength to take a chance on love.

"Listen here, smartass. Love doesn't make you weak. You're stronger as a couple than you are apart. If he's the right man, he'll know how to bring out your strengths. He'll make you a better person. If you lose yourself, then you weren't strong to begin with. Man the fuck up and take a chance for once. Prove you got a set of balls on you like you always claim."

Mike was challenging me and being all philosophical and shit. I turned toward Joe, hoping he'd have something better to say. "And you?" I challenged.

"What he said," Joe replied with a smile and a wink.

I looked over at Anthony, who was staring at the ceiling, avoiding eye contact with me. "Anth, I know you have something to say. Tell them they're wrong."

Slowly, he brought his eyes to mine and shrugged. "You know I think relationships are bullshit, Iz, but I think James is a great guy."

"When did everyone jump off team Izzy and hop on the James train?" I asked, ready to pull my hair out.

Before anyone could answer, Terri walked back into the work area. "Sorry," he coughed, plopping his ass back in the chair.

"No worries, Ter. You rescued me," I said as I picked up the gun and got back to work.

Terri was a big-ass biker around fifty, and he had an old lady at home. He'd been coming to the shop for a couple of years and

I knew some things about him, but we didn't spend much time chatting like two old friends.

"Ter, let me ask you something before you disappear into your Led Zeppelin haze."

He placed the headphones around his neck and leaned forward, displaying his back. "Sure thing, kid. Shoot."

"You're married, right?"

"Twenty years."

"You happy?"

"Well, yeah, or I wouldn't be married anymore."

"She a pushover?"

"What?"

"You like your woman weak?"

He shook his head, turning slightly to look over his shoulder at me with his unibrow arched inward. "Babe, I don't do weak."

"Is your wife a 'yes, sir' kind of woman?"

"She's the toughest woman I know."

"You seem like a badass dude, yet you're with a tough chick. Why?"

"I said that I don't do weak. I wanted a partner. If I just wanted someone who would fill my bed, I would've stuck with club whores, kid."

"I thought tough guys liked weak," I said, placing the needle against his skin and starting on the heart I'd woven with the skull.

"Weak pricks like weak chicks. I want someone to keep me on my toes. You have some fucked-up thoughts on men, babe."

I thought about his words, letting them sink in before I spoke. "I have four brothers who act like the missing link between modern-day man and cavemen," I said, laughing to myself as I pictured them beating on their chests.

"They're men and not pussies like boys are today. Video games, manscaping, and metrosexuals have fucked up society. We're raising a generation of pansy-ass motherfuckers. Your brothers are solid dudes. I'd want them at my back when shit went down."

"Huh," I said, knowing that his words were true. My brothers always had my back and were there when I needed them. I'd never feared shit because of them.

"We done?" he asked, holding his headphones in his hand.

"Yep," I answered, not looking at my brothers as I continued to work. I knew they were all smiles with shitty "I told you so" looks on their faces.

Opinions were like assholes—everybody had one.

# CHAPTER 15
# PLAYING DIRTY

JAMES

FOUR HOURS HAD PASSED since I'd sent Izzy the message asking her what she didn't like. She could've been writing a goddamn novel to describe everything that drove her ass crazy. Just when I was about to lose my shit, my phone beeped.

*Sexy Fugitive: Sorry. I had an early client and it took for fucking ever... HUGE piece of work covering his entire back.*

At least I knew her quietness hadn't been intentional.

*Me: I thought you were giving me the brush-off... again.*

*Sexy Fugitive: I don't even know where to start, James.*

*Me: Anywhere you want, beautiful. Tell me one thing you didn't like.*

I was possibly inviting disaster.

*Sexy Fugitive: You're bossy.*

I laughed as I read her words. Izzy was a bossy little thing too. She wasn't a patsy for anyone, especially someone with a dick between their legs.

*Me: Only when I need to be.*

*Sexy Fugitive: So all the time basically you feel the need.*

She was a ball buster. Her brothers had raised her right and hadn't sheltered her.

*Me: When I feel the need to protect something important, then yes.*

*Sexy Fugitive: I'm capable of protecting myself, James.*

*Me: Never said you couldn't, but I'd rather be your shield and take the brunt of anything thrown your way.*

A few minutes passed and I waited, sipping on a beer as I let ESPN play in the background. Seventy-two hours ago, I'd walked out of her house and waited for her to make the first move. It hadn't come, but I'd been man enough to suck it up and take the first step.

*Sexy Fugitive: You're cocky.*

*Me: Wait a second here. Are we listing your traits or mine?*

She had cocky down pat. The girl had the shit in spades.

*Sexy Fugitive: Don't be an ass. We're talking about you.*

*Me: Confused me there for a second. I am who I am just like you are who you are... Smug, bossy, and beautiful.*

*Sexy Fugitive: Flattery will get you nowhere.*

*Me: I know. You like the challenge as much as I do.*

*Sexy Fugitive: Bullshit. You're infuriating.*

*Me: And it makes you wet.*

*Sexy Fugitive: You can't be serious.*

*Me: I'd never joke when talking about that sweet-ass pussy of yours, Izzy.*

I had a hard-on just thinking about her. It took everything in me not to hop on my bike and have this conversation face to face.

*Me: Touch yourself. I'm sure you're wet right now.*

Her reply was swift and made me laugh. She didn't like the thought of me being right.

*Sexy Fugitive: Fuck off, James.*

*Me: If you were here, I'd have you on all fours, begging for more.*

*Sexy Fugitive: Maybe I'd want to be on my back and looking in your eyes.*

*Me: Lying through your teeth, doll. You'd be slamming yourself against my cock, taking all I had to give.*

*Sexy Fugitive: STOP.*

My dick throbbed, aching for release. My balls had to be blue with the way they felt. Bastards may burst at any moment. I needed inside Izzy and I didn't want to wait. I knew that if I jerked off, it wouldn't fucking help. My hand didn't compare to her milking the life out of my dick.

**Me: Panties soaked?**

**Sexy Fugitive: I didn't wear any today.**

She didn't understand how her trying to shut me the hell up was a total cocktease. I loved it. I could go out and find some nameless woman who would lay herself out and offer her pussy to me to relieve the ache deep in my balls. I didn't want that. I only wanted her. After having a few tastes, I was hooked. No one else would ever compare.

**Me: STOP.**

**Sexy Fugitive: I'm almost dripping thinking of you jamming your hard, long cock inside me.**

She was the devil.

**Me: STOP.**

**Sexy Fugitive: My fingers don't feel as good as your dick driving into me.**

I closed my eyes, rubbing my hard-on through my jeans as I thought about her fingering herself. I refused to let myself come until I was buried deep inside her.

**Me: You're wicked.**

**Sexy Fugitive: Spank me.**

I thought that she needed a visual. I unzipped my jeans and pulled out my cock. Gripping it from the base in one hand, I snapped a picture and sent it to her. *Let her choke on that.*

I gave my cock a quick squeeze, trying to stop the ache before I shoved it back in my jeans. Tonight, I'd need an ice bath to quell my hard-on.

**Sexy Fugitive: You don't play fair.**

**Me: When it comes to you…no fuckin' way.**

**Sexy Fugitive: I have a client. Gotta go.**

**Me: Think of me when you touch yourself tonight.**

**Sexy Fugitive: Arrogant asshole.**

I left it at that. I had her.

# CHAPTER 16
# MOTHER KNOWS BEST

IZZY

"WHAT'S TROUBLING YOU, ISABELLA?" Ma asked as she sat down next to me at her kitchen table.

James and I had been texting for the last twenty-four hours—a constant volley of messages to drive each other insane. I didn't know what I wanted anymore. The world seemed to be conspiring against me when it came to James. Was I the only one who thought we were a terrible idea?

"James," I whispered without looking at her as I rubbed the smooth wooden table with my fingertips.

Placing her hand over mine, she stopped my nervous motion. "Izzy, look at me."

I met her soft, kind eyes. My mother was and would always be my best friend. I looked up to her and how she lived her life. From the outside, people would assume that she didn't run the show, but make no bones about it—she was the boss of this family.

"What are you so scared of?" she asked, stroking the back of my hand with her thumb.

"He's just so…"

"Perfect for you?" she asked, smiling wide.

"Ma, are you crazy?" I asked, flabbergasted by her question.

"I know when a man is smitten. I've seen you with other men, Izzy. No one got the reaction out of you that James did."

"Isn't that a bad thing, Ma?"

"Oh, honey, no. Your father still gets a rise out of me. It's what keeps us going after all these years of marriage. Without the fire between us, we would've ended long ago."

"But you and Pop love each other."

"Fiercely," she said, staring out the window as she watched my dad tend the garden. "Even after all these years, he makes me batshit crazy."

"Pop isn't bossy like James."

"Isabella, you look at your father through rose-colored glasses. Salvatore was the bossiest man I've ever met."

"Not Daddy," I said, following her eyes to watch him as he handpicked some tomatoes.

She laughed, patting my hand. "Child, that man made your brothers look soft. I've worn him down throughout the years. Don't tell him that, though."

I giggled, thinking of my mother laying into my dad. "I remember what you told us before Suzy and Joe were married."

"Men like to think they have all the power, but we really know who rules the roost."

"Ma, if you start talking about sex, I'll puke right here."

"James will make you happy."

"He makes me miserable. What if I become one of those women who changes for her man?"

She shook her head, turning her attention back to me. "Izzy, baby. I raised you to be strong and independent. That'll never happen. A man like James needs someone who is his equal. I can see it in his eyes when he looks at you."

"What do you see?" I asked, wondering how I missed all the signs.

"He looks at you like your father looked at me when we dated. Hell, he still looks at me that way now."

"Like a piece of meat?"

"Like a challenge worth the fight, baby girl."

"I don't know, Ma."

"Have I ever given you bad advice?"

I thought about it for a moment before I answered her. Shaking my head, I said, "No."

The door opened as Dad walked in. "Baby girl, what are you doing here?"

"That happy to see me, Daddy?" I asked, jumping to my feet to kiss him.

"I'm always happy to see my favorite child."

I slapped him on the shoulder and smiled. "You say that to all of us."

"You're my favorite daughter," he said, setting the tomatoes on the counter.

"Your only daughter."

"You mince words. Give me a hug," he demanded, holding out his arms.

I buried my face in his chest, wrapping my arms around my dad. Even at his age, he was still toned and muscular. It was in the male genes in the Gallo family. They didn't breed them small.

He stroked my hair and spoke softly. "What's troubling you, Isabella?"

"You and Ma are scary," I said, moving from his arms to look up at his face.

"Why?" he asked with knitted brows, lines creasing his forehead.

"She asked the same exact question."

"What was your answer?"

"James."

"Ah. I like that man."

I rolled my eyes, releasing my grip from my dad's shirt. "Who doesn't?"

"I know you're sweet on him too, baby girl."

"Dad—"

He put his finger against my lips. "I always have your best interests at heart. No one will ever be good enough for my baby girl, but James is a man's man. I know he'll protect you when shit gets bad. I won't ever have to worry about your safety."

CHELLE BLISS

"I'm kind of old for you to worry, Daddy," I grumbled, smiling and rubbing his face.

"You'll always be a little girl in pigtails to me, Isabella. The little tiny thing playing with her Barbies in her room or trying to tackle her brothers in the backyard when they played football. You may be a woman, but I don't see you that way. I just can't." He sighed, brushing a hair away from my face.

"I love you, Daddy."

"Love you too, baby girl." He leaned forward, kissing me on the cheek. "What did you say, my love?"

My mother sniffled, rubbing her eyes as I turned to look at her. "I said the same, sweetheart."

"There is just too much loving going on in this room. I need to go."

"Where are you headed off to today?" my pop asked as I grabbed my keys.

"I have to work and then I'm headed out with the girls tonight."

"Mia and Suzy?" Ma asked.

"Yep. It's a girls' night out. The boys are all going to play poker at Joe's place while we have drinks."

"Just be careful," he said as I kissed him quickly.

"I will, Daddy."

"Call me tomorrow, dear," my ma said as she walked me to the door.

"I will, Ma. Love ya."

"Love you too, my sweet child."

After we kissed goodbye, I headed to my car feeling entirely different than what I'd felt when I'd arrived.

Maybe I needed to give James another chance. Either that or I needed my head to be examined. I'd think about it over drinks.

***

I downed another shot of Patron, sucking on a lemon before I wiped my lips. My legs felt numb from the three shots I'd already ingested.

148

"Izzy, you may want to slow down," Suzy suggested, sipping her virgin something or other.

"I got this shit," I said, slurring my words as I threw the lemon on the napkin in front of me. Picking up my phone, I typed out a little message to James.

**Me: What are you wearing?**

I giggled, figuring I'd turn the tables on him. He wasn't the only one who could send nudies.

"Okey-dokey," she whispered, rubbing her belly and frowning. "I can't carry you out of here tonight."

**Cocky Bastard: How much have you had to drink?**
**Me: Enough.**
**Cocky Bastard: Clearly you've reached your limit.**

"What?" I asked, missing what Suzy had just said.

"I can't carry your drunk ass out of here," she repeated.

I blinked, my vision partially clouded and my mind a little muddled. "Mia can do it," I slurred, laughing before I typed another message.

**Me: You're always so serious. Do you even know how to have fun?**

I set my phone down on the table, resting my head in my hand.

"Bitch, I'll roll ya out, but I sure as fuck am not carrying you anywhere."

"Whore." I laughed, moving my head to rest on the table.

"I think we should get the check," Suzy said, touching my chair.

I lifted my head, squinting toward her to bring her face into focus. "Don't you dare! We're not done here."

"What's crawled in your snatch and died tonight?" Mia asked, polishing off her martini.

"James." I smiled, the dopey grin spreading across my face. I felt heat creep up my neck and settle in my cheeks. My entire body overheated. I pulled at the scoop neck on my shirt, trying to cool off.

**Cocky Bastard: I think I showed you a good time not so long ago. Let me remind you.**

Suddenly a picture of his cock, piercing and all, popped up on my screen. I blushed as I stared at it, almost in a trance.

"He has your panties in a wad," Mia teased, raising her hand to get the attention of the waitress.

"He hasn't been in my panties since last weekend," I croaked with a frown as I scrubbed my hands across my face.

"Missing him?" Suzy asked with a cocked eyebrow.

"I kicked him out of bed." I set my phone down on the table and looked at my girls with a giant-ass smile. I was proud that I'd kicked his ass out of bed.

"You did what?" they asked in unison, moving backward as if I'd slapped them.

Mia leaned forward, confusion all over her face. "Back the fuck up. You kicked him out of bed?"

"Shameful," Suzy muttered, shaking her head and staring with her beady blue eyes.

"I did," I yelped, slamming my hand down on the table. I tossed my head back and giggled, thinking that the entire situation was funny. I stopped when I realized that I was the only one laughing. "What?" I asked, calling over the waitress.

"Why the fuck would you do that?" Mia asked.

"Hello? James is a bossy fuck."

"He's sexy too."

I smirked and looked at Suzy. "I know."

"Are you going to be a hardass your entire life?" Mia asked, handing over cash to the waitress and shooing her away.

"I wasn't being a hardass."

"No, you're being a pussy," Mia spat.

"Am not." I stuck out my tongue at her and snarled.

"And a child."

"I'm drunk," I blurted, burping and covering my mouth.

"Have you at least talked with him?" Suzy asked, taking another sip of her drink.

"When is that baby going to pop out so you can drink with us again?" I asked, leaning over the table and poking her belly.

"More months than I wish to count."

"It better have a pussy, dear Suzy. No more cocks in this

family." I sat back down just as the waitress approached. "Ahh, perfect timing," I howled as I grabbed the drink off her tray and set it in front of me without spilling a drop.

"We want it to be a surprise," Suzy said, smiling.

"Surprises suck," I shot back. "To pussy!" I yelled, holding my glass high before taking a sip. To my shock, it wasn't what I'd ordered. "What the fuck is this?" I asked, looking at the drink.

"I cut your ass off," Mia replied.

"You're such a party pooper."

"You'll thank me tomorrow."

"Are you going to see him again?"

I turned my head to look at Suzy as her words registered with me. My brain had to work overtime to process each phrase. Clearly Mia had been right in cutting off my drinks.

"Who?" I asked, swaying in my chair.

"For the love of God," Suzy whined, looking toward the ceiling.

"Is he there?"

"Who?" she asked.

"I dunno…God?"

"Jesus, girl. Get your shit together," Suzy scolded me, biting her lip to stifle a laugh.

"Why? We leaving?"

"Are you going to see James again?" Suzy said, leaning forward, almost resting her belly on the table.

"You don't have to be so serious," I said, blinking slowly and opening my eyes wide. I felt like I was sitting there with my eyes closed, looking through slits.

"Mia, I'm gonna choke her ass out. You talk to her." Suzy leaned back in her chair as she glared at me.

"James, Izzy. Are you going to see him again?"

"Fuck," I muttered, trying to look at my phone, but my eyes were almost crossed. "We were texting and he said I'm to call him as soon as I get inside tonight and he'll be over after work tomorrow or at least that's what he said."

"I like him," Suzy said, a sappy grin on her face.

"You would," I said, resting my head in my hand. I felt like I had a bowling ball rolling around in my head. I just wanted to lie down for a bit.

"Come on, princess. It's time to get you home. You're going to need your beauty sleep if James is coming over tomorrow," Mia said, grabbing me under the arms from behind.

I slapped her hands away. "I can walk."

"Fine, tough ass. I want to see this shit on those heels."

"I'm a pro," I bragged, trying to climb off the high-top chair.

"I'm filming this shit to blackmail you later," Mia said, pulling the phone from her purse.

"I'll kill ya," I said as I slipped, grabbing the table for support. I steadied myself and turned to her. "Mia, put that shit away and help me."

"You're one crazy bitch."

"You girls love me anyway." I smiled, wrapping my arm around Mia as she helped me to the door.

I must've passed out in the car, because before I knew it, I was sitting on the couch in my living room with Mia and Suzy.

"Gimme your foot," Suzy demanded, bending down in front of me and touching my leg.

"What are you doing?" I asked, giving her my leg without hesitation.

"Helping your hot-mess self get undressed," she crowed, unstrapping my shoe.

"I can do it," I argued, falling back into the comfy cushions. "Just leave me here."

"Don't you want to go to your bed?" Mia asked, standing behind Suzy.

Mia looked like a giant Greek goddess from where I sat. Her long hair moved as if a soft breeze were circulating in the room. Clearly, I was three sheets to the wind and way beyond my limit.

"No, don't move me," I begged. "Everything just stopped spinning."

"Fine." Suzy stood and smoothed her pretty pink maternity dress.

"Are you sure, love?" Mia asked, tilting her head and staring at me.

"Please just leave me here. Go home to your bossy-ass men and leave me in peace."

"Love ya, Iz," Suzy said, patting my leg.

"You're a crazy whore," Mia said with a small laugh as she bent down to kiss my cheek. "I love ya too."

"I love you bitches, but if you don't get the fuck out, I'm gonna scream."

They threw their hands up as Mia said, "We're going. I left aspirin and water next to you. You're going to need them."

"Fuck off, bitches."

The sound of their heels grew softer as they walked toward the front door before I heard the lock engage.

I sighed, happy to be alone in peace as I let my heavy eyelids close and drifted off to sleep.

***

"Wake up, beautiful," I heard a man say in my dream. "Isabella." The deep voice rang in my ear.

As I felt something touch my lips, my eyes flew open to see a pair of green eyes staring back at me.

I blinked, clearing my vision. The alcohol must have clouded more than just my eyes, because he looked like... Fuck. For the life of me, I couldn't remember his name.

"Am I dreaming?" I asked, reaching up and grabbing his cheek.

"You have to come with me," he demanded, letting me clumsily paw at his face.

"No," I said. My head fell back. I was too tired and drunk to deal with this fucked-up dream. "Lemme sleep."

"Thomas needs you," the man said, waking me from my dream.

"What?" I asked, sitting straight up and blinking rapidly.

"Come on, girl. He's hurt and asking for you," the thick, gravelly voice whispered in my ear.

CHELLE BLISS

"Oh my God," I cried, pushing myself off the couch only to fall back down against the cushions.

Thomas needed me. He was hurt. Thomas needed me. He was hurt. His words kept ringing in my ears as I tried to stagger to my feet.

"Let me help you up," Green Eyes said, wrapping his arms around me as he lifted me from the couch. "Hurry, Isabella. We don't have much time."

"What the fuck are you waiting for?" I asked, laying my head on his chest as he carried me from the house. "I need to get to my brother."

Those were the last words I spoke before passing out in Green Eyes's arms.

# CHAPTER 17
# NAGGING FEELING...

JAMES

I COULDN'T SLEEP. It was two a.m. and Izzy still hadn't called. I didn't know if she was just being difficult or if I should listen to the nagging feeling in the pit of my stomach.

Everything had been going smoothly since we'd started texting each other on Wednesday. We had worked out some issues and come to a general understanding. I knew shit would be rough, but this was fucking ridiculous. She couldn't possibly be so cruel to not call. She had to know I'd be out of my fucking mind.

I dialed her number, letting it ring until her voicemail picked up. I tapped end and redialed, but still nothing. Tomorrow, I planned to drive up to her place in the late afternoon and whisk her off to dinner, but I couldn't wait. I had to know where the fuck she was. I'd probably get kicked in the fucking balls, but I'd go out of my mind if I didn't know she was at home, safely sleeping in her bed.

I grabbed the keys to my bike and started toward the door, but stopped. I tossed the bike keys on the table near the door and picked up the keys to my 1969 GTO. She had power and speed and I needed both right now.

I sped down I-75 headed toward her house. I gripped the steering wheel, my fingers damp with sweat. I tried to control my breathing and nerves as I drove. Working myself up wouldn't help get me there any quicker.

What if something was wrong? My stomach turned as I thought about the possibilities. My mind, maybe, was a little too imaginative. If something bad had happened, I would've heard by now. Being in law enforcement and seeing all the bad shit in the world doesn't help keep one's imagination at bay. Every sick crime scene flashed through my mind, replacing the victim with Izzy.

My blood turned cold the closer I got to her house. I hit redial over and over again until it went right to voicemail. I knew what that fucking meant. Either she had turned off her phone, it had died, or someone else had turned it off for her. There weren't any other options.

I slammed my fist down on the steering wheel, pressing my foot down against the pedal to pick up speed. I didn't have time to waste with worrying about the cops pulling me over. They'd have to chase my ass down and follow me to her house if they wanted to catch me.

My heart jumped out of my chest as my phone rang. When I looked down at my phone, I expected to see Izzy's number flash across my screen, but it wasn't her. I pressed speaker, placing the phone on my dash.

"What the fuck?" I barked as the call connected.

"Where the fuck is Izzy?" Thomas asked, breathing heavily.

"I'm on my way to her now. What the fuck is going on, Thomas?" I gripped the steering wheel so hard I could have snapped it from the dashboard.

"Flash just called me. He said Izzy was in danger. Somehow Rebel found out who she was. He knows who I am too. Find her, James, and do it now!" he roared, a loud slamming noise filling the air.

"I'm pulling on her street now," I growled, looking around the neighborhood as I sped down the road.

"I don't know who knows what at this point, brother. Find my goddamn sister."

"On it," I barked, fear gripping my insides.

"Call me back. I'm headed that way with Flash in tow."

"Give me five," I replied, stopping the car in her driveway. I tapped end, jumped from the car, and ran up her front steps.

Turning the doorknob, I realized that it was locked. I reared back and kicked in the door.

"Izzy?" I thundered, flipping on the light in the entry.

With no sign of her, I walked down the hallway to her bedroom, but it was empty. Her bed hadn't been touched.

"Izzy?" I continued yelling, running from room to room, but she wasn't there.

A lump formed in my stomach and I felt like throwing up. Izzy was gone and Rebel fucking knew about her and Thomas.

I walked toward the front door and something on the floor caught my eye. Turning, I saw a single shoe lying on the floor and her phone on the coffee table.

I ran from the house, dialing Thomas as I jumped back in the car. "She's gone," I bit out, slightly winded and in a total panic as I started the car.

"Gone or missing?" he asked, anger oozing in his voice.

"One shoe on the floor and her phone on the coffee table. She's missing."

"Fucking Rebel," Thomas muttered, his breathing growing harsh and loud. "Flash and I are an hour out. We need to figure this shit out and what our next move is."

"Fuck," I hissed, trying to think of where they would've gone.

"Stay the fuck there and make calls. Do not leave in case she shows up. We'll be there in sixty."

"Hurry the fuck up!" I snarled, and hung up as I climbed out of the car.

Once back inside, I dialed Bobby and began to pace. *Ring. Ring.* Where the fuck was he? *Ring.* I didn't have time to wait for his lazy ass to pick up the phone. *Ring.*

"Hello," a groggy voice said.

"Bobby, wake the fuck up. Izzy's been taken and Thomas's cover may have been blown."

"Wait, what?" he asked through a yawn.

"Jesus, fuck. Thomas called me tonight. Said Izzy was in danger and that Rebel found out who he is."

"Fuck," he spat, a loud thump sounding on the other end of the phone.

"Get your ass out of bed," I growled, ready to jump through the phone and choke his ass.

If my life—or Izzy's, for that matter—depended on this asshole, we were in fucking trouble.

"I'm up. Let me make some calls and get back to you," he said, disconnecting the call.

"What the fuck?" I yelled, my voice echoing through the house.

I called everyone I knew—local law enforcement in Leesburg, DEA, and FBI. All were working to bring down the MC, but the problem was that no one communicated with each other.

No one had seen Rebel. They'd lost track of him when he left the compound hours ago and he hadn't been spotted since.

Just when I was about to start climbing the fucking walls, I heard a car outside followed by two sets of footsteps up the stairs. Reaching for my gun, I drew as Thomas and Flash burst through the door.

"What the fuck did you find out?" Thomas asked, looking around the room.

"Nothing. No one knows shit," I ranted, running my fingers through my hair.

"Flash made some calls on the way here. Everyone is searching for them. They can't get far without us hearing about it."

I glared at Flash. "Did you open your fucking mouth?" I asked, charging toward him.

His mouth dropped open and his eyes grew wide as he stepped backward to avoid my grasp. A set of arms grabbed me from behind, pulling me away.

"Calm your shit down," Thomas ordered.

"Thomas, he's the only douche who knew who you were!" I roared, prying his hands from my body.

"Listen, fucker," Flash snarled, moving toward me. "I went

into Rebel's room to leave a package on his bed and I found a file sitting in plain sight."

"What a fucking clusterfuck," I hissed, scrubbing my face in my hands. "What was inside?"

"A picture of Izzy with her full name and address and a complete file about Thomas."

"Think he told others?" I asked, looking at Thomas.

He shook his head and winced. "I don't think so. No one seemed to act any differently. Rebel was the only one missing at the compound when Flash called me."

"Did you at least grab the fucking file?" I asked Flash.

"I'm not a fucking moron."

"When did you know about this?" Thomas asked, stepping in between Flash and me.

"When you called." As soon as the words left my mouth, I knew my mistake.

"What the fuck do you mean when I called you?" He glared at me, invading my space. "How the fuck did you beat us here?"

"Well, I—"

"You didn't give that file to Rebel, did you?" Thomas asked, standing nose to nose with me.

"Fuck, man. No fucking way!"

"James, I'll fucking kill you if I find out you sold me out, and if Izzy's hurt, I'll bring your ass back from the dead and kill you again."

"You don't even know how your words slice right through me."

"Who else could have given him that information?"

"It wasn't me," I insisted, turning toward Flash.

"Fuck, dude. You know I love Izzy. I wouldn't risk her life. I told you that man to man, James."

"What the fuck am I missing here?" Thomas asked, looking between us.

"James has a thing for your sister," Flash told Thomas.

There went any hope of explaining it when the time was right. *Let's add more gasoline to the flames.*

"What?" Thomas screeched, turning toward me, red-faced, with the veins of his neck popping out.

"*Thing* isn't really the right word," I said, looking him straight in the eyes.

"You're going to start talking as soon as we get her back safe."

I nodded, knowing that I should've already been straight with him about my feelings for Izzy. Thomas deserved to know how I felt about her and that I wasn't using her for sex. Flash had made it seem tawdry and sordid, but it was nothing like that.

My phone rang, breaking the uncomfortable silence as Thomas and I stared at each other. I lifted the phone to my ear without losing eye contact.

"Yo," I barked, chewing the inside of my lip.

"I got some news," Bobby said, the sound of papers moving in the background.

"Hit me."

"Rebel was spotted with a female at a motel in Bushnell. I just got the tip," he said, then he covered the phone and spoke to someone. "Sorry. The wife."

"Text me the information. We're heading that way," I said before disconnecting the call. "Motel in Bushnell," I said, grabbing my keys from the table and running toward the door. "Move your shit, Flash. We're taking my car."

As we climbed in the car, Thomas shotgun and Flash in the back, I threw my phone to Thomas. "Handle it," I said, starting the GTO and taking off toward Izzy. Thomas rattled off the address to the motel while tapping the screen on my phone.

"Should we call backup?" Flash asked, leaning forward and sticking his head between us.

"No," I snapped, gripping the steering wheel tighter. "Sit the fuck back. I don't need your face all up in my shit."

"Asshole," Flash mumbled. "How do you want to handle this, Blue?"

"We're going to find out who else knows and then we're going to kill the motherfucker," Thomas said, not looking up from the phone screen.

"Shouldn't we arrest him?" Flash asked, his eyes wide as I watched him in the rearview mirror.

"Fuck him. He deserves to die after taking Izzy," I said.

"What the fuck is this shit on your phone?" Thomas asked, holding out my phone and staring at me.

"What the hell are you talking about?" I asked, glancing at him out of the corner of my eyes but not daring to take my focus off the road.

"This shit with my sister, motherfucker."

"We're friends," I said calmly, wishing we weren't having this conversation.

"There's some shit in here that can't be unseen," Thomas bit out, growling as he continued to scroll.

"Stop fucking reading it, then."

"A fucking cock shot? Really? What the fuck? That's my little sister and you're sending her pictures of your junk?"

"Give me my goddamn phone," I growled, reaching over as I tried to rip it from his grasp.

"After we kill Rebel, I'm kicking your ass."

I nodded. "I deserve it."

If she were my sister, I'd do the same. I'd want to beat the living fuck out of anyone who touched her or harmed her virtue. This was Izzy, and I wasn't her first, but I planned to be the last damn man she ever bedded.

"Shut the fuck up and drive!" he shouted, tossing the phone back into my lap.

We drove in silence as we made our way to Bushnell. The highway was empty during the dead of night, a streetlight near an exit the only change in scenery.

As we pulled off the highway, Thomas spoke first. "This is how this shit is going to happen. I'll get the information from the desk clerk while you and Flash make sure no one leaves the motel."

The closer we got, the faster my heartbeat pounded in my chest. All the horrible things I'd imagined when I thought she hadn't made it home safe amplified. Knowing that she was in the hands of Rebel, an MC vice president, made my fucking stomach churn.

"Okay," Flash said, pulling himself forward.

"Then when I get the room number, you'll wait outside"—he turned to face Flash—"and James and I will go inside and deal with whatever clusterfuck we find."

"But I want to go inside too," Flash whined.

"Man the fuck up. We need someone to keep an eye out in case others show up."

"Fine," he snapped, slapping the front seat before he slumped in the back seat.

"Fucking pussy," I mumbled, trying to stop myself from turning around and punching him in the face. "Who's getting Rebel?"

"Let me deal with Rebel. You get Izzy out of there," Thomas said, turning to look out the window.

I flipped off the headlights as we approached the motel. The contents of my stomach began to churn inside me. Sweat dotted my brow as nerves racked my body. Jesus, I was so scared of what we might find inside. I'd kill the motherfucker with my own bare hands if he'd hurt her.

Thomas went inside as Flash and I watched the motel, making sure no one left.

"You got a problem with me?" Flash asked, my eyes flickering to him in the rearview mirror.

If looks could kill, he'd be a dead man. "This shit is all your fault," I said, my voice laced with anger.

"How the hell is this my fault?" he asked, glaring at me.

"You thought it was a great idea to bring her to Bike Week," I spat out, wishing I could wrap my hands around his pencil neck.

"I thought we could have some fun. How did I know all this shit would happen?" he asked, running his fingers through his hair.

"Don't they teach you anything at the mighty FBI? You don't fucking mix personal and business. Ever."

"James, wouldn't you call sleeping with Izzy a conflict of interest there, buddy?" A smug grin spread across his face.

"Fucker, I didn't bring her into my world. I went to her, never the other way around."

Thomas walked out of the office, motioning to us to follow. I grabbed my gun as I climbed out, and we both ran toward him on quiet feet.

"Room 103. Guy inside said he only saw Rebel and no one else," Thomas informed us, pulling the magazine from his gun and looking at it. "Ready?" he whispered, stopping before the room and jamming the magazine back in place.

We nodded, removing the safeties from our guns as we approached the room that hopefully held Izzy.

Thomas motioned to Flash to stand in the parking lot, pointing to his eyes and then around the exterior of the building. Flash was to be our lookout. Thomas lifted his chin, standing off to the side as I used my leg and reared up, kicking in the door.

Charging into the room, I looked around and saw Izzy lying on the bed, unconscious. My heart sank as I ran to her. A heat and searing pain sliced through my arm as a loud bang filled the room. My body jerked sideways as I reached for her.

I didn't look or stop to help Thomas; he could handle Rebel without a doubt. He'd given me a task and I'd follow it—save Izzy and get her the fuck out.

I carried her outside as another gunshot went off. She looked like an angel, resting and blissfully unaware of the shit going down. As I laid her on the hood of my car, I grabbed her face and placed my ear near her nose. She was breathing and reeked of liquor. I lifted her arms, studying every surface of her body. She was unharmed and had simply passed the fuck out.

"Watch her!" I yelled at Flash before running back into the room.

Kicking the door closed, I took in the scene before me. Thomas had Rebel on his knees with the gun to his head. Rebel was bleeding from his leg, his hands behind his head and his chin up in defiance.

"I want to know how you found out about me," Thomas

roared, his hand almost shaking as he held it to the top of Rebel's head.

"Go fuck yourself," Rebel sneered, spit flying from his mouth as he spoke.

I stepped forward, wondering what I should do next. I was torn between my duty to the DEA and my feelings for Izzy. Rebel knew information that could end her life and Thomas's.

Thomas raised his hand, smacking Rebel with the butt of his gun. "You want to get out of this room alive? You better start fucking talking."

"You're a traitor and a fucking rat. You might as well kill me, because I'll put your ass in the ground otherwise. I'm dead either way," Rebel bit out, wincing from the pain. "I brought you in and helped you move up the ranks. Fucking shoot me, you pussy."

"Who. The. Fuck. Knows?" Thomas said, moving to stand in front of Rebel with the gun still trained on his head.

"Fucking sucks not knowing something, doesn't it, *Blue*?" Rebel growled, kneeling and bleeding all over the floor.

Thomas moved quickly, pointing the gun at Rebel's shoulder and pulling the trigger. Rebel's body swayed backward before he righted himself.

"First chance I get, I'm going to taste the pussy on your beautiful sister." Rebel laughed.

I closed my eyes, seeing red as my stomach turned at the thought of Izzy being in danger. Fisting one hand at my side with my gun still in the other, I fought the urge to push Thomas out of the way and shoot the motherfucker in the head myself.

"I bet she tastes as fucking sweet as she looks." Rebel smiled, bringing his hand to his face and licking his fingers.

I couldn't stand the shitty look on his face. I didn't want to listen to him talk about Izzy anymore. Lunging forward, I pushed Thomas out of the way, and Rebel's eyes grew wide.

I pulled the trigger, watching Rebel's body fall back in a heap on the shaggy green carpet. Leaning over his bloodied body, I spat in his face. "Rot in hell, motherfucker!" I shouted, a growl rising in my throat.

"What the fuck?" Thomas asked, hitting my arm.

I looked at him and shook my head. "You two would never be safe with that motherfucker around. He deserved to die."

"I didn't get the information out of him," Thomas groaned as he sat on the bed.

"No one knew. If they did, he would've had backup here with him. He had to know we were going to come after him."

He sighed, setting his gun next to him on the bed. "You're right. Fuck, this complicates shit with the club."

"Only thing it does is move you up higher in the ranks, brother," I said, sitting next to him and staring at Rebel's body as the blood almost reached my boots. "What do you want to do with the body?" I asked, debating if we should bury him somewhere along the highway or make it look like a setup.

"You take Izzy home and Flash and I will handle it," Thomas said, standing from the bed as he stuck his gun in his waistband. "Is she okay, James?"

"Izzy?" I asked, nodding. "Yeah, she's just passed out. Hopefully she won't remember a damn thing."

"Fuck. No one can know about Rebel's death. Got me? No one besides the few people we called. Especially Izzy. Do not tell her." Thomas moved toward the door and walked out.

I stood and rubbed my face with my hands. When had my life gotten so fucking difficult? Everything used to be so damn simple.

Thomas was hovering over her, checking her for injuries when I stepped outside.

"I checked her. She's fine," I said, pushing him away and scooping her into my arms. "I'll get her home."

He nodded, glaring at me as I held his sister in my arms. She nuzzled my neck as tiny whimpers fell from her lips.

"Shh, doll. Sleep," I whispered in her ear as I held her body tightly.

"Flash!" Thomas yelled, causing Flash to jump.

"What?"

"Get your ass in the room. Let's get Rebel and get the fuck

out of here. James is taking Izzy home," Thomas said, motioning toward the motel room.

Flash looked at Izzy and me, then nodded at Thomas before disappearing into the room.

I laid Izzy in the front seat. "You be careful, brother," I said as I gently closed the car door, trying not to wake her.

Thomas stepped closer, standing toe to toe with me. "I'll text you when it's done. Keep her safe," he said, holding out his hand to me.

"You're okay with this?" I asked, taking his hand in mine.

"Fuck no. I'm still going to kick your ass when everything is said and done, but for now, you make sure she's okay."

"I'll wait until she wakes up and then I'll head back up to make sure shit doesn't go down in the MC."

"No, you stay clear until you get the all-clear from me. Do not come back. Stay with her and don't leave her side. Do you understand me?"

"I can't leave you without backup," I said, shaking my head. I didn't like it one bit.

"I'll be fine, James."

"I can't bear the thought of losing you, Thomas. You're like a brother to me, man."

"I don't have time to stand here and argue with your stubborn ass. Let me ask you this: Do you love her?" he asked, lifting his chin and motioning toward his sister with his head.

My feelings for Izzy ran deep—deeper than they had for anyone ever before. Was it love? To be truthful with myself and him, I replied, "Yes."

"Then keep her safe, James. I can handle the club, and Bobby will be around for help. Flash too. Now get the fuck out of here and take her home. Make sure she's sleeping."

"Not a problem," I said, smiling and turning my back to get in the car.

My head jerked to the side, pain shooting across my jaw as his fist connected with my face. I turned quickly, gaping at him.

"What the fuck was that for?" I asked, rubbing my jaw.

"Keep your dick in your pants," he said before leaving me

standing outside with a stupid-ass grin on my face. "Get your fucking arm looked at too."

"I'll patch up my arm when I get her home," I said, touching the wound on my arm. It wasn't anything I hadn't dealt with before. I could patch it up with a first aid kit and a knife.

I pulled away as he closed the door, leaving them behind and speeding toward Izzy's before she woke.

# CHAPTER 18
# DREAMS

IZZY

I SQUINTED, covering my eyes as I cracked open an eye. Everything in my body ached. My head throbbed and my stomach churned—both casualties of having overindulged the night before. Reaching out, I grabbed a spare pillow and yanked, trying to cover my face. The pillow didn't move, stopped by something heavy. Turning, I saw him. I had to still be fucking drunk.

Rubbing my eyes, I looked to my side again and saw James sprawled out and naked at my side. The sheet had slipped below his waist, showing off a very erect and hungry-looking cock.

I turned away, staring at the ceiling and wondering exactly how fucked up I had been. I didn't remember him coming over —or even inviting him, for that matter. I bit my lip while trying to remember the events of the previous night.

I remembered leaving the club with help from Mia, and the girls bringing me inside. I didn't remember the car ride at all. Although hazy, I remembered them leaving me dressed on the couch before I heard the door close.

How the fuck had James gotten here? Did I have sex with him again and this time didn't actually remember it?

Covering my face with both hands, I played the night before back like a movie. Drinks, home, sleep...and then Green Eyes.

I'd thought I'd dreamt him showing up in my house and scooping me off the couch, but I hadn't.

The churning in my stomach increased as liquid climbed my throat. After rolling out of bed, I ran to the bathroom and slammed the door. I grabbed the toilet, not bothering to lift the lid before I emptied the contents that were coming out one way or another.

Heaving over and over again, I prayed for something cool and comforting. As the urge to throw up passed, I rested my head against the cool plastic toilet seat. "I'll never drink like that again," I whispered. "Just make me feel better and I'll swear off alcohol forever," I promised God, even though I knew it was a vow I wouldn't be able to keep.

Moaning, I sprawled out on the tile floor, resting my cheek against the cold surface. I hated being cold, but right now, it was the only thing I craved. My body was covered in sweat and I felt like I was on fire. When I closed my eyes, the only sound I heard was my breathing as I wished for death or sleep. Anything was better than how awful I felt.

"Up you go, beautiful," James said as he scooped me into his arms.

"Leave me here," I whispered, wishing for the cold tile instead of the heat from his body. "I wanna die."

"Shh. I'll make you feel better," he whispered, feathering kisses against my forehead.

"Don't even think about sex," I groaned, lifting my head to look at him.

He wrinkled his brows and smirked. "I'm not an asshole, doll. It wasn't even a thought in my mind."

"What's that poking me in the ass?" I said, laying my head against his chest.

"My dick has a mind of its own." He laughed, gently placing me in my bed and pulling up the blankets.

I touched his arm, running my fingers along the bandage. "What happened?" I asked, looking up at him.

"Nothing for you to worry about, Izzy. Just a small wound," he said, cupping his bicep in his hand.

169

I kicked at the sheets, using all my energy to keep the heat at bay. "I'm so fucking hot. I don't want blankets," I whined, moving the sheets off my body and sprawled out stark naked.

"Kinda hard not to think about fucking you when you're lying like that, Izzy," James groaned, pinching the bridge of his nose and shaking his head.

"Stop looking and make yourself useful." I closed my eyes and motioned for him to go away.

"What would you like, mistress?" he asked, a lightness in his voice.

"Fetch me something cold, and medicine for my head." I dismissed him with my hand as the corners of my lips twitched. I wanted to laugh but stayed in character. The playful side of James was something I hadn't really experienced before, but I sure as fuck liked it.

"How about I grab a giant fan and keep a cool breeze flowing across your skin?"

I opened my eyes, taking in the sight of James standing at the end of my bed, naked as the day he was born, with a smile on his face.

"Leave me in peace. Go fetch my things," I demanded, throwing my arm across my face to block out the light.

"Right away."

I moved my arm, making space enough for me to watch him walk away. I giggled softly as his beautifully naked ass strutted toward the door. He looked over his shoulder and winked, catching me peeking at him. I didn't have the energy, or else I would've thrown a pillow at him before he walked out.

I rubbed my face, trying to calm the throbbing in my head. It felt like the drummer from Anthony's band was inside, banging away on the cymbals.

The bed dipped, and I opened my eyes to see a smiling James staring at my flesh like a rabid dog. "Down, boy," I teased, pushing myself up on my elbows. "The last thing I'm thinking about is sex."

"Fuck," he muttered, handing me the aspirin and water. "It's all I can think about when I'm around you."

"Do men ever grow up?" I asked before placing the pills in my mouth and taking a gulp of water.

"I sure as hell fucking hope not." He took the water from my hand and set it on the nightstand.

Lying back down, I sighed and closed my eyes. His fingertips began to trail a path up my arms, moving gently across my skin. The light touches made goose bumps break out across my body. Shivering, I sucked in a breath as he drew a tiny circle on the space between my breasts.

"James," I whispered, my breathing altered by his movements. "Why are you here?" I opened my eyes to look at him.

He smiled as he guided the hair away from my face. "You didn't call me like I'd asked. I was worried, so I jumped in my car and headed over."

"What if I were with someone?" I asked, biting my lip.

"Wouldn't have happened," he said, lying down next to me, resting his head in his hand.

"How do you know?"

He cupped my pussy, gripping it in his hand. "This right here is mine."

"Actually, it's attached to me," I said, smirking at him.

"I thought we'd cleared this shit up already."

"That you're a caveman pig? Yes, that we've agreed upon." I laughed, grabbing my head as the pounding made me wince.

"God's paying you back for those nasty words." He snorted, increasing his hold on my core. "You agreed to let me back in, and 'in' means the entire package. No one else touches what's mine, especially when it's attached to your body. It's the only thing I care about."

"James, you're getting all mushy. I don't do mushy."

"I know, doll. You like it rough." He laughed, dragging his hands from between my legs to my thighs. He began to trace small circles down my legs before starting the same path upward.

"Shut the fuck up," I whispered. "Hey, how did you get in?"

"Broke the door down," he said matter-of-factly.

"What the fuck? Jesus, you could've knocked."

"Iz, you didn't hear me bust open the door, so you sure as fuck weren't going to hear me knock."

"I'll get you a key so you don't have to break any more of my shit."

He grabbed me by the waist, pulling me against him.

"You're so fucking hot," I shrieked, trying to inch away.

He nuzzled my neck as his hand mindlessly stroked my ribs. "Tell me how you really feel."

Using the last bit of strength I had, I slapped him on the shoulder. "You're still a cocky bastard."

His face grew serious as he looked down at me. "Izzy, I want to tell you that I—"

I covered his lips and shook my head. "Don't," I said, swallowing hard, afraid of what he was going to say.

He smirked and spoke against my finger. "I think you should brush your teeth." He broke into laughter, the entire bed moving under his weight.

I closed my eyes, thankful and a little bit hurt that I'd jumped to the conclusion that he had been about to profess his undying love to me. We weren't ready, and I sure as fuck could barely think the words, let alone say them. I cared for James. No one fucked me like him. He had the mix of animalistic sexuality that I hadn't known I'd wanted.

"Fuck off," I snapped, lashing out at him as I rolled from the bed. "You're not smelling as fresh as a daisy either."

"Better than vodka vomit," he replied, covering his mouth as he laughed.

"Patron," I said, hanging my head and vowing to never drink tequila again. "He and I go way back."

"Tortured love affair?" he asked as his eyes followed me in the mirror next to the bathroom door.

"Story of my fucking life," I said, smiling at him.

He stretched out across the mattress, looking at home in my room. Closing the door, I turned and looked at myself in the mirror. "Fuck," I muttered, moving my face closer to get a better look at my reflection. Smashing my cheeks, I blinked twice, hoping it was just the alcohol affecting my vision. No such luck.

I looked like death. Heavy black bags had formed under my eyes with my mascara smeared all around them, framing them and drawing attention to the nightmare.

I grabbed a washcloth and a bar of soap and washed all evidence of the night before away. Brushing my teeth, I tried not to gag. Toothpaste and vomit didn't make the task easy. I cupped my hands together to pool water in my palms before bringing it to my mouth and swishing it around.

When I went back into the bedroom, I still felt like shit, but at least I thought I looked better.

"Let's talk, Izzy." He patted the mattress next to him and motioned to me with his hand.

I rolled my eyes, pain shooting through my head by the simple movement I'd done a million times. "Now? I'm too sick to talk."

"It's the perfect time to talk."

"Ugh," I whined, sliding in next to him. "Why?"

"'Cause you aren't as big of a smartass when you're like this, and I need you to be serious for a few minutes."

"Oh boy," I whispered.

"Just shut it, woman." He placed his finger over my mouth. "I'll talk, and you pipe in when you don't agree."

"So no talking?" I asked, knowing that wasn't going to fucking happen.

"If that's possible," he said, and laughed.

"Not a fucking chance."

He rubbed his eyes, trying to hide the smile on his face. "Izzy, I want to give this a shot between you and me." He paused.

I stared up at him and blinked.

"I know I can be demanding—"

I giggled, covering my mouth and quickly turning my face back to stone.

He sighed and continued. "I *am* demanding. I need control in the bedroom. It's hard to explain it."

"Are you a swinger?" I blurted.

"Fuck no. What kinda shit do you have in that head?"

173

I shrugged and waited for him to go on.

"I don't want to control your life. I want a partner, but inside the bedroom or anywhere I'm taking you…I'm the boss."

"Okay. I don't have any complaints when it comes to you and sex."

"Good," he said, and smiled, lightly touching my cheek. "Are you into kink?"

I smiled. Kink should be my middle name, but I'd play dumb for his sake. "Like what?"

"Why did you call me master when we had sex?" he asked with one eyebrow cocked.

"Felt right, and I was being a total smartass. I've been to a kink club in Tampa with my girlfriends once or twice to check shit out."

"What?" he asked, his eyes growing wide.

"You know. We were curious. There was so much talk on the news about submission. We wanted to see what all the fuss was about." I shrugged, feeling my cheeks turning pink as heat crept up my neck.

"Did you do anything when you were there?"

"James, I may have been easy for you, but I don't just fuck around with every cock that comes my way."

He sucked in a breath. I thought I'd given him a little too much information.

"Let's just say it was eye opening."

"Did you like what you saw?"

"Let's say it piqued my interest."

"Did it make you wet?" he asked, running his knuckles down my cheek before resting his hand on my neck.

"Some things." I smiled, heat spreading throughout my body.

"Which things?"

"Have you been to one of those clubs?" I asked, throwing the question in his court.

"I have."

"Really?" I whispered as images of James dominating women flooded my mind. "Tell me more. Do you like to hit women?"

"Fuck, I'm not a sadist, but I like to dominate women sexually."

"Women or me? I don't think I could handle you doing shit to other women."

He laughed, rubbing his nose against my cheek. "I want to dominate you, Izzy." He nipped my ear. "No one else."

"Not in a club either," I said, turning to face him.

"Never. I don't want anyone seeing what's mine."

"I'm willing to try everything once."

"You're a natural submissive, Izzy," he said, smiling at me.

I reached up, laying my hand against his forehead, and laughed. "Are you feeling okay? One thing I'm *not* is a submissive, James."

"You didn't say no when I told you to strip and handcuffed you to the bed."

"I liked stripping for you. It was sexy."

"And the handcuffs?" he asked, touching my wrists where the cuffs had been.

I closed my eyes, remembering the feel of him overpowering me and being unable to stop him. It sent a tingle through my body and made my pussy convulse. I opened my eyes and shrugged.

"It was all right," I said, pursing my lips.

"Sweetheart, I remember how hard you came when I tied you up. Don't lie to me," he said, running his finger across my bottom lip.

"Arrogant," I whispered, licking his finger with the tip of my tongue.

"I'm right. There's a difference."

"I can already see how it's going to be," I said, pouting, crossing my arms over my chest.

"I ask only three things, Izzy."

"What?" I asked, removing the fake pout from my lips and replacing it with a smile.

"You're only mine, no other men. Secondly, don't run away. The last thing I ask is that we get tested, you get on the pill, and no more barriers between us. I need to feel all of you."

"Sounds like a hell of a lot more than three," I teased. I gnawed on my lips, looking around the room as if I were debating the three things he'd asked. I sighed before I replied, "I can do that."

"Try not to bust my balls too much, 'kay?"

"Only when you're being a total asshole. I'll save it for those special occasions." I smiled, a giggle escaping my lips. "So when people ask me who I am—and they will, trust me—do I say I'm your submissive?" I asked, and pulled at my lip, waiting for him to answer.

"You're my girlfriend, Isabella."

"So I'm not your submissive?" I asked, still fidgeting.

He lay back, covering his face with his hands. "You're so difficult."

"You have no idea. I'm just getting started, Jimmy."

He jumped up, jostling the bed, and started to tickle me. I laughed uncontrollably with tears streaming down my face. Grabbing for his hands, I yelled, "I can't breathe!" as he pawed at my ribs.

He stopped, his face quickly sobering. "Are you okay?

"Psych!" I screeched, jumping on top of him and straddling him.

"I can see this shit won't be easy," he mumbled, pushing his hardness against me and laughing.

"Nothing in life that's worth having ever is," I whispered, leaning over and kissing him.

# CHAPTER 19
# WILD WILD LOVE

JAMES

"I'M ON MY WAY, doll. You ready for me?" I asked, climbing on my bike and placing the key in the ignition.

"I'm already naked," she said, her laughter tickling my ear.

"Fuck," I muttered, scrubbing my face with my hand. "I already have blue balls."

"Hurry or I'll start without you." She laughed and hung up.

I stared at the screen, shaking my head. She was the biggest pricktease I'd ever met. I shoved the phone in my pocket, started the bike, and took off.

I spent every possible moment I had free with Izzy. Working with Thomas to take down the Sun Devils and living an hour away didn't leave us much time together. I knew things would change eventually, but for now the distance worked. With her phobia of relationships and my overly bossy attitude—her words, not mine—the time we spent apart helped calm her fears. It had been a month since Izzy finally agreed to be mine.

We talked on the phone, texted nonstop, and Facetimed. I was able to convince her to masturbate while I watched, and it was the sexiest damn thing I'd ever seen. By the time I was able to see her, my cock ached, my balls were blue, and I couldn't control myself. We didn't spend too much time with clothes on when I visited.

I thought about how she tasted, the smell of her skin, the feel of her hands as I drove to her house. By the time I parked my bike, my hard-on had become as hard as granite.

"Shit," I mumbled, climbing off my bike and adjusting myself. I grabbed my stuff and headed for the promised land.

I didn't bother knocking. She may be a tease, but I knew her ass was naked and waiting, just like she said before she hung up on my sorry ass.

"Izzy," I shouted, throwing my bag down next to the couch.

"Back here," she yelled.

I headed toward her bedroom, unzipping my pants as I walked. As I turned the corner, entering her room, I stopped dead.

"What the fuck?" I said, my eyes growing wide. I blinked and shook my head, wondering if I was seeing things.

"Ya like?" she asked, smiling as she twirled.

"What—" I was stunned. She had on a corset that hugged her every curve as her breasts spilled out the top. Black thigh-highs, a matching garter belt, and a G-string, with black stilettos.

"I wanted to do something different." She giggled, walking toward me.

"I can't—" I said, feeling my cock about to break off in my pants.

"You don't like it?" she whispered against my lips, palming my dick through my pants.

"Jesus," I hissed. "I fuckin' love it."

She pushed against my chest. "Wait, I got something else." She walked next to the bed, opening her nightstand and pulling something from inside.

"What?" I asked, a little worried about what she was adding to the outfit. Anything more and I'd explode in my pants.

"These," she whispered, holding up two sets of handcuffs and a crop. Her smile was wide, almost touching her eyes. "I thought we could get a little adventurous."

"Doll, I'm going to show you adventurous." I beckoned her with my finger.

"No way, James Caldo. This is my show."

"I'm not following," I said, wondering when she thought she had the reins.

"You want my sweet pussy?" she asked, sliding the crop up her legs and stopping at her G-string.

"More than I want air," I replied, pushing my pants down. "Get your ass over here."

"I'm in charge tonight, Jimmy," she drawled, hitting her leg with the crop.

"What?" I asked, shaking my head.

"I get to boss your sexy ass around. That's the deal. I get to play too."

"Fuck," I said, my balls aching for release. "Whatever you want, doll. I just need to be inside you." I walked toward her, kicking off my pants.

"Not so fast, mister," she growled, holding the crop out and hitting me in the chest. "I didn't tell you to strip yet."

I bit my lip, keeping the laugh I felt coming from escaping. "Izzy," I said.

"Strip, and make it good or I'll have to give you ten lashes." She grinned, sitting on the bed and leaning back.

I couldn't bring myself to correct her on the type of impact a crop inflicted. "Yes, Izzy," I growled, slowly lowering my pants to my ankles.

"Mistress," she croaked, the corner of her mouth turning up.

"Mistress?" I asked, stopping my movement and staring at her.

"I like the sound of it." She shrugged, causing her tits to pop out of the corset a little more.

I continued with my striptease, dancing around the room and teasing her the best I could. It didn't take long for me to undress, since I only had on jeans and a t-shirt.

"Such a letdown," she whispered, shaking her head and pursing her lips.

"Hey," I said.

A loud slap echoed in the room as I felt a pinch on my hip. Looking down, I saw the crop retreating from my body. "You did it too quick." She laughed.

179

"I did not," I said.

She swatted me again and giggled.

"You hit me one more time for no reason and I'm going to take you over my knee and spank your ass," I growled, stalking toward her.

"James," she murmured. "I didn't say you could touch me."

"Izzy, I'm about two seconds from coming just looking at you. Get your ass naked and suck my dick."

"Tsk, tsk," she said, placing the heel of her shoe against my abdomen. "Get on your knees and eat my pussy," she commanded, pointing to the floor between her legs with the crop.

That was an order I'd gladly follow. I dropped to my knees, pulling her body forward, and ripped the G-string from her body. Placing her legs over my shoulder, I leaned in and licked her. She flinched and whimpered, "James."

I held her waist, keeping her in place as I latched on to her wetness. Groaning, I devoured her as she writhed under my hands.

"Harder," she chanted, pushing her pussy against my face.

I obeyed, driving her closer to the edge. I listened to her breathing, waiting until the right moment to pull away.

"Don't stop," she demanded, looking at me with an evil glare.

I smirked, going back to feasting on her as I inserted two fingers into her depths. Curling my fingers, I stroked her from the inside and licked at her clit like a man possessed. All I wanted to do was jam my dick inside her. I'd give her this moment to feel in control before I took over.

"Yes, yes!" she shouted, her entire body growing rigid. "Fuck," she hissed, trying to pull away.

I didn't relent, sucking harder while flicking her with my tongue. "Another," I murmured against her pussy, sending her spiraling into a second orgasm.

I backed away, wiping her juices from my face. "Your play-time is over, doll," I growled, pulling her off the bed like a rag doll and impaling her with my dick.

"James," she screeched as I filled her, throwing her head back and gasping.

"So fuckin' good," I groaned, pausing to gain my bearings. "Don't move," I said, holding her back in my hands.

"You don't have a condom on," she whispered, looking at me with large doe eyes.

"We're clean, babe. I needed to feel all of you. It's been too damn long since I've been inside you," I said, grabbing her by the waist and easing her off my shaft.

She blinked, a small smile spreading across her face. "Okay," she whispered.

Still kneeling, I slammed her back down on top of me, repeating the motion until I felt my balls about to explode. I stilled, not ready to come, and grabbed her face.

"I've missed you," I murmured, bringing my lips to hers.

"I missed you too," she whispered, staring in my eyes.

I kissed her, holding her body tight, still planted deep inside. Breaking the kiss, I licked a trail down her neck to her breasts, still spilling over in her corset. Looping my tongue inside, I pulled her nipple from its restraint and sucked. Her pussy convulsed, milking me and matching the rhythm of my mouth.

Unable to restrain myself any longer, I pulled her off me, letting my cock free from her vise. I thrust my hips as I yanked her body down, slamming into her.

"Fuck," I hissed, my body on the verge of orgasm. I kept battering her pussy, driving myself toward the release my body needed. Finally feeling her core gripping my cock, I hammered into her at a quicker pace. Sweat trickled down my back, and my body and balls overheated as she clawed at my skin.

My vision blurred and shivers raked my body as I came. "Izzy," I gasped, unable to catch my breath.

As my world came back into focus, I saw Izzy pouting. "What's wrong, doll?" I asked, nuzzling her neck.

"I wanted to be the boss," she whined, crossing her arms in front of her chest as her bottom lip trembled.

"Jesus," I mumbled, rubbing my nose against her soft skin. "We have all weekend," I said, moving back to look at her.

"Promise?" she asked. "I really want to beat your ass with this thing." She snickered, smacking the floor with the crop.

I shook my head, laughing as she smiled innocently. "You're too much."

She bounced, stroking my semi-erect dick with her inside. "Yes," she shouted, slamming down on top of me.

"Keep doing that shit and I'll show you how to really use that."

"Oh?" she asked, her eyebrows moving toward her hairlines.

"I have so much to teach you."

"I can be a really good student," she said, batting her eyelashes at me.

"I'm sure you were anything but, Izzy." I laughed, holding her under the ass and climbing to my feet with her legs wrapped around me.

"James," she whispered.

"Yeah?" I asked, setting her on the bed and collapsing next to her.

"I really did miss you." She buried her face in my side, hiding her eyes.

I grunted, unsticking her from my body. "When this shit with your brother is all over, I want you to live with me," I said, staring down at her.

"With you?" she asked, pursing her lips.

"Ah, yeah. You didn't hear me wrong, doll."

"Babe," she said, reaching up and touching my cheek, "I'm not leaving this house."

"Fine, I'll move in here," I said.

"Don't you think it's too soon?"

"You want someone else?" I asked.

"No."

"Miss me when we're apart?"

"Yes."

"Love how I fuck you?"

"Uh, yeah. Dumb question."

"Lo—"

She placed her hand over my mouth. "You can move in here."

I laughed, falling on to my back. She was easy. Say any word that started with "lo" and she freaked the fuck out. I knew it was the best way to get her to agree.

"Wise girl," I mumbled, feeling her pulse under my lips as I kissed her neck.

"Just remember I'm the boss," she moaned as I bit down.

"You're the queen of the castle, but I'm master of the bedroom."

"Okay," she whispered.

"Or any other room I want to fuck you in."

"Okay."

"Why are you so agreeable tonight?" I asked.

"I think you literally fucked me stupid." She giggled.

"I'm leaving my shit here this weekend."

"Okay."

"Izzy, you're fucking killin' me here. You never just say okay to *everything*." I brushed a few stray hairs that had fallen across her face. "What gives?"

"I'm scared," she confessed, covering her eyes.

"Of me?" I asked as I peeled her hands away from her face.

She nodded, biting on her bottom lip. "Yes," she whispered.

"Isabella, don't ever be afraid of me."

"What if I lose myself?" she asked, opening her eyes and stared at me.

"You're too strong for that to happen. I'd never let that shit happen either. I love you for the fireball you are. Your sassy mouth and sharp tongue make my dick hard."

She laughed, "Your dick is always hard."

"Only because of you."

"What if we fight?"

"Makeup sex, doll. It's fucking fantastic," I whispered in her ear.

She turned to face me. "James, what if something happens to you?"

"I'm not going anywhere."

"You don't know the future," she said, closing her eyes and breathing deeply.

"I waited all my life to find someone that lights my fire like you do, Izzy. Nothing can put out that flame. Come hell or high water, I'll spend eternity lo—" Her hand flew to my mouth. "Stop doing that," I hissed, pulling her hand from my face.

"Don't say it."

"As I was saying," I said, holding her hands above her head, "I'll spend eternity by your side and worshipping you."

"Why me, James?"

I looked at her, taking a deep breath before speaking. "Your brother talked about you all the time. I felt like I knew you before we met. That night at the reception when I saw you and you threw your attitude at me...I can't explain it. In that moment I knew I wanted no one else but you."

She smiled, blinking slowly. "But I ditched you." She grimaced.

I laughed, running my hand down her arm. "I wouldn't have expected anything less."

"Really?" she asked, her eyebrows knitting together.

"Really. I figured you'd run away. When I touched you for the first time, it was like fireworks exploding under my skin. I never felt that with anyone before, Izzy. Never in my entire life," I said, grabbing her hand and linking our fingers. "I knew I'd have you again and that someday I'd get you."

"Liar."

"You didn't feel it?"

"Fuck," she mumbled, looking down before bringing her eyes to mine. "Yes. Why the hell do you think I ran out of there?"

I chuckled, pulling her against me. "I told you I love a good chase. I knew you couldn't resist me."

"It's kinda hard when you keep finding ways to pop into my life."

"Divine intervention," I whispered, crushing my lips to hers.

"Bullshit," she muttered into my mouth.

"Izzy," I said, pulling her lip between my teeth.

"Yeah?"

"Shut the fuck up and suck my cock," I growled, pushing her head down toward my dick.

Her eyes flickered as a grin spread across her face. "Yes, master," she teased, climbing down my body.

# CHAPTER 20
# TIME KEEPS ON TICKIN'
JAMES

***Two Months Later***

"JAMES," Mrs. Gallo crooned, holding out her arms to me. "It's been far too long since we've seen you."

Izzy cleared her throat as her mother nuzzled against me, rubbing her hands down my back. "Ma, really? Must you paw him?"

Mrs. Gallo pulled back, sticking her tongue out at Izzy. "I'm just giving him a hug, dear."

"Looked like more than a hug."

"She's always been so sensitive," she said to me, ignoring Izzy.

"For fuck's sake," Izzy said behind me.

"Watch your language, Isabella."

"Oh, she notices me all of a sudden." Izzy's voice was laced with sarcasm.

"You should hear her, Mrs. Gallo. She has the dirtiest mouth I've heard on a woman." I looked over my shoulder and winked.

"It's her brothers' fault. Her father and I didn't teach her to speak like that." Mrs. Gallo shook her head, peeking over my shoulder at Izzy.

"Oh please, Ma. I've heard you drop more F-bombs than anyone I know. Give up your Mother Teresa act."

"She's a mouthy one, isn't she? How do you deal with her?"

"I'll whip her into shape, Mrs. Gallo." I turned to Izzy with a smile so large my cheeks hurt.

"You do that, dear. Lord knows her father and I didn't do a good enough job."

"What the hell?" Izzy muttered, pushing past us to get into the house.

"Thanks, Mrs. Gallo."

"For what, James?"

"Busting her balls for once." I laughed.

"Oh," she said. "I've been doing it for years." She smiled, laughing and looping her arms with mine. "Any news on Thomas?" she asked as we entered the foyer.

"He's well, but I can't say much else. I'm sorry."

She nodded, her face beaming from the smile on her face. "No worries. Any news is better than no news. It's been a tough couple of years."

"It shouldn't be much longer." I couldn't give her a time-frame, but after Rebel's death, things had been kicked into over-drive. The MC was heading for a cliff, they just didn't know it yet.

"James, how the hell have you been, son?" Mr. Gallo asked, holding out his hand as he approached when Mrs. Gallo headed toward the kitchen.

"Couldn't be better, Mr. Gallo." I shook his hand, watching as Izzy followed her mother while giving me the evil eye.

"Don't mind her. All the ladies are touchy in this house lately."

"Must be the heat," I said. Wondering where to take that topic of conversation, I decided to switch course. "How are your Cubbies doing?"

"There's always next year." He shook his head and sighed. "Someday before I die, I'd like to see a championship. The rest of the men are watching the game. Join us?" he asked, tilting his head and smiling.

I liked Mr. Gallo. He was my kind of man. Strong and protective, but he knew how to laugh. He loved his wife. That was evident the last time I was here. He cherished her, and I wanted their kind of relationship with Izzy. I hoped maybe someday we'd get there.

"Sure." I peeked into the kitchen on the way, seeing Mrs. Gallo and Izzy talking at the kitchen table. "Hey," I said as I walked around the couch to find an open spot.

They all waved, keeping their eyes glued to the television. Suzy was the only one to look at me and smile before she patted the seat next to her.

Joe turned toward her, making a face. "Here," he said as he stood and lifted Suzy, depositing her in his spot.

I sat, feeling slightly uncomfortable, and looked around the room without moving my head. The couch dipped as Joe sat between Suzy and me.

I gaped at him. My eyebrows drew together as a confusion spread across my face.

"Just lookin' out for what's mine. You got me?" he asked, raising his eyebrow at me.

"I do."

I could see why Izzy wanted to run away from me. All the men in this family were cavemen. We were cut from the same cloth.

Joey's head jerked forward, and I turned to see Izzy standing behind him.

"What the fuck was that for?" he asked, turning to glare at her.

"Being a jerk." She snickered, crossing her arms over her chest.

"Jesus. You're lucky you're my sister."

"Izzy, doll, I've never seen your room," I said, changing the subject.

"What?" she asked as she turned toward me.

"I want to see your room. Did your parents change it?"

"Nope. Looks exactly like it did the day I moved out."

"Show me," I blurted, getting up from the couch.

"Ma!" Izzy shouted. "How much longer for dinner?"

"Thirty minutes!" Mrs. Gallo yelled from the kitchen.

"Is it okay, Daddy?" Izzy asked, looking at her dad.

"You're a grown woman."

She laughed, drawing her lips into her mouth. "They like you," she said, pulling me by the arm up the stairs.

"Ya think?"

"I've never been allowed to bring a boy up to my room," she mumbled as we hit the top step.

"I like the sound of that."

"That doesn't mean I haven't had a boy in there, though, James. Don't get too excited."

I stopped, pulling her into me as she grabbed for the door handle to what I assumed was her bedroom. "Have you ever fucked a *man* in your childhood bedroom?" I murmured against her lips.

She sucked in a breath, blinking slowly. "No," she whispered.

I covered her hand in mine and turned the doorknob, opening the door. "You're not scared?" I asked as I closed the door, locking it.

"Of what?"

"Getting caught," I said, starting to undo my zipper.

She shook her head. "Nope. They won't look for us. They think you walk on water." She laughed.

Picking her up, I walked toward the bed, placing her on her back. My hand glided up her leg, taking the bottom of her dress with it. I smiled as I realized that she'd listened this morning and hadn't worn panties.

"I didn't want them ruined," she said, wrapping her arms around my neck.

"Smart girl." I rubbed my nose against hers as I cupped her mound. "You're already wet." I dipped a finger inside, watching her eyes close.

She moaned softly, pushing her head back into the blankets.

Covering her mouth with my free hand, I hissed, "Shh. Quiet."

Moving my hips, I placed my dick close enough to grasp it with my hand and slam it into her body. She gasped, biting down on my fingers.

"Fuck," I muttered.

"Not so easy to stay quiet, is it?" she said, smiling underneath my palm.

"Quiet, girl," I commanded, slapping her hip before I slid my hand underneath her ass.

She opened her mouth, pulling my fingers inside with her tongue. I pounded into her as she sucked my fingers. The extra sensation made my vision blurry, and I picked up the pace.

She moaned, sending vibrations through my fingers straight to my balls. Staring down at her, I watched her tits bounce out of the top of her dress. She looked so fucking beautiful underneath me as I possessed her. Moments later, my world exploded as I pushed inside her one last time before collapsing.

"Damn it," I growled, swallowing as I tried to catch my breath.

She wrapped her legs around me, holding my body in place. "I didn't get to come," Izzy whined, kicking me in the ass.

"You'll get yours." I smiled, pushing myself up.

"Who's the selfish one now?" she teased, unwrapping her legs from my body.

I stuffed my dick back in my pants and zipped it up, returning my outfit to its original state. I held out my hand, helping Izzy off the bed.

"If you're a good girl, I'll let you play mistress again tonight," I whispered, brushing my lips against her mouth.

A smile spread across her face as her blue eyes blazed. "Only if I can use the whip again," she said, clapping her hands as she bounced.

"I've created a monster." I laughed, picking her up and tossing her over my shoulder before I swatted her ass.

"Mmm, I liked that." She giggled before biting the sensitive spot just below my shoulder blades.

"Fuck, Izzy," I growled, slapping her ass a little harder.

"You better watch yourself, Jimmy. I'm gonna get you later," she said through her laughter as we descended the stairs.

I pulled her body down, letting it slide against mine until we were eye to eye. "You already got me, Izzy Gallo. Bring it." I cradled her face in my hands and kissed her hard, demanding entrance into her sweet mouth.

I finally felt at peace and secure with Izzy. Although we hadn't professed our undying love to each other, I could see the sadness in her eyes every time I had to say goodbye and head back to Leesburg to work. We spent a couple of days every week together, but it was becoming harder to stay apart.

My phone rang in my pocket, echoing throughout the hallways. I sighed, pulling it from my pocket. "I gotta take this. It's work."

She nodded and walked away as I hit answer.

"Yeah?"

"Get your ass back here now," Bobby barked, his breathing fast and hard.

"What the fuck, Bobby? It's my day off, man," I whispered, trying to not draw the attention of the family.

"The bust. Thomas called. It needs to happen tonight. It's all hands on deck, James. Wipe the pussy off your face and stick your dick back in your pants. You have two hours to get the fuck back here and be ready."

"Are you sure?" I asked, pinching the bridge of my nose as panic started to grip me.

These were the final hours of the thing Thomas and I had been working years to accomplish. This was our chance to bring the MC to its knees and bite off the head of the snake. One fuck-up and everything could go wrong.

"You got a dick?"

"Yeah. Dumbass question."

"Well, so is questioning my orders. Get the fuck off the phone, kiss your lady goodbye, and get the hell back here ASAP." A loud bang in my ear caused me to pull the phone away from my head before the line went dead.

"Izzy!" I called, waiting for her to come back so I could spill the news.

"Yes, Jimmy," she answered as she walked in with a confused look on her face.

"I gotta run, doll." I kissed her on the forehead.

She gripped my arms, staring into my eyes. "Everything okay?"

"Yeah. I got called into work. Tell your folks I had to run and that I'm sorry."

"I wanted to play mistress tonight." She stuck out her lip, pouting at me.

"I'll be back in a couple of days and we can play mistress all you want."

"Jimmy." She pulled me closer, her grip tightening around my biceps.

"What, Izzy?" I leaned forward, resting my forehead against her.

My heart ached from having to say goodbye. I'd told her I'd be back in a couple of days, but I didn't know when I'd see her again. With the case wrapping up, I could be buried under a sea of paperwork and court dates.

"Promise me everything will be okay?" she whispered with sad eyes.

"I promise," I lied. I couldn't promise a goddamn thing except that I would do everything in my power to be back in her arms as quickly as possible.

"Bring him home to my parents and yourself back to me." She leaned forward, tenderly kissing my lips.

"I will. We'll be here together before you know it," I said, kissing her one last time, inhaling and memorizing her scent and taste. "Izzy, I lo—" She placed her finger against my lips.

"Don't," she whispered. "Tell me when you come back to me."

I nodded and released her, touching her hand until my fingers slipped from hers as I walked out the door. She waved from the doorway as I jumped in my car and sped off to the one thing that could bring me back to her forever.

We needed to put an end to the Sun Devils MC and I needed to bring Thomas home safe.

---

*Please turn the page to read a short novella about the night Izzy and James met. Enjoy!*

# RESISTING

## A MEN OF INKED NOVELLA

I belong to no one. It's the way I've chosen to live. Master of my own destiny, finding my way through this bullshit thing called life. I learned from a young age how to get my way. Being a woman isn't a weakness. It's the opposite.

I've spent my life being surrounded by four overbearing brothers, but I've never been a wallflower. Independent and unwilling to be tied down, I grabbed life by the balls and lived it to the fullest. I was enjoying myself, minding my own business at my brother's wedding.

Then wham!

# CHAPTER
# ONE

IZZY

I'M A SIMPLE WOMAN. I grew up in a house with four brothers and loving parents who have remained married even after more than thirty years together. They showered us with love and affection. I'm the youngest of their children.

I have four very annoying older brothers. They're overprotective, and even though I'm an adult, that's never changed. They chased every man I ever liked (fuck the L-word) away as they screamed bloody murder and ran for their lives. Some would call the Gallo men alphas, but not me. I call them pains in my ass.

They helped mold me into the woman I am today. I don't take shit from anyone. I know how to throw an amazing right hook, just the right angle to knee a guy in the balls so he'll never have children, and how to keep my mouth shut.

A couple years ago, we opened a tattoo shop together. We simply named it Inked. Our family has money, but we were raised to not sit on our asses like spoiled brats. We get up each day and go to work. It's our goal to stand on our own two feet. So far, we've been successful. Even though we fight like cats and dogs, we love each other fiercely and are very careful whom we let into our little Gallo Family Club.

Thomas, my eldest brother and an undercover DEA agent, is the only one who doesn't work in the shop. He's a silent partner,

197

and we pray that, one day, he'll get sick of his undercover work and settle down. He's been working inside the Sun Devils MC for some time. Moving up the ranks, he's made his mark and is on the verge of bringing the entire club to its knees.

Joe is one badass motherfucker. He's kinda my favorite, but I'll never tell him that. Shit, I'm not stupid. He's an amazing artist and tattooist, and will be an amazing father. A while back, he rescued a little hot blond named Suzy. She's sweet as pie and used to be innocent. His badass biker ways ruined her, but naturally, I rubbed off on her, too. Some of his friends call him City because he was born in Chicago. The name fits him, but he'll always still be my Joey.

Mike is our shop's piercer, and he's built like a brick shithouse. He trained for years to be an MMA fighter. He was moving up the ranks and making a name for himself. That was until he literally knocked the woman of his dreams on her ass. He traded in his fighting days to help the love of his life, Mia, with her medical clinic. I'd almost say that he lost his balls somewhere along the way, but that would just be my jaded, fucked-up perception of love talking.

Anthony. What can I say about him? He's my partner in crime most of the time. He and I are the single ones out of the group. Thomas doesn't count, because we never know anything about his life. Anthony wants to be a rock god. He wants ladies falling at his feet, professing their love, and freely offering their pussies to him with no strings attached. It makes me laugh, because honestly, he's already arrived if those are his criteria. He's stunning. One day, someone is going to steal him from me and I'll end up being a lonely ol' biddy.

Then there's me—youngest child who still uses the word *daddy.* I'm not talking about some sick fuckin' fetish shit either. I melt into a puddle of goo when my father's around. I've always been a daddy's girl. I don't think that'll ever change.

I live by no one's rules—well, maybe my daddy's at times— and I try to cram as much fun as I possibly can in my one shot at this life. I don't make apologies for my behavior. I shoot straight and tell it like it is. I never want to be tied down. Fuck convention. I don't need a husband to complete me a la Tom Cruise in *Jerry Maguire*.

Men are only good for a few things. One—they're handy when you have a flat tire or some other thing that requires heavy lifting. Two—their cocks are beautiful. Three—did I mention cock? Four—fucking. Wait… that's still cock-related.

I take it back. They're only good for two things in life: lifting heavy shit and fucking. Walks of shame are for pansy asses. I proudly leave them hanging, walking out the door, and I make no apologies for it. I'm not looking for a prince charming or knight in shining armor. I want to be fucked and then left the hell alone.

That is where my life was headed. I was blissfully happy and unencumbered. Life was grand—one big fucking party and I was the guest of honor.

Ever have a man walk into your life and alter your entire universe?

I'm not talking about the small shit. I'm talking about the "big fuckin' bang." You're minding your own business, enjoying yourself, and then *WHAM*. Everything you think is right suddenly spins on its axis and bitch-slaps you in the face.

The party came to a screeching halt the night of my brother's wedding.

He changed everything. He fucked it all up.

World altered. Party over.

James Caldo became something bigger.

I couldn't resist him.

# CHAPTER
## TWO

IZZY

"EVERYONE'S ASS better be at my house tomorrow at two," Joe said as he finished cleaning his station.

"Yeah, yeah." Anthony kicked back and sipped a beer.

"Don't give me that shit. Be there on time."

"Is Suzy cooking?" Mike emptied the trashcan, not turning around to look at Joe as he waited for an answer.

"Fuck no," Joe said, breaking out into laughter.

We all knew that Suzy couldn't cook. God love her, and Lord knows she'd tried, but it wasn't in her DNA.

"Thank fuck," I huffed out, walking to the backroom to grab a cold one.

"Dude, someday you have to teach her to cook," Mike said, shaking his head.

"Fuck that. She doesn't need to learn how to cook. It's not why I love her."

"We all fucking know that," Anthony said, rolling his eyes as he rolled the beer bottle between his hands.

"Shut your fucking mouth. You're talking about my fiancée."

"Uh huh," Anthony muttered, wiping the drops of beer from his mouth.

Moments like this I loved. Sitting around, shooting the shit, and just laughing made me happy. I loved my brothers and their women, but I liked having them all to myself.

200

"I couldn't give a shit about Thanksgiving dinner, Joe. I'm waiting for the bachelorette party," I said, smiling as I walked toward my station. Then I kicked my feet up, leaned back, and took a sip.

"Izzy," Joe warned, glaring at me from his chair.

"Oh, shove it, mister. It's a girls' night and we're going to have fun. Don't tell me you boys are just going to sit around and watch sports all night. I know what the fuck happens at bachelor parties. What's good for the goose is good for the gander."

"What the fuck does that shit even mean?" Mike snorted.

"Dumb fuck," I mumbled against the rim of my Corona.

"What the hell did you just say?" His voice boomed as he turned to stare at me.

I gave him an innocent smile. "Love you."

"Dude, I can't believe you're getting married in a week. What the fuck? I never thought you'd be the first to be tied down," Anthony said, getting up from his chair. "I'm grabbing a beer. Anyone else want one while I'm up?"

I picked up my phone to scroll through my Facebook newsfeed. "Nope," I said.

To my delight, there was a message from Flash. We grew up together and I think I've known him forever. We used to play doctor when we were alone. It was the first time I ever saw a penis. As we grew up, the quick peeks turned into touching—then fucking when we hit high school.

Flash and I had an understanding. Neither of us wanted to be tied down, and we weren't exclusive. He was my booty call when I had an itch that needed to be scratched. He moved away a couple of years ago, and since then, every time he was in town, I would get the call offering a quick fuck and an even quicker goodbye. It was a match made in heaven.

*Flash: Whatcha doin' baby?*

He was the only person in the world I let call me baby. It was patronizing and I fucking hated it. Typically, it would earn a man a punch to his junk, but when Flash said it, I let it slide.

*Me: Getting ready to head home. U?*

201

"Izzy, are you listening to me?" Joe asked, casting a shadow on me as his big body blocked out the light.

I shook my head as I looked up at him. "What?"

"Do not have naked men at the bachelorette party."

"What's a little peen between friends?" I asked, laughing in his face.

"You know I love you, Izzy. I never judge you, but do not have *peen* at my soon-to-be wife's party." He put his hands on his hips and tapped his foot.

"Pfft," I said, standing up. "You having pussy at yours?" I asked.

"No."

"Fucking liar!" I shouted, hitting him in the chest with my finger.

He looked down, watching me as I poked him. "I mean it, sister. I don't want any nasty-ass stripper touching my woman."

I kept poking him. "Do you hear yourself?"

"I ain't fuckin' deaf and neither are you. I never ask for much, but this is non-negotiable. I believe Suzy told you she didn't want one."

"Suzy doesn't know how to have fun." I waved him off as I tossed the empty bottle in the trash.

"Suzy does. She just prefers my dick. She doesn't need some greasy male dancer touching her."

"Joe," I said, sliding my arm around his waist, "the stripper is only there for the other girls, not for Suzy."

"Bullshit," he mumbled, kissing the top of my head. "Please, Iz. For me."

I puffed out a breath, moving the hair that had fallen in my eyes. "Fine, Joe. As long as you're happy," I lied.

There was no way in hell I'd throw a bachelorette party for my soon-to-be sister-in-law and not have a stripper. If the boys got to see snatch, then fuck yeah, we were seeing peen.

"Thanks, baby girl," he said, squeezing me tight.

"Any time." I looked up and smiled. Releasing him, I stuck out my tongue at Anthony as I sat.

He winked, knowing I was full of shit, and started talking with Mike about the big Thanksgiving football matchups. I tuned out, picking up my phone as I waited for us to close the shop.

**Flash: *Interested in a little company tonight?***

I tapped my phone as I thought about his offer. Did I want to see Flash? I didn't have to be up early the next day, but then again, I never had to be up early. I hadn't had sex since the last time he'd dropped by, and that was over a month ago. I could use a good fuck.

**Me: *Hell yeah. Get your sexy ass to my place. Meet ya there?***

**Flash: *On my way. Be there in 30.***

I stood, shoving the phone in my pocket. "I gotta go, boys."

"Where the hell you runnin' off to?" Mike asked, stretching out and looking comfortable.

"None of your business. I got shit to do," I said as I grabbed my purse out of the backroom.

"Two o'clock tomorrow, Izzy," Joe said as I reached for the door handle.

"Got it!" I yelled over my shoulder, leaving my brothers behind, and headed home.

———————

"Yo!" Flash bellowed as I heard the door slam shut.

"Back here," I replied, before spitting out my toothpaste.

He walked into the room and said, "Get your sweet ass over here and gimme a kiss, baby."

I turned toward him, glaring as I wiped the leftover paste from my lips. "You must have me confused with someone else." I winked at him and laughed.

He smiled, leaning against the doorframe with his arms crossed. "I know exactly who I'm talking to." Then he closed his eyes and puckered his lips.

I threw the washcloth at him, hitting him square in the face.

His eyes flew open as the cloth fell to the floor. "What the fuck was that for?"

"You're not the boss of me, Flash," I said, putting my hands on my hips as I stared at him.

His eyes softened as he pushed off the doorframe. "I've missed you," he whispered, trying to wrap his arms around me.

"Flash," I warned, pushing him away. "I'm not your girlfriend."

"A guy can dream, can't he?" He brushed his lips against my temples, finally gaining a firm grasp around my body.

He felt nice. I'd never admit it, but I did like Flash. I loved him, but no way in hell was I *in* love with him.

"Might as well shoot for the stars." I giggled, snuggling my face into his chest and inhaling. My nose tickled. His normal smell was missing and seemed to have been replaced by something offensive and stinky as fuck. "Flash, you smell like shit," I said, pushing him away.

He lifted his arms, sniffing his pit as he wrinkled his nose. "Fuck," he muttered, pulling off his shirt. "Let me grab a shower and I'm yours." He kicked off his shoes and unzipped his pants. Bending over, he pushed down the jeans and tossed them to the side.

"You're mighty comfy here, aren't you?" I asked, taking my turn to lean in the doorway and stare at him. He was rough around the edges but beautiful. His smile was killer, but he wasn't the boy I'd had a crush on when I was a kid.

As he reached in the shower, turning on the water, he turned to me and smiled. "I can fuck you smelling like shit." His back stiffened as he stood straight, cracking his knuckles. "As long as I get some pussy, I don't give a fuck what I smell like."

"Get your dirty ass in the shower," I groaned, ready to rip my hair out but itching to touch him.

He laughed, climbing in the shower. Flash was always cute, but as he'd aged, he'd turned into a ruggedly handsome man. Less and less of his skin was visible, replaced by tattoos that decorated his body like a storyboard—most of the work I'd done over the years. He'd been my best test subject when I was learning my craft. Stupid fucker, if you ask me. I wouldn't let some newbie put ink that soap couldn't wash off on my body. He was tall, a couple of inches taller than I was, and lean. He wasn't overly muscular or bulky, but he fit between my thighs like a glove.

"You starin', baby?" he asked, his voice muffled by the water.

I blinked, pulling my eyes away. "Fuck no. Hurry your ass up," I said, stomping out of the bathroom.

I pulled back the blankets as I waited for Flash. His whistling filled the room, along with the plops of water that cascaded off his body, hitting the shower floor. I stripped off my clothes, fell on the bed, sprawled out, and stared at the ceiling.

I used to get so excited when he said that he was dropping by for a little while. Not so much anymore. I kept telling myself, "It'll pass," but it never did. He'd grown more loving and tender, and both of those freaked me the hell out. It ain't my bag.

Years ago, I'd be jumping up and down on the bed, waiting for the big, bad Sam, a.k.a. Flash, to come toss my apples. Now, it was—

"Ready or not, here I come!" he yelled from the bathroom, interrupting my thoughts.

"Yippee," I muttered, rolling my eyes as I leaned up on my elbows.

He strode into the room stark naked and dripping wet. "You look edible." He stopped at the foot of my bed and stared down at me. "I think you need to come, Izzy. You're wound tight tonight. Let me help you out." He grabbed my feet and yanked my body to the edge of the bed.

"Up for the challenge?" I asked, raising an eyebrow as I placed the bottom of my feet on his chest.

"Babe, really?" he asked, holding my ankles.

"You think you're that good at eating pussy?" I laughed, trying not to hurt his male ego.

"I munch like no other."

I knew the man tried to be sexy, but ew. He wasn't. "Show me whatcha got. If you're a good boy, I'll give ya some pussy."

He rubbed his hands together before placing my foot on his shoulder. "I'm going to eat it like it's my last fucking meal."

I melted into the bed, feeling his hot breath on me as he inhaled.

"Better than fresh-baked apple pie."

"Less talking, more eating, Flash." I threw my arm over my face, blocking out all light as he placed his mouth on me.

Moaning, he sucked my clit into his mouth, making my eyes roll back into my head.

"Fuck," I hissed, drawing in a sharp breath.

He mumbled, the vibration penetrating my skin, as he drew me deeper into his mouth. Sinking into the bed, I reached down and grabbed his head.

"Right there, Flash," I pleaded, grinding my pussy against his face.

He gripped my thighs, pulling me closer as his tongue traced tiny circles around my clit.

Shivers raked my body. He knew exactly how I liked it. Many years of fooling around had given him that advantage over other men. His fingers slid through my wetness, causing my body to clench in anticipation.

"You missed me, baby," he murmured against my pussy, his hot breath lashing my clit like a whip.

"Flash," I warned, pushing myself against his face. "Shut up and eat."

"Mmm hmmm," he mumbled, closing his lips around my clit, sucking gently.

Needing something more, I touched my nipples, rolling them between my fingers. Waves of pleasure came over me as I stared at him. Moaning and writhing underneath his touch, I closed my eyes and rode the crest, waiting for it to come crashing down and wash away the stress.

The warmth of his mouth, the flicks of his tongue, the pressure of his sucking, and my fingers on my breasts had me screaming within minutes.

"Fuck," I mumbled, my body growing limp as I sagged into the mattress.

"Damn," Flash groaned, licking his lips as he pushed himself up. Resting on his heels, he stroked his shaft and stared. "Baby, I can't wait to tap that pussy. I've missed you and being deep inside you."

I giggled, grabbing my sides as I rolled over. "Oh my God. When did you turn so wishy-washy?" I asked, gasping for air.

"Fuck you, Izzy. I know you fucking love me," he said as he started to lean over me.

"Wait," I said, putting my feet against his chest, pushing him away. "We're friends, Sam. Nothing more." I needed him to understand this. He and I would never be any more than what we were right now—fuck buddies.

We didn't go for drinks like girlfriends to talk about our lives. He never took me to dinner, unless you count the shithole bar in town as a restaurant, or McDonald's. We didn't hold hands, walk along the beach, or snuggle. We fucked and he left. Plain. Simple. No feelings involved.

"I know, Izzy." He swallowed hard, his Adam's apple bobbing, as he looked down at me. "I meant as a friend. I've known you my entire life."

"Just as long as we're clear, Flash." I slid my feet down his chest, rubbing against his hard length before I opened my legs to him. The look on his face was closer to a little boy losing a puppy dog than one about to fuck my brains out. "Come here and kiss me already," I said, holding out my arms to him.

A small smile spread across his face as he leaned over me, placing his arms under my body. "I thought you'd never ask," he said with a chuckle.

I'd known Flash long enough to know that there was something more he wanted to say, but he always held back. I loved him. Don't get me wrong. We'd gone to kindergarten together, but I wasn't in love with him. I never would be, either.

I grabbed his face as he hovered over me. "Hey," I whispered, "I'm happy you're here."

His eyes lit up as he rested his forehead against mine. "Thanks, Izzy. It's just so hard at times."

"What is, babe?" I asked, moving my arms around his shoulders.

"Being part of the Sun Devils MC. I feel so lonely."

"Get yourself an ol' lady," I replied.

He rolled his eyes, pushing himself up on his elbows. "They're bullshit."

"Come on. I'm sure there's someone you're sweet on, Flash."

"She's not—"

"Babe, listen to me. Everyone needs someone. You need to fill that void."

He sprawled out on the mattress, putting his hands behind his head. "It's not that simple, Izzy."

Resting my head in my hand, I placed the other on his chest. "I know. You have a big heart, and any girl would be lucky to have you, Sam."

He didn't like anyone calling him that anymore, but I was always the exception to the rule. I only used it to help drive home the point. He needed to finally comprehend that he and I would never be a "we."

"Not the one I want, though," he mumbled, blowing out a breath.

My heart hurt for him, but I just couldn't give myself to him in that way. "I'm sorry. You know I love you, but not in that way. You'll always be one of my best friends. You need to forget about me and find someone who's going to love you the way you deserve to be loved."

"Yeah, maybe." He closed his eyes as he laid his hand on top of mine and stroked my skin. "No woman will ever measure up to you, though, Isabella."

"I know I'm pretty fanfuckingtastic, but I'm not the one. She'll fall into your lap when you least expect it," I said as I nuzzled my face against his chest.

"What about you?" he asked, kissing the top of my head.

"What about me?" I looked at him.

"When are you going to find someone to love?"

"Aw, baby. I have my family. I don't need anyone else."

"We all do, Iz. When are you going to stop lying to yourself?"

I winked at him, laying my head back down against his skin as I twirled his dark chest hair in my fingers. "I have as much love as I can handle. I don't want to be tied down. I'm happy with my life. The last thing I am is lonely."

"Liar." He laughed, pulling me flush against his side. "Can we just sleep like this tonight?"

"Snuggle?" I asked, wanting to run out of the room.

"I just want to feel close to someone tonight. Please, Iz. I'm so comfortable like this. I don't want to sleep on the couch."

I bit my lip, feeling shitty about always doing that to him. Having him sleep in my bed always felt too intimate for me to handle. "Fine," I said, hoping I wouldn't regret it later. "Don't get used to it."

"Thanks," he whispered, burrowing his nose in my hair. "Night."

"Night," I mumbled as I closed my eyes.

An overwhelming sense of guilt came over me as I lay in his arms. Flash loved me, and had voiced it many times over the years. I'd always set him straight. Tonight felt different, though. It was as if I'd had a knife and jammed it in his heart. I felt like such a cunt for telling him I wouldn't love him—not in that way, at least.

We'd sworn that it wouldn't be any more than a physical friendship. He'd promised me years ago that he wouldn't fall in love with me. Sam had given me that amazing smile while speaking the words I'd wanted to hear but meaning none of them. I felt the end near for us, because I couldn't handle having to kill his heart and hurt him every time we were together.

Hurting someone, no matter the reason, sucks—especially when they're a friend. Someone who has been by your side and had your back since you were a little girl is an important person. He meant the world to me, but I could never settle down and spend my life with Flash.

I needed to let him down easy, and that wasn't my strong

suit. I always spoke my mind, and sometimes I came off as brash or unkind.

I curled into his side, letting my old friend drift to sleep while I mulled over my future without Flash weaving himself in and out of my life through the months. I needed to move on. More importantly, he needed to move on and find himself someone to love.

As long as it wasn't me.

# CHAPTER
# THREE

IZZY

"MORNING, BEAUTIFUL," Flash whispered in my ear as I hugged my pillow, facing away from him.

"Morning," I said, groaning as I stretched.

I wasn't a morning person. I'd slept like shit with Flash in my bed. He'd been a hog and snored no matter how much I'd elbowed him to move. The noise just kept coming. I'd thought about pinching his nose, but I'd also thought that'd earn me an elbow to the face by accident. So I'd covered my head with my pillow, faced away from him, and prayed for him to shut the fuck up.

"Sleep well?" he asked, stroking my arm lightly as goose bumps broke out across my skin.

"Ugh," I whined, turning toward him. "No."

"I slept like a fuckin' rock." He smiled, brushing the hair out of my eyes.

"Yeah, I know," I mumbled.

His slow blinks and sappy smile made my stomach turn. He wasn't staring at me like a piece of meat or a hit-it-and-quit-it kind of thing. His face screamed that he loved me, and it freaked me the fuck out.

"So, what do you want to do today?" he asked, his eyes searching my face.

I bit the inside of my lip. "It's Thanksgiving, Flash. I'm going to spend the day with my family."

"Fuck," he muttered as he stared at the ceiling.

"What?" I asked, pulling the sheet over my breasts as I sat up and rested against the headboard.

"I forgot it's Thanksgiving."

"I'm sure your parents are expecting you."

"No, they're out of town. I'll just do what I came here for and head back to the clubhouse."

*Fucking great. I don't want him to be alone on a holiday. No one deserves that.* "I'm sure Joe wouldn't mind if you came to dinner. He cooks for an army, just like my ma."

"You wouldn't care?" he asked, looking over at me with puppy-dog eyes.

"No. You know everybody, and my mom has always liked you."

"Your mom is the best damn cook. That's one of the reasons I liked you as a kid. Your mom fed everybody."

"You liked me because I let you feel me up in eighth grade." I laughed, hitting him in the face with my pillow.

"Yeah, that too." He grabbed me by the arms, pulling me down on top of him.

"Flash," I warned.

"I know, Izzy. I'm just a cock to you."

I hit his shoulder hard, making my palm sting. "Fucker, you're a friend, but your cock is mighty fine."

"My cock could use some attention."

"So could my pussy."

"Listen, you greedy little cunt. I ate you so fucking good last night and what did I get?"

"You just said what you got. You got to eat my pussy."

"Izzy," he said, grabbing my shoulder. "My balls are gonna burst. You gotta help a guy out here."

I crawled on top of him, straddling him, and felt his dick already hard underneath me. "Flash, what do I get if I let you?"

"Woman," he said as he swatted my ass. "You'll get to come on my 'mighty fine cock,' as you called it."

"I want two," I demanded, grinding myself against him.

He shivered as a small moan escaped his lips. "Anything you want."

I looked at the ceiling, resting my index finger against my lips as I moved my hips. "Well, my house could use a good cleaning," I teased.

"You'll get what I give you," he growled.

"Oh, I like big, bad biker Flash." I laughed, leaning back and pushing the tip of his cock farther into my wetness.

He tossed me through the air, and I landed on the bed and bounced. I snorted as I laughed. He grabbed the condom off the nightstand and moved his body between my legs.

"I'll show you big, bad biker Flash."

"Shit better be good."

"You talk too fucking much," he said as he rolled the condom down his shaft. "I always do you good, Izzy. No one does it better."

On a consistent basis, he was the best, but I'd had better one-night stands. There's something about the explosion of passion that happens when two strangers get together and there's an undeniable attraction. Clothes get torn, bodies get bruised, and everyone walks away with exactly what they wanted to begin with—a quick fuck, no strings attached.

"Gimme those lips," he said, leaning over me as he stuck the tip of his cock inside me.

"No," I whispered, turning my head.

He stopped all movement. "No?"

"Your breath." I laughed, but it was more than that. It felt too personal, and the last thing I wanted was anything that involved feelings.

"Gotcha," he replied as he jammed his dick inside me, causing me to cry out in pleasure.

"Jesus," I mumbled, pushing my head into my pillow and arching my back to give him better access.

"So fuckin' good," he whispered, rocking back and forth.

I sighed, letting myself get lost in the pleasure and blocking everything out. As his thrusts grew more punishing, I dug my fingers into his skin, trying to ground myself.

Closing my eyes, I listened to our moans as he moved. The sound of our bodies connecting filled the room, mingled with our breathing. He drove me closer to the edge. Each thrust hit my clit, bringing the orgasm just within reach.

Within minutes, I was flying off a cliff. A kaleidoscope of colors filled my vision as the orgasm that tore through me stole the air from my lungs. Flash had that ability. That's one reason why I always welcomed him into my bed.

"Oh God, yes!" I screamed, meeting his thrusts as the orgasm waned. I wanted more, needed more. I wasn't done, and neither was he.

He stared down at me, his eyes blazing as he gritted his teeth, chasing his own release. Picking up the pace, he grabbed my ass and tilted my hips, causing him to slide in farther.

"Right there!" I screeched, kicking my feet against the bed.

"Fuck," he hissed, his momentum quickening to an impressive speed.

Moments later, his movement stuttered as he groaned though his release. Sweat dripped from his chin, landing on my breast and sliding down to rest in between my tits.

The very last thrust he gave me sent me over the edge. The second orgasm was just as intense as the first and left me a puddle of jelly.

We lay there panting, sweaty, and exhausted. Trying to gulp air as if we were fish searching for water as we flopped in a new atmosphere. I wanted to fall back asleep. My eyes felt heavy as the tiredness I felt went bone deep.

Just as my breathing slowed and my mind started to turn off, my phone beeped.

"Fuck," I muttered, reaching out and feeling around my nightstand. Cracking one eye, I brought the phone to my face, too tired to open both.

***Joe: Be on time today.***

I rolled my eyes, tossing the phone to the floor. Yawning, I moving away from Flash and snuggled with my pillow. I had hours until I needed to be there for dinner. It was a holiday, for shit's sake, and I needed rest after having listened to Flash snore all night.

Comfortable and sated sleep took me quickly. Everything faded away.

"Izzy," a voice said inside my dream, but I ignored it. "Izzy," the voice repeated.

"What?" I mumbled, annoyed to have my darkness interrupted.

"Izzy," Flash said, shaking my shoulders. "What time do we have to be at your brother's?"

"Two," I muttered, placing the pillow over my head.

"It's one thirty, babe."

I jumped from the bed, my heart racing at the thought of being late. "Fuck. Why did you let me sleep so long?" I grabbed my jeans off the dresser, slipping them on and quickly fastening them. Then I turned to see Flash staring at me. "Get your ass up. We gotta go."

"Is someone scared of her brother?" He smiled, stretching out across my bed.

"No. I just don't want to hear bullshit about being late."

"Pussy." He laughed, climbing off the bed.

"If you ever want my pussy again, you'll move your ass." I threw his dirty clothes at him before he could react. They hit him square in the chest and fell to his feet.

"What the fuck, dude?" he asked, holding out his hands.

"Put something on. You can't go like that," I said, waving my hands up and down.

"My clothes are outside."

I crossed my arms over my chest, highly irritated at this point. "Flash, move it. Stop fucking around. Get your shit and get ready. I'm leaving in ten with or without you."

"Fine," he said, pulling on his jeans before stomping out the door as I walked into my closet to grab a cami.

It was bad enough that I was bringing Flash with me. Joe hated him. Fuck, all my brothers hated him. Hopefully, with it being a holiday, they could put aside their bullshit and welcome

215

him inside. I could hope, but I knew the reality. I'd be playing interference the entire day to stop fists from flying.

Exactly ten minutes later, I grabbed my keys off the counter and threw on my heels. Then I stood by the front door, about to walk out, when Flash rounded the corner looking as good as biker Flash could. His outfit wasn't fancy, but it would do. Time to get the clusterfuck over with.

# CHAPTER
# FOUR
IZZY

THANK goodness Anthony showed up when we did. I wouldn't have to hear Joe's mouth about being the last one to dinner.

"Hey, Anth."

Anthony hugged me, moving in closer to my ear and whispering, "Why the fuck did you bring him?"

I looked at Flash, giving him a smile before responding to Anthony. "He didn't have anywhere else to go." I batted my eyelashes at him as he backed away and gave Flash a once-over.

"Joe is going to shit a motherfucking brick." Anthony winked and grinned.

"Just thought I'd keep the day interesting."

"Hey, man," Flash said as he walked up to Anthony with his hand outstretched.

"Long time no see, Sam." Anthony grasped his hand, shaking it for longer than normal.

"Yeah." Flash flinched from the handshake. Then he flexed his hands as Anthony released him. "It's Flash now."

I rolled my eyes and shook my head. *This shit should go over real well with my family.* Anthony looked at me, and I shrugged before pinching my nose.

"Stay behind me," I said, looking at Flash and pointing at the ground.

"Why?"

"'Cause Joe won't punch me when he sees you, but by all means," I said, motioning in front of me with my hand. "Go ahead in front if you want a fist in the face as a greeting."

Flash grimaced and sighed. "I don't know why your brother doesn't fuckin' like me."

"Maybe 'cause you've been fucking his little sister for years."

Flash mumbled something under his breath, moving to stand behind me as we approached the door. As Anthony knocked, I fidgeted with my hands, praying that the day didn't turn into a clusterfuck.

"Fucker hated me before that," Flash snarled behind me.

Anthony's fists didn't relent as he pounded on the door.

"Why don't you just open it?"

"This isn't Ma's and I don't just walk in without being told it's okay," he said, landing another blow.

"Pussy," I whispered, moving around Anthony and walking inside.

Flash laughed, following behind me as Anthony grumbled.

"Smells damn good in here." I inhaled deeply.

"Hey, sis," Joe said, walking over to hug me.

"I brought someone. I hope you don't mind." I smiled, looking up into his eyes. I knew I was laying it on thick, but I was just trying to cushion the blow.

"Who?" Joe asked, looking over my shoulder. "Really?" he growled in my ear, grabbing my shoulder.

"Come on, Joey. He didn't have anywhere else to be. He was in town and I told him he could spend the day with us. I know you made enough food for an entire army." I batted my eyelashes at Joe.

"He's here now." Joe shook his head, staring down at me. "Next time ask, Izzy."

"Okay," I whispered against his chest, giving him a squeeze before ducking under his arms.

Joe held out his hand to Flash as Anthony walked by and

grimaced. "Nice to see you again, Sam," Joe bit out through gritted teeth.

"I go by Flash now."

I cringed at his response. I always knew Flash wasn't the most intelligent man, but to reply to my brother in that way was just plain idiotic—or he had a death wish.

"Whatever," Joe said, rolling his eyes. "Welcome to my home." He pulled Flash closer. "If you hurt my sister, I'll fucking bury you. Got me?"

"Easy now, City. I wouldn't dream of it. We're just friends." He stood toe to toe with Joe, gripping his shoulder.

I swear to fuck that all I could see was a train wreck. I thought I was standing in the middle of a Looney Tunes cartoon. There had to be a big kaboom coming at any second. Joe and Flash wouldn't be parting on a happy note, but hopefully they could keep their hands to themselves for Thanksgiving.

"I don't care who the fuck you think you are or what MC you're in. You're still Sam to me and I can still whip your ass. Just so we're clear." Joe glared at him.

Suzy's arms slid around Joe as she looked at Flash. "Everything okay, baby?" she asked.

"Just perfect, sugar. This is Sam, Izzy's friend."

She released him, holding out her hand to Flash. "Hi, Sam. I'm Suzy. Nice to meet you," she said, smiling.

"It's my pleasure, Suzy." He pulled her hand to his lips and gently kissed it. "You have a beautiful home."

"Thank you, Sam."

Joe growled. Honest to motherfucking god, the man growled. I knew that my brother was a caveman, but this was beyond the realm of normal behavior. Flash looked at Joe, his lips turning up in a half-smirk before he turned back to Suzy.

"Joe's a very lucky man. I hope you don't mind me crashing the party." Sam looked to Joe with a shit-eating grin before he looked at Suzy.

Yep—death wish.

"Not at all. Come on in and make yourself at home," Suzy

said with a smile before stepping aside and wrapping her arms around my big brother.

"Let's go say hi to my parents, dumbass," I said to Flash, grabbing his shirt and pulling him toward the living room.

"Why the fuck am I a dumbass?" he asked, looking at me with a furrowed brow.

I stopped, turning to face him. "Starting shit with my brother," I whispered, glaring at him.

"Dude, I gotta stand up to the guy. I can't be a doormat. Show no weakness."

"You're a fucking moron." I laughed. "Ma," I said, entering the room.

"Happy Thanksgiving, baby girl." She wrapped her arms around me.

I have the best fucking mother in the world. She had to be the best to raise us as children and come out without a scratch. We didn't make shit easy for her.

"Happy Thanksgiving, Ma." I kissed her cheek before releasing her. "I brought Sam with me." I turned to him and smirked. "He would've been all alone today."

"Aww, Sam, it's so good to see you. How have you been?" she asked as she moved toward him with open arms.

This was pure Mama Gallo. She welcomes everyone and doesn't hold a grudge. I, on the other hand, hold on to shit for too long and always wonder what angle the person is working when they are being nice.

"Mrs. G, looking amazing as always." He hugged her, lifting her off the ground.

She giggled as her face turned pink. "Oh, Sam. Put this old woman down."

"You're not old, Mrs. G. You never will be. You haven't aged a bit since I saw you last."

Flash may be a dumbass and a douche some of the time, but he knew how to talk to the ladies. He'd fine-tuned that skill since we were teenagers. I was immune to his charm.

My pop rose to his feet, moving toward Flash with his arm extended as he offered his hand. "Sam, good to see you, kid.

How the hell have you been?" Pop asked, smacking Flash on the shoulder with his free hand.

I turned to look at my brothers. Snarls and glares were the Gallo boys' preferred mug of choice today. I knew deep down that this would be the longest fucking holiday of my life.

There wasn't a cock in the world worth this much bullshit at a family holiday. I just wanted to laugh and bust a few balls. I didn't want to play referee.

"Yo, Joe, is dinner almost ready?" I yelled, plopping down on the couch in an open spot. If everyone had their mouths full, they couldn't be spouting nonsense.

Suzy came flying out of the kitchen, adjusting her sundress as she walked. Her face was flushed and her lips looked swollen. "Food's ready. Go sit down while Joe and I bring everything to the table, please." She turned around and ran into the kitchen.

Flash held out his hand, helping me from the couch.

I smiled at him. "Thanks," I whispered, climbing off the couch.

"Any time, babe. Only thing better than tasting you is Thanksgiving dinner." He licked his lips as a small grin played on the corner of his mouth.

"Jesus. Not smooth, man. You need to work on your lines if that's the best you have," I said to him as we followed behind everyone else to the dining room table.

"What the fuck is wrong with my lines?"

"Totally not sexy. Does that shit work on the club girls?"

"I don't need lines with those ladies."

"Lucky for you then or you wouldn't be getting any pussy. *Ever.*"

---

"Why the fuck were you gone so long?" Flash asked as we walked into the kitchen. His face was red and he was on edge.

Suzy, Mia, my ma, and I had been upstairs in the war room. It's what we referred to the room as, anyway. It was filled with information about Suzy's wedding. Everything was planned

221

down to the last details. She's anal that way. She's a total over-achiever who has never done anything by the seat of her pants. She has plans for her plans. There's no room for error.

Suzy and Joe were getting married in a week. I had been elected to be in charge of the bachelorette party and nothing else. Thank Christ. I didn't want to be responsible for any fuck-ups. I am not a planner. I've winged shit my entire life.

"We were talking and got a little carried away."

Flash ran his fingers through his hair, making it a bigger mess than it'd already been. "I felt like you threw me to a pack of wolves."

I looked around the room, taking in the sight of my brothers and Pop sitting around the living room. I knew they could be ruthless, but they were harmless.

I ruffled his hair. "Stop being a drama queen."

"Izzy, why do they hate me so much?"

"They don't," I said, sitting next to him at the kitchen table.

"Bullshit," he murmured. "Joey wants to cut my fuckin' throat."

"Nah." I shook my head as I bit my lip. "He just wants you to know where you stand."

"What's his issue?"

"Where would I even begin?" I laughed. "Joe is protective of everyone in this family, especially me. You're in an MC, and for that reason alone, he'd hate you being around me. He knows you fuck me, and that makes him want to rip your cock off and shove it down your throat."

Flash's face paled and his Adam's apple bobbed as he swallowed roughly. "You know I'd protect you, Izzy. You may not be mine, but I'd never let anything happen to you."

"I know, Flash, but Joe doesn't. Let's have dessert and we'll be out of here in a couple of hours. Aren't you happy you came to Thanksgiving Gallo style?"

"Hell yeah." He burped, rubbing his stomach. "The food alone was worth all the trouble."

Suzy walked into the kitchen, giving me a devilish smile as

she looked between Flash and me. "Hey, guys. Ready for dessert?"

I nodded my head, smirking at her. "Yeah. I have to get Flash home soon."

"Aww, really? I wanted to play cards or something." Suzy pouted and stomped to the counter to grab the pumpkin pie.

"We can stay," Flash interrupted before I could reply.

I glared at him, not really in the mood to play cards with the family. "Fine. We'll stay."

His smile grew wide as Suzy yipped and jumped up and down. "Heck yeah! I'm so excited!"

As she walked out of the room, I kept my eyes glued to Flash. This was going to be a very long evening.

"What time do you have to head back?" I asked him, hoping it was sooner than later.

"I'll leave whenever we get back to your place. I just have to be back tonight. I don't have a curfew, Izzy." He laughed, standing and walking to the counter to grab the other pie.

I put my head on the table, lightly smashing it against the surface. I hated bringing anyone with me to family dinners, even Flash. I always felt a sense of being restricted or tied down. They were two things I never wanted to feel.

I avoided relationships like the plague. I never begrudged anyone happiness, but togetherness wasn't for me.

# CHAPTER
# FIVE

IZZY

TEARS STUNG the back of my eyes as I stood in the bridal suite at the church and stared at Suzy. She looked amazing. I'd worried this day wouldn't come, especially after the bachelorette party.

I'd kind of fucked up. She'd said no to male strippers, but shit... I never listen. Joe had flipped when he'd caught the scent of the guy as it lingered on her skin that night. Their entire relationship had almost exploded into a million tiny pieces, but their love was too strong. Plus, Joe had decided to take the stick out of his ass and apologize to her for acting like a complete caveman asshole.

I'd marked that shit down on my calendar because it wasn't likely to ever happen again. Gallo men aren't quick to take the blame for shit. They grunt, smile, and move on.

"She looks stunning, doesn't she?" Mia asked, nudging me in the shoulder.

I slowly nodded, unable to take my eyes off her. "She does." I turned to Mia with a small smile. "When am I going to see you in a wedding dress?"

"Oh," she said, her cheeks turning pink. "I'm just waiting for Mike to ask me."

"Haven't you two talked about marriage?"

"He's mentioned it a time or two, but I'm not pushing it on

him." She shook her head and sighed.

"I need another sister-in-law. You're like my sister already, but I need it official and on paper." I smiled, happy that there were finally some females inside the family circle after years of dealing with the boys.

She laughed, tossing her head back, and held her stomach. "You're more demanding than my mom," she said, wiping the corner of her eyes.

"Hell yeah. I've gone too many years surrounded by testosterone. I need vadge in this family."

Mia and I stood side by side and stared at Suzy as she fussed with her dress and checked her makeup before moving closer to the mirror.

"You look beautiful, Suzy," I said, walking toward her.

The dress had a form-fitting bodice with a thick ribbon and a flower around the waist. The V-shaped neckline plunged just far enough to show off her chest. The bottom was comprised of loose tulle that kissed the floor and shifted when she walked. Suzy always looked amazing, but today she glowed.

"I'm so nervous. Why am I so nervous?" she asked, turning toward me and taking a deep breath.

I grabbed her hands, wanting to avoid messing up her dress. "You're going to be fine. Everything is ready. Don't stress."

"What if he changes his mind?" Her eyes grew wide as she said the words.

I shook my head, my mouth set in a firm line. "You can't be serious. My brother is so in love with you. Why would you even think that?"

"I don't know. I feel panicked."

I touched her forehead, thinking she had to be sick. "No fever," I said as I removed my hand. "Calm the fuck down, Suzy. Joe loves you. I've never seen him so sure about anything or anyone in his life."

She blew out a breath, touching her stomach and smoothing the fabric. "I know," she said, looking down at the floor.

"Are you sure, though?" I asked.

"I love him," she stated firmly.

"Is it enough?" I asked, cocking my eyebrow.

"Izzy, you're such a Debbie Downer on love," she said, laughing. "I can't wait until you find 'the one.'"

I doubled over in a fit of giggles. "You must clearly be ill. I don't want 'the one,'" I said, making air quotes. "I'm perfectly happy being single. The last thing I want is a ball and chain to tie my ass down."

"Uh huh," she said, looking in the mirror again.

"Izzy, when are you going to stop lying to yourself?" Mia interrupted.

"You two bitches need to slow your roll. I'm not the dating type, let alone the marrying kind."

"It's time." Ma clapped her hands as she sang the words.

"Someone do my veil. I'm too nervous!" Suzy shrieked, shaking her hands.

"I got it," I said, stepping in front of her and reaching behind to take the thin material. Then I placed it over her face, smoothing it to not block her vision. "Good?" I asked before moving away.

"Yes," she replied. "It's now or never."

"Suzy, you two were meant for each other. I may not want it for myself, but I have no doubt there's no one else out there for my brother."

"You're right, Izzy. Let's do this crap."

I chuckled, trying to cover my mouth. "You don't always talk like a Gallo, but you're one at heart."

She giggled nervously, moving toward the door. I grabbed her short train, not wanting it to get stuck on anything. When Suzy's father saw her, his face lit up like a Christmas tree.

"There's my girl," he cooed, holding out his arms.

"Hey, Dad." She wrapped her arms around him, trying to avoid touching his tuxedo with her face.

He backed away and stared at her. "You look beautiful, Suzette," he said, holding her shoulders and taking her in.

"Thanks," she said, linking her arm with his.

The music from inside the church filled the corridor where we stood. Nerves filled my belly as it flipped inside my body. I couldn't imagine how Suzy felt. Some would say that I love to be the center of attention, but having hundreds of pairs of eyes staring at you as you try to walk in a pair of five-inch heels and not fall on your face has to be daunting.

As I started down the aisle and smiled, I knew that no one was really looking at me. Their eyes were trained on the back of the room, waiting for a peek at the bride.

Joe nodded at me as I moved into the pew and then turned to watch Suzy. He glowed. When Suzy came into view, his face lit up, his eyes grew wide, and a giant smile spread across his face.

I never thought he'd fall so head over heels for anyone like he did for Suzy. I would've never put the two of them together and thought, *Fuck yeah, that'll work*, but for some odd reason, it had. Her innocence had captured his attention, but we all knew she was a freak underneath that put-together-teacher exterior.

Joe looked handsome in his tuxedo. His hair was freshly cut and styled, his face cleanly shaven. Sun-kissed skin made his blue eyes stand out. All of my brothers looked killer today. Rarely did they all dress up, but weddings were the exception. Joe was the first out of the five of us to be married, and we knew it would be a while before another wedding would take place.

Mike and Mia had met months ago and were the next in line. That would only happen if my brother could get his head out of his ass and pop the question. Anthony and I were the two hold-outs on relationships of any sort. We were the free birds of the group.

I turned, taking in the sight of Suzy as she glided down the aisle. I could see the smile on her face even through her veil as she locked eyes with Joe. They were in a trance, staring at each other as she made her way toward the altar.

When Suzy stopped at the altar, the priest said, "Who gives this bride away today?"

"I do," her father answered, releasing her hand and lifting her veil. Then he placed a chaste kiss on her cheek before stepping back.

Suzy and Joe mouthed some words to each other, which

looked like "I love you," as they held hands. After, they made their way to the center of the altar and stood with the priest.

I sat back, watching the beginning of their happily ever after. I wiggled my nose, stopping the tickling sensation from the tears that threatened to fall.

Even someone such as myself, someone against the entire institution of marriage, could grow misty-eyed at a wedding. I couldn't have been happier to have Suzy officially become a member of the Gallo family. It only took twenty-something years for me to finally have a sister.

Today would be a new beginning. The Gallo family would be forever changed.

# CHAPTER
# SIX

IZZY

STANDING in the reception line had to be the most mind-numbing experience of my entire life. Greeting people I didn't know, welcoming them, and thanking them for coming to my brother's wedding—totally fucking exhausting.

Then there were the people who liked to pinch my cheeks like I was still a five-year-old girl. It took everything I had not to slap their hands away and keep a smile glued to my face. By the time the line waned and I was able to hit the bar, my face hurt from my fake smile and my feet were screaming for relief.

I kicked off my shoes, pushing them under the bar and held my hand up to the bartender.

He sauntered over with a giant smile on his face. "What can I get you, darlin'?"

I leaned against the bar, putting my face in my hands, and stared him down. After the hour of awesomeness that was the receiving line, I wanted a drink and nothing more. I didn't feel like flirting or small talk.

"Jack, straight up," I said without cracking a smile.

"Single or double?"

"Double, please."

As he walked away to pour my drink, I turned and took in the room of people. The wedding was massive. Between Suzy and my ma, I think they had all of Tampa Bay crammed in the room.

"God, I need a drink," Mia said as she walked toward me.

"As bored as I am?" I asked as I leaned back, taking the pressure off my feet.

"At least you know all those people," she replied, motioning toward the bartender.

"The fuck I do. I know maybe half, and even then, I'm sketchy on their names."

"There's a small army here," she said. "Martini, please. Make it dirty with two olives."

"Someone looking to get a little buzzed, like me?"

"Just need to take the edge off," Mia replied. "Weddings make me itchy."

"Like you're allergic?"

"No, Izzy." She shook her head and laughed.

"Well, what the fuck? Clue a sister in."

We turned toward the bar, picking up our drinks and clinking them together.

"I feel I'll always be a bridesmaid and never a bride."

"You have Mike." I sipped the Jack, letting it slide down my throat in one quick swallow.

Mia sipped her martini and winced before her lips puckered. "I could be an old hag before he finds just the right way to ask me to marry him."

"Fuck tradition. Ask him already."

"He'd die," she said, bringing the glass to her lips and looking at me over the rim.

I held up my hand, snapping my fingers for a refill. "He'll get over it. Make a deadline, then. If he doesn't ask by a certain date, then you ask him."

"Maybe," she replied, setting her drink on the bar. "I wouldn't walk away if he doesn't ask. I love him too much."

"He loves you too, Mia. It's really sickening how often I have to hear about you." I laughed, tapping my fingernails against the wooden surface as I waited for my drink. "I love you, of course, but Jesus. The man talks about nothing else except for you and the clinic."

She hit my shoulder, causing me to laugh. "Would you rather him talk about Rob and working out all the time?"

Rob was my brother's trainer before he quit fighting. Rob and I had had a "thing" for a short time. It'd ended badly. Mostly for him, though, since my knee had found its way to his balls and he'd ended up on the floor.

"Well, lesson one is don't refer to women as bitches."

"I'm sure he learned his lesson," she said, and laughed. "I've heard more than once about your wicked, bony-ass knee. I think he still has a thing for you, Izzy."

I turned, holding my glass near my lips. "Ain't no way in hell am I ever dating him. Never. Ever. He's a total asshole."

Mia's laughter turned into a fit of giggles as she held on to the bar to maintain her balance. Tears streamed down her face and her dark eyes twinkled in the lighting. "I know he is. Total douche, but he has a soft side."

"Mia, stop trying to get me to hook up with Rob." I sipped the Jack Daniel's, the feeling of the first shot already making its way through my system. My legs felt a little wobbly and my core warmed. "I don't want a boyfriend and I certainly don't want him."

"Someday, Izzy, you're going to meet that guy. One who makes your belly flip and toes curl. The electricity between you two will be undeniable. You just haven't met the right one."

"He's like a unicorn, Mia. Totally fictional bullshit."

She shook her head, finishing the last sip of her martini. "He's not. You just haven't found him yet. I feel those things when I'm with Michael."

"You're obviously mentally impaired," I chortled.

"I can't wait to see the day someone has you all in a fluster. You're going to be totally fucked."

"Mia, babe, there ain't no man tough enough to handle all this," I said, motioning down my body.

"Uh huh," she clucked, her shoulders shaking from laughter. "I can't wait to see the damn day."

"It's dinnertime, ladies," my ma sang as she walked through the bar area. "It's time to take your seats."

"I could use a little food and a damn chair," I said, wondering how I'd make it to the table with my feet feeling like someone was rubbing hot coals on them.

"Me too," Mia said, following behind me.

We both walked gingerly toward the table that was placed on the dance floor and facing the entire room. I felt almost like a zoo animal as I sat down and looked around the large ballroom.

I ate my food and chatted with Mia throughout the dinner. Joe and Suzy were interrupted so many times with clinking glasses that I didn't have any idea if they were able to consume half their meal. It was cute, and at some point, I thought Joe would tell them to use their fucking forks to eat, but he didn't.

Suzy did that to him. She chilled him out at times when he was ready to burst. I knew he wanted the day to be special, and did everything in his power to make sure it was perfect. Even held his tongue when I know he had to be biting it so hard that he drew blood.

"I'm hitting the bar again after dinner," I told Mia, hoping she'd join me.

"I'm in," she replied. "Until Michael drags me on the dance floor."

"I wish you luck with that." I laughed, placing the last bit of pasta in my mouth.

I didn't get up immediately. My mother would have given me the stink eye if I'd looked too eager to run to the bar. I sat there staring at the crowd, smiling, and making small talk with the others at the table. Sipping my wine, I counted the minutes until I could stand again on my aching feet and drink myself into oblivion.

Weddings, even my brother's, were bullshit. There was no fucking way in hell I'd be standing on the dance floor later, knocking over girls to get a bouquet of flowers. I wasn't looking for some symbolic nonsense that I'd be the next one walking down the aisle and giving up my freedom. Fuck tradition.

# CHAPTER
# SEVEN

IZZY

AFTER DOWNING countless drinks and chatting up Mia and all the long-lost family members who'd shown their asses at the wedding, I turned to see a very red-faced Suzy enter the ballroom. Joe stood by her side, but he looked calm—besides the small smirk on his face.

"Hey, sister," I said as I walked toward her. "I'm so excited to be able to say that and it be true. I've always wanted a sister." I wrapped my arms around her, squeezing her a little too tight.

"Can't breathe," she whispered.

"Man up," I said, releasing her.

"I'll be back, ladies. I'm going to grab a drink at the bar with my boys," Joe said before he kissed her cheek and left us alone.

"Where's your sister?" I asked, looking around the crowd.

Suzy had a sister, but they weren't close. The Gallos were closer to her, and more of a family than hers would ever be. I felt bad for her, but it made me love her more.

"Don't know and don't give a shit either." She shrugged and looked at the floor.

"You know you've turned into a badass with a potty mouth, Suz."

She smiled, shaking her head. "City. It's all his fault."

"I'd like to think I played a part in it, too." I laughed.

"You're always getting me in trouble, Izzy."

233

"Me?" I asked, holding my hand to my chest.

"Always."

A man cleared his throat next to us and we both turned in his direction. "Excuse me, ladies. I don't mean to interrupt."

"Well then don't," I slurred, looking the stranger up and down. Handsome, well built, great hair, and totally doable. Maybe I shouldn't have been such a bitch, but then again, Jack was talking after I'd consumed more than necessary.

"Don't be rude, Izzy," Suzy said, turning to face him. "How can I help you?"

"I'm a friend of Thomas's, and he asked me to drop off a gift on his behalf." The man held out an envelope and waited for her to take it.

I took this moment to study him further. His muscles bulged underneath his suit as he held out his hands. His eyes were green, but I couldn't tell the shade. His jaw line was sharp and strong.

"Is he okay?" I asked. I hadn't seen my brother in so long, and information wasn't freely flowing lately. He worked under-cover for the DEA and was in deep with an MC in Florida. I wanted him home, safe and sound.

"He is, and he's very sorry he couldn't make it," he said, looking down at me.

"Don't mind her," Suzy said to him, her eyes moving from me to him. "Thomas is her brother."

"Ah, you're *that* Izzy," he said, his lips turning up into a smile. "I've heard a lot about you."

What the fuck did that mean? I snarled, not entirely liking the shit-eating grin on his face. "And you are?" I asked, holding out my hand for him to take.

"James." He slid his hand along my palm and stilled. "James Caldo."

"Never heard of you, Jimmy," I said, trying to knock him down a peg. I didn't like that he had heard of me, with his "*that* Izzy" comment, and I'd never even heard his name.

He brought my hand to his lips and placed a kiss just below my knuckles. "Perfect."

His lips scorched my skin. An overwhelming sense of want came over me. I felt the urge to jump into his arms and kiss his very full lips. My toes curled painfully in my shoes as I stared at his mouth against my skin. As he removed his lips from my hand and brought his eyes back to mine, I wiped all evidence of want from my face.

Suzy coughed, ruining my fantasy and bringing me back to reality. "Thanks, James. I'll give this to Joseph for you. Why don't you stay and enjoy the wedding?" She smiled at the man.

"What?" I asked, turning toward her. Suzy played dirty. Her angel act was just that—an act.

"We have plenty of food, and I'm sure the Gallos would love to talk with you about their Thomas," Suzy said, grinning like an idiot.

I gave her the look of death. What in the fuck was wrong with her?

"You can keep James company tonight, Izzy. You didn't bring a date."

*She did not just say that.* If it weren't her wedding, I swear to shit I would've smacked her. I could feel my cheeks turning red as his eyes flickered to mine.

"I'd love to stay. Thank you. Izzy, would you like a drink?" he asked, still holding my hand in his.

"Only because Suzy would want me to be a gracious host," I said, looking at her out of the corner of my eye.

"I don't want to put you out or anything. I'm a *big* boy and can handle myself. I just thought you could use a drink to unwind a bit. You feel a little tense, and that mouth of yours could get you into trouble."

Obviously, he was full of himself. Trust me when I say I can smell a cocky bastard from a mile away. I grew up with enough of them to sniff them out across a room.

"I don't need a babysitter, Jimmy, but I'll take the drink."

"It's James," he said, squeezing my hand.

"You two kids play nice," Suzy said before she waved and walked away.

"Bitch," I mumbled under my breath as I turned back toward the bar.

"Excuse me?" he asked, gripping my arm as he pulled me backward.

I stopped and faced him. "Are you going to release me anytime soon?"

"Highly unlikely." He smirked.

"Jimmy, listen. I don't know what your deal is or who the fuck you think you are, but no one touches me without permission."

With that, he released me, but not before squeezing my arm. "You'll be begging for my touch."

I glared at him, floored by his cockiness. "Obviously you know nothing about me then." I left him in the dust.

I leaned against the bar, feeling him behind me as I motioned to the bartender. At this point in the evening, I no longer had to verbalize my order. He knew it.

"Like what you see?" I asked as I kept my eyes forward.

"Your brother didn't do you justice."

Resting my back against the bar, I asked, "What exactly do you think of me?"

He smiled, stepping closer as he invaded my personal space. He brushed the hair from my cheek, running his fingertip down my face. "You're prettier in person. You are tough as nails, just like your brother said, but I can see the real Izzy underneath."

I snarled, feeling all kinds of bitchy. "There's no hidden me underneath. This is who I am. I make no apologies for my bitchiness or candid comments."

"Oh, little girl, you're so much more than a smart mouth." He leaned in, hovering his mouth just above mine.

I held my breath, silently debating if I wanted him to kiss me. I had to be crazy. There was nothing about this man I liked, besides his face. His words were infuriating, his attitude was obnoxious, and the fact that he thought he had me pegged made me want to slap his face when he spoke.

His eyes searched mine as I stood there not breathing and just keeping myself upright against the bar.

"You're an asshole, Jimmy."

He didn't back away. Instead, he held his ground, pressing against my body. "It's James," he murmured.

I swallowed hard, my stomach flipping inside my body like I'd just gone down the giant hill on a roller-coaster. "Still an asshole," I whispered, my tongue darting out to caress my lips and almost touch his.

"Doll, I never claimed to be nice." His lips were turned up into a grin so large that it almost kissed his eyes.

"Can we drink now?" I asked, wanting to move our bodies apart. The heat coming off him was penetrating my dress and causing my body to break out into a sweat. The pop and sizzle I felt inside was more than just the alcohol. James, the asshole, did naughty things to my body, and I needed distance between us.

"Don't you think you've had enough?" he asked without moving out of my personal space.

I placed my hands against his chest and pushed. He didn't budge or falter as I pushed again.

He tipped his head back and laughed. "Is that all you got?"

"Fucker. First off, I have more, but I don't want to cause a scene at my brother's wedding. Second, I haven't had enough. You aren't my father and you don't get to tell me when to stop drinking. Last time I checked my driver's license, I was old enough to make that choice for myself." I crossed my arms over my chest, trying to put some space between his torso and mine.

"Let's get one thing straight, Isabella." His hot breath tickled the nape of my neck as he put his mouth against my ear and spoke. "I will have you in my bed tonight."

I rolled my eyes and pursed my lips, trying to hide exactly how excited that statement had made me. I didn't want to date the man, but shit, I wanted to fuck him.

"You're quite sure of yourself, *Jimmy*." I emphasized his name, knowing it would drive him crazy.

"There are things I'm very sure of."

"Like what?" I spat.

"From the moment I saw you, I knew I wanted to be inside you. When I touched you, I felt something, and I know you felt it, too. There's something between us. I think I need to fuck you out of my system."

"Is that the best line you have?" I hissed, feeling his lips against my ear. I groaned, closing my eyes to let the feel of his mouth on my skin soak into my bones.

"I don't need lines, Izzy," he growled, with his teeth caging the flesh of my ear.

My toes curled inside my heels; I felt him all over my body. No one had ever affected me in this way.

"I'm down for a challenge."

"Doll, there's no challenge with a willing participant."

I pulled back, feeling his mouth slip from my skin, and looked him in the eye. "I was referring to your ability to keep up with me."

Again, he laughed and held his stomach. "Izzy, Izzy. Baby, if you can walk right in the morning without still feeling me inside you, I'd be shocked. I have no doubt I can keep up with you. You'll never be the same after I've fucked you."

"You better buy me a drink, then. I'll go easier on you." I smiled, turning my back to him and facing the bartender. Then I snapped my fingers, pointing in front of me as he smiled and grabbed the bottle of Jack.

Over my shoulder, James called out, "Make it two." He placed one hand on the bar to my right and stood to the left of me. His forearm pressed against my back, holding me in place and leaving me no escape. "What shall we drink to?" he asked.

"My brother," I replied. Thomas was our link. The connection that James and I shared. "What did he say about me?" I asked.

James smiled, turning his head to face me. "That you're his favorite sister."

"Jackass, I'm his only sister."

"I know." He laughed. "He told me you're hard to please."

I shook my head. "I'm not. I'm just picky and I don't settle."

"Can't fault you there. He's proud of you."

"For what?" I asked, looking at him, stunned.

"He's proud of the strong woman you've grown into, and I'd have to agree with the little bit of you I've experienced."

"Ha," I said. "I learned everything I know from my four brothers."

The bartender placed our shots on the bar and started to walk away.

"Hey, can we get two more?" I asked before he could get too far.

He nodded and grabbed the bottle, making two more drinks.

I lifted my glass, waiting for James to pick his up before I spoke. "To Thomas." I tipped my drink, clinking the glass with his before downing the liquid.

I watched over the rim as James swallowed it and didn't wince. His features were so strong and manly. I mean, what the fuck was that? I'd never thought of any one as manly. *Maybe I shouldn't have another drink.*

"Tell me who you really are," James said as he placed his empty glass on the bar.

"What you see is what you get," I said before I licked the Jack off my lips.

"I know there's the Izzy everyone sees and the real woman underneath."

"James, what you see is what you get."

"Are you always so hard?" he asked, brushing his thumb against my hand as it rested on the bar.

"I don't know. Are you always so damn nosy?"

"I think you haven't found the right man to tame your sass."

I turned to glare at him. "Hold up. I need a man, is that what you're saying?"

"No," he said, shaking his head. "I think your tongue is so sharp because you haven't found the man who makes you whole. Someone who crawls inside you so deep that you finally figure out who you are, what you were always meant to be."

"What the fuck?" I asked, scrunching my eyebrows in confusion.

"It's for another day, doll. Sometimes, we just need someone to bring out our true nature."

CHELLE BLISS

"Either I've clearly had too much to drink or you're talking out of your ass. I'm going to go with option two."

He cupped my face in his hand, rubbing the spot just behind my ear with his fingertips. "Sometimes, we don't know who we really are until we find the perfect partner to bring it out."

"Jimmy, I think we were talking about one night. You and me fucking each other's brains out and then walking away. Now, you're talking crazy if you think I need you in my life to complete me. I'm certainly not Renée Zellweger and you're no Tom Cruise. I don't need any man to complete me. I'm quite happy with my life."

"Fine. Tell me who you are." His stare pinned me in place.

Swallowing, I didn't take my eyes off him as I thought about my reply. I'd never had to explain myself to anyone. "Who are you, James?"

He shook his head, a small smile on his face, as he laughed softly. "I'm a protector."

I cut him off. "Do you think I need protecting?"

"I don't know," he replied.

"I have four older brothers who have made it their life's mission to make sure I'm protected. It's the last thing I need in my life."

"Can I finish?" he asked, taking a deep breath and tilting his head.

"Yes," I said, gulping hard and searching for some moisture in my now parched mouth.

"As I was saying, I'm a natural protector. That's why I joined the agency. I'm loyal to the core. I know what I want in life, and I never give up until I get it. There's nothing better than a good chase. Once I have my mind set on something, I'll stop at nothing to get what I want."

"Am I your goal?" I asked, smirking and feeling a little playful.

"What if I said yes?" James asked, moving his face closer to mine.

"I'd say you better have a new game plan."

240

"Are you a secret lesbian?" he teased, the corner of his mouth twitching.

"No! Fuck!" I hissed. "I mean, more power to anyone who loves vadge, but I'm all about cock, baby."

He closed his eyes, his breath skidding across my face as he blew the air out of his lungs. "If you talk about cock one more time, I'm taking you upstairs and fucking you until you can't scream anymore."

"That sounds creepy."

His chest shook as a laugh fell from his lips. "You have to be the most difficult female I have ever met."

"Maybe I'm more woman than you can handle," I purred, running my hand down his chest. Underneath my fingertips, I could feel his muscles flexing. I splayed my palm against his shirt, letting my hand rest against his rock-hard pec.

"Doll, I'm more man than you've ever had. That I can guarantee."

The air between us crackled. Like it did in the movies. Sparks were probably visible to any guest milling around the bar area.

"Izzy," Mia said, interrupting my moment with James.

I blinked slowly, looking over his shoulder and smiling at her. "Hey, Mia."

"Who do we have here?" she asked, a grin on her face.

"Mia, this is Jimmy, Thomas's friend."

His eyes flashed before he turned to face her. "Mia, it's nice to meet you. I'm James." He held out his hand, waiting for her touch.

"James, I'm Mike's girl." She slid her hand into his palm, shaking it slowly.

"I'd say you're more than a girl." He pulled her hand to his mouth and placed a soft kiss on the top.

She laughed, her cheeks turning red. Did he have this effect on all women? "You know what I mean," she said, batting her eyelashes.

Thank Christ Mike wasn't here to see Mia blushing and flirting with Jimmy boy.

"Mike's a very lucky man," James replied, releasing her hand.

I sighed, rolling my eyes before glaring at Mia. "Where's Mike, anyway?" I asked, feeling a bit jealous of his flirting.

I was bothered that he was flirting with her, but why? I shouldn't have been. I didn't like him. I wanted to use him. That was all. I wanted to have my way with him for one night and walk away unscathed. Jealousy wasn't an emotion I was used to experiencing, and I sure as hell didn't know how to deal with it.

"He's dancing with his ma," she replied, winking at me and mouthing, "Wow," as James turned to look at me before returning his attention to her.

"Would you like a drink, Mia?"

She smiled, nodding. "Always."

James motioned to the bartender as I walked to stand next to Mia.

"He's sexy as fuck," Mia whispered in my ear.

"He's an asshole, though."

"Nah, he couldn't be. He seems to be a perfect gentleman."

"Maybe you shouldn't have another if you think he's not a total prick."

"You're just too damn hard on men, Iz."

"He's cocky, Mia. He makes Mike and Joe seem like teddy bears."

"I like him," she said, her eyes raking over him.

"Hey, slutty Aphrodite, you're taken."

"I can look, *putana*. I'm not dead. I can tell you like him."

My mouth dropped open. "What?" I whispered. "I do not."

She smiled, nodding at me. "You do."

"All right, ladies," James said as he held out two glasses of Jack.

"To love," Mia said. "And passion."

"For fuck's sake," I blurted, bringing the cup to my mouth.

"I'll drink to that," James said, holding me in place with his stare.

I didn't respond as I slammed back the drink, letting it slide down my throat. Instead, I started to picture sex with James.

242

There was a simmering tension between us. An animal attraction that was undeniable. I wanted to slap him and fuck him at the same time. I wanted to let loose and show him what Izzy Gallo really had.

"Thanks for the drink, James. I'm going to find Mike. You two have a fun night," Mia said, winking and smiling as she waved and walked away.

"Traitor," I mumbled, turning to face James.

"You want to fuck me?" James asked, taking the drink from my hand.

"What?" I asked, wondering if he would be so bold.

"You in or you out?" he growled with his hand on my hip, gripping it roughly with his fingers.

"I don't even know you," I replied, as his hold on me felt like a branding iron under my dress.

"What do you want to know?" he asked, still touching my body.

"You could be a bad man." That sounded stupid and childish, but I was trying to not seem too eager to jump in the sack with him.

"Would your brother send me here if I were a total asshole?"

He had me there. "No," I admitted.

"Do you know everything about every man you sleep with?" he asked, running his free hand down my arm.

"No."

"Do you want to fuck me?"

I bit my lip, blinking slowly and processing my thoughts. Did I want to? Fuck yes, I did. Was it a good idea? Hell no, it wasn't a good idea. But then again, mistakes sometimes leave the biggest mark in one's life.

"Maybe," I squeaked out.

He released my hip, moving his hand to the small of my back. "Ready?" he asked, cocking an eyebrow.

"Now?"

"Are you scared, little girl?" he teased.

"Of you?" There wasn't a man on this planet who scared me. The fear I felt was from within. It was pointed directly at me. A man wasn't the issue. James was, and the way my body reacted to him had me on high alert.

"Yeah," he said, the side of his mouth turning up into a grin I wanted to smack off his face.

This was where I should've called a time-out. The words I should've spoken didn't come out of my mouth.

"James, I have four older brothers. You hardly scare me."

"But they want to protect you and love you. While I, on the other hand, want to bury my dick so far inside you that I ruin you for eternity."

"You say such beautiful things." I'd be lying if I didn't admit to myself that he made my pussy clench with his words.

"You in or you out?"

"The real question, Jimmy, is am I going to let you in?" I turned back toward the bar and signaled for another drink.

*Let the games begin.*

# CHAPTER
# EIGHT

JAMES

WHAT THE FUCK was wrong with me? This wasn't how I normally treated a woman I'd just met. There was something different about Izzy, though. I'd felt like I knew her the moment we met. Thomas had filled my head with stories about his little sister and made her bigger than life. Seeing her in person only drove the point home that she was different than other women.

If he'd heard how I was talking to her, he'd have my nuts in a vise, making sure I'd never be able to get another hard-on in my life. I needed to slow my shit down.

"I'm a patient man, and you'll be in my bed before the night is through."

She laughed, her head falling back as her teeth shone in the light. "I can't leave yet," she said, grabbing her drink and swirling the contents inside. "I have to do all the bridesmaid bullshit."

"I can tell by your comment that you believe in true love."

"Fuck love. Don't get me wrong. I'm thrilled for Joe and Suzy, but the shit isn't for me. Don't say it," she warned, her eyes turning into small slits as she glared at me.

"What? That you just haven't met the right man?" I stood next to her at the bar and leaned my arm against the wooden surface as I faced her.

"Yes. It's not about that. Love makes shit messy," she explained before bringing the glass to her lips.

"Can I get a beer?" I asked the bartender as he walked by, and his eyes flickered to us.

His eyes raked over Izzy, and I saw the hunger burning inside them. I felt an overwhelming urge to rip them from his skull just so he couldn't eye-fuck her again.

He looked to me and snarled as he reached in the cooler, popped the top of a Yuengling, and placed it in front of me. Grabbing the cool bottle, I let my fingers slide over the wetness. Then I wished I could squelch the internal burning I felt for Izzy.

"You sound like a woman who came from a broken home. Thomas speaks very highly of your parents and the love they feel for each other. What turned you off love?" Bringing the bottle to my lips, I watched her as she swallowed hard and played with the glass in her hand.

"It's not love that I have an issue with. It's the battle that ensues because of it."

After pulling the beer from my mouth, I shook my head, trying to make sense of her statement. "What battle?"

"The one every girl I've ever known has gone through. They have to decide how much of themselves they're willing to lose to be with the man they love."

"That's bullshit."

"There isn't a female I know who didn't change after being in 'love,'" she said, making air quotes and rolling her eyes.

"Maybe they brought out the real woman who was always lurking at the surface and too scared to show."

"You can have your opinion, James, but I know what I see."

"Ladies and gentlemen," a man called through the microphone. "If we could have the bride and groom on the dance floor and all the single ladies and gentlemen join them."

"You going?" I asked with a cocked eyebrow.

"It's stupid," she said before taking a sip of Jack.

"You're such a party pooper. Get your fine ass to the dance floor."

"Or what?"

246

I smiled, shaking my head slowly. "Let's place a bet."

"Whatcha got in mind, Jimmy?" Izzy cooed, rubbing the lapels on my suit jacket with her fingers.

"If I catch the garter, then we ditch this place and head to my room. No questions asked and no lip from you." I'd knock every motherfucker on the dance floor over to get the garter and have Izzy underneath me within an hour.

"Okay, and if I catch the bouquet, then I don't have to go anywhere with you. You leave and I get to spend the rest of the night in peace." She tilted her head, waiting for me to accept that challenge.

"Fuck yeah. I'm game," I said. Then I gulped the last bit of beer as she downed her drink and placed it on the bar. Setting my hand on the small of her back, I guided her away from the bar.

She stood stiff next to me as we watched her brother use his teeth to remove the garter from underneath the dress of his new bride. The crowd cheered when he appeared from the dress victorious. Twirling the small scrap of material in his hands, he raised his arms in victory.

"You ready to lose?" I asked, looking down at Izzy.

"One thing I'm never good at is losing, Jimmy."

"Single gentlemen first. All others please clear the floor," the DJ said as everyone moved away, leaving about fifteen of us to jockey for the garter.

I looked around, sizing up the competition. I was the biggest besides Michael, Izzy's brother. I took my spot to the side, knowing I could move quickly in front of the crowd and snatch the material before it turned into a free-for-all.

As the DJ started the countdown, Joe turned his back, practicing his throw, and the men moved with his motion. I readied myself as my heart hammered in my chest louder than a drum at a Metallica concert. I kept my eyes locked to his hand as he moved, waiting to see it fly through the air.

As his hand jerked back, the material flew through the air only feet to my right. I moved quickly, stepping in front of everyone else, and snatched it easily. The wedding attendees cheered as I turned to Izzy with a sinful smile, and nothing but seeing her ass in the air, waiting for my dick filled my mind.

"Fucker," she mouthed at me as I walked toward her.

"It's all on you now. Better catch that bouquet," I said, running my index finger down her cheek.

She closed her eyes, swallowing hard before opening them. Inside her baby blues was a fire burning so hot that I could see her pupils dilate as she looked at me. She nodded before making her way toward the crowd of women now standing at the ready.

She whispered to Mia, and their eyes flickered to me. A giant smile spread across Mia's face as Izzy glared at me. Winking, Mia tipped her chin in my direction as her smile grew wider. I said a silent prayer as Suzy readied herself with her bouquet and turned her back on the crowd. Mia bent at the knees like an athlete waiting for the gunshot to sound.

Silently, I prayed that Mia could take Izzy down and make sure she didn't grab the flowers. I wouldn't want to lose a bet to Isabella Gallo, and certainly not one as important as this. I didn't need a bet to bed a woman, but I had a feeling Izzy needed to feel like the choice was out of her hands. She needed an out. Needed something to tell herself to make it all okay to spend the night with me.

I should have felt guilty about the bet, but I didn't. Not one fucking bit.

The countdown began, my heart matching the drum roll blaring through the speakers. "Come on, Mia," I whispered.

My palms grew sweaty as I formed my hands into a tight fist, trying to shake out some of the nervous energy. If Izzy caught the fucking bouquet, I'd have a very long night filled with fantasies and jacking off like a twelve-year-old boy.

As the flowers traveled through the air, Mia held out her arm, pushing Izzy backward. Mia jumped in the air, Izzy looking at Mia in horror. The flowers grazed Mia's fingers, sailing over her head to the woman standing behind her.

The redheaded beauty closed her hands around the flowers, jumped up and down, and squealed.

"Fuck," Izzy hissed, turning to me and glaring in my direction.

I smiled, shrugging as I held up the garter and twirled it in my fingers. "You're mine," I mouthed before licking my lips.

The hunger I felt inside when looking at her was unlike anything I'd ever felt before. I'd lusted after women in the past, but the want for her was so intense that I wasn't even sure one night with her would be enough to satisfy the craving.

She turned to Mia, saying a few things, with her hands flapping around. Clearly Izzy was angry, but all Mia did was shrug and smile. Then Izzy turned her back, quickly moving toward me.

"Mia totally fucked me," she said as she stood in front of me, looking up into my eyes.

My lips curved into a smile as I stuffed the garter in my jacket pocket. "I don't care how I get you, but tonight, I'm the only one fucking you, doll."

"Fine," she said, standing with her legs shoulder width apart and her arms crossed over her chest.

"I'll give you one out. Kiss me, and if you feel nothing, I'll let you out of the bet." It could all blow up in my face, but I couldn't be a total prick. I didn't want her to be an unwilling participant.

"Just one kiss?" she asked as her face softened.

"Yes," I said, holding her face in my hand and running my thumb across her bottom lip.

"I'll take you up on that offer, but I don't welsh on my bets."

"It's your only out. So use it if you need to or else we're going to my room. No more waiting."

"Come on," she said, grabbing my hand and pulling me toward the ballroom exit.

I laughed as I followed behind her, letting her lead me into the corridor.

"Over there," she said as she pointed down the hallway near the elevator bank.

"Anywhere you want, doll."

The crowd thinned as we walked to a small cutout near the bathrooms.

"Why don't we go outside for a moment? Grab some air," I said. I didn't want to kiss her outside the bathroom. There were too many wedding guests and it was not sexy at all.

"Are you pussying out?" she said as she stopped and turned to face me.

"Fuck no. I just don't feel like kissing you outside the bathroom. I've never been a pussy a day in my life."

"Fine, but fuck, these shoes are killing me," she said as she reached down and pulled one off her foot. When she removed the second one, she sighed, closing her eyes like she'd had a weight lifted off her shoulders. She shrank by at least three inches, making me feel even bigger than I was.

"Are *you* pussying out?" I asked, teasing her for taking a moment to enjoy the newfound freedom of being shoeless.

"You're fucking crazy. Just know that, once my lips touch yours, there's no turning back. Come on, Jimmy boy. Show me what you got," she said as she pushed open the exit door in the hallway.

We stepped outside, into the cool night air, into privacy. The back of the hotel was deserted as the parking lot light flickered above us.

"So now what?" she asked, turning to face me.

I looked down at her, taking in her body before staring into her eyes. I didn't respond as I stepped into her space and pulled her toward me. Holding her neck with one hand and her back with the other, I molded my body to hers. Pushing her against the brick façade, I hovered my lips above hers.

Her eyes were wide, the deep blue appearing black in the darkness. Her warm breath tickled my lips as her breathing grew harsh. I waited a moment, letting the anticipation build, knowing that the kiss would alter everything. There would be no turning back.

I crushed my lips to hers, feeling the warmth and softness, tasting the Jack as I ran my tongue along the seam of her closed mouth. A small moan from her filled my mouth, causing my dick to pulse. Pulling her closer to me, tipping her head back farther with the grip on her neck, I devoured her mouth.

Her hands found their way to my hair, trying to grab hold, but the cropped cut made it impossible. She dug her nails into my neck, kissing me back with such fervor that I knew I had her. Sliding my hand down her dress, I pulled the material between my fingers and hiked it up enough to touch the skin above her knee. Then she broke the kiss, backing away as she stared at me and tried to catch her breath.

Before she could respond or tell me to stop, I plunged my tongue into her mouth, stripping her ability to speak. Her hands found their way into my suit jacket, gripping my back and kneading the muscles just above my ass. I ground myself against her, pinning her against the wall as I kissed her like a man possessed.

The ember of lust that had filled my body when I'd first touched her turned into an out-of-control wildfire. She shuddered as my fingers slid up her inner thigh, stopping just outside her panties. I rubbed my finger back and forth, touching the edge where the lace met her soft flesh. Her body grew soft in my arms as she moaned into my mouth.

Not waiting for approval, I pulled the material aside and dipped my fingers into her wetness. I slid my fingers up, circling her clit with my index and middle finger. A strangled moan escaped her lips as my touch grew more demanding. She pushed herself against my fingers, wanting more pressure from my touch.

Gliding my fingers down, I inserted a single finger inside her pussy. She was tight, slick, and ready. Her inner walls squeezed against my digit, sucking it farther inside. Moving my thumb to her clit, I finger-fucked her, bringing her to the brink of orgasm without breaking the kiss. She held on to my shoulder, digging her nails in so hard that I could feel the pinch through my suit jacket.

Just as her breathing grew more erratic and her pussy clamped down on my finger, I pulled out. She sucked in a breath as her eyes flew open.

"What the fuck?" she hissed as she glared at me.

"You want to come, doll?" I asked, sticking my finger in my mouth and groaning.

This was just as much of a fucking tease for me as it was for her. To taste her and feel her against me made my body blaze with need and want, and I wasn't sure one night could extinguish the flame.

"What kind of question is that?" she snapped.

"It's simple. If you want to come, you'll follow me to my room or I walk away and never look back."

She placed her hands against my chest, slightly pushing me away from her. Staring into my eyes, she stated firmly, "No strings attached."

"I didn't picture myself getting down on one knee and proposing." I instantly regretted the words. It wasn't that I wanted to propose, but I didn't want her to feel cheap and disposable. Then again, she'd set the stage for that type of statement. Izzy Gallo didn't want to be tied down and didn't want to have to explain shit to her brother. I liked my life and balls too much to tell him that I wanted her in my life.

"Music to my ears," she said, dropping her hand to my chest, sliding it down my abdomen and grabbing my dick. "Let's see if you're as good as you claim, Jimmy."

"Babe, I'm going to rock your world so fuckin' hard you're going to get down on one knee and propose to *me*."

She threw her head back and laughed. Her beauty was amplified when she smiled. With a small burst of giggles breaking free, she tried to speak. "You obviously think highly of yourself." She squeezed my hardness and bit her lip, stifling the laughter.

"I'm done talking," I said as I pulled her toward the door. "Time to put up or shut up, doll."

"I like a challenge," she replied as she touched the door handle.

Reaching in front of her, I placed my hand over hers. Pulling the door open, I waited for her to step inside. When she walked, she shook her hips, and the movement made it almost impossible to keep my hands to myself. I nestled my palm against the small of her back, helping her toward the bank of elevators.

"Last chance to chicken out," I teased in her ear.

"I may have a pussy, Jimmy, but I'm sure as hell *not* one."

"Usually, a mouth like that I'd say is crude, but hearing you talk dirty just makes me want to jam my cock inside to quiet you," I whispered, trying to avoid the attention of the people passing by us.

As soon as the elevator doors closed, I had her against the wall. I claimed her mouth, her tongue sweet from the Jack lingering on the surface as I devoured her. Caging her face in my hands, I stole her breath and replaced it with my own.

When we reached my floor, I broke the kiss. Her body was still as her eyes fluttered open, and her breathing was ragged. I grabbed her hand, pulling her toward my room, a little too eager to feel her skin.

The chemistry was off the charts. As soon as the door closed behind us, I pushed her against the door, capturing her lips. The need I felt to be inside her bordered on animalistic as our heavy breathing and panting filled the room. I grabbed the purse she had tucked under her arm and tossed it over my head, removing any distraction.

I dropped to my knees, looking up at her, and said, "I need to taste you."

She was a vision. She had on thigh-highs that connected to a garter belt and lace panties.

She didn't reply, but she did spread her legs. I cupped her ass, ripping the thin lace material from her body and bringing her forward before I swept my tongue against her skin. I could smell her arousal. I wanted to worship at her altar.

I lifted her with my hands, placing her legs over my shoulders as I feasted on her. I sucked like a starved man, licking every ridge and bump as she chanted, "Fuck yeah," and "Oh my God." I didn't relent when she came on my face, her legs almost a vise around my head. I dug in deeper, sucking harder as I brushed her asshole with my fingertip. Her body shuddered, the light touch against the sensitive spot sending her quickly over the edge for the second time.

I gave her a moment to catch her breath before I peeled her off me and stood. As soon as I did, her lips captured mine; the tiger inside her had been unleashed. Her tongue danced inside my mouth, intertwining with mine. She wrapped her legs around my waist, digging her pussy into my already hard and throbbing cock.

The wetness from her pussy soaked through my dress shirt, searing my flesh. I walked toward the bed, unzipping her dress and resting my palm against her back. I wanted to rip her dress off, take her fast and hard, but I knew I needed to take my time with her. This would be my only shot to have Izzy Gallo, and I wouldn't waste it. I wanted to spend all night inside her and hear her scream my name.

My first instinct kicked in as I pulled her dress down her shoulders. She released my hair, removing her arms from the small scraps of material that encased her. Holding her body with one arm, I slid my other hand up her side and cupped her breast. Rolling her nipple between my fingers, I pulled her body closer and left no space between us. I toyed with the hoop piercing, gently tugging on her nipple to see her pain threshold.

Her breathing grew erratic as her body shuddered against mine. Biting her lip, I moaned into her mouth as I tried to keep myself upright. I had never kissed someone and felt weak-kneed, but with her, it was like my first kiss. World ending. Life altering. Completely fucked up.

She sucked the air from my lungs, capturing my moans as she rubbed her core against me. Unable to wait any longer, I reached between us and plunged my fingers back inside her. Her body sucked them in, pulsing around the length as I dragged them back out. Curling them up, I rubbed her G-spot with each lash of my digits.

Her fingers moved to my shoulders, digging into my flesh as I brought her close to coming. Claiming her mouth, stealing each other's air, and driving each other absolutely mad, I knew I was fucked.

That's the thing about sex. Touching someone for the first time is so intense that you feel like you'll never be the same. I felt that way with her in my arms and my fingers inside her. I knew I'd be changed forever. Izzy was my equal. Her wit, sass, and sexuality couldn't compare to any other woman I'd ever met. How could I go back to average when I'd had spectacular?

I removed my fingers, hearing her hiss at the loss of friction. I shrugged off my suit jacket; my body cooled, but not my need for her. I laid her down, her chest exposed and the bottom of the dress a mess as I pulled off my tie and started to open my shirt.

A small smile crept across her face as she fondled her tits. Taking a deep breath, I tried to calm my insides as I watched her touch herself. Giving up on the slow-ass fucking buttons, I ripped my shirt open, and the buttons flew everywhere.

Fuck slow. I needed relief. I needed her.

The smile melted from her face as I stared down at her. She pulled at her nipples, her eyes raking over my chest. Moving forward, I unzipped my pants. I grabbed her ankles, yanking her to the edge of the bed. Unable to wait any longer, I pushed down my pants, letting my cock spring free.

Her eyes traveled down my body, landing on my dick. Then her eyes perked up and the corner of her mouth turned into a devilish smile.

"Impressive," she said as she cupped a breast in each hand and squeezed.

"Fuck," I hissed, realizing I didn't have a condom.

What a fucking idiot. I hadn't planned on taking her to bed, or else I would've been prepared. This hadn't been in the cards for this weekend, but I'd take the jackpot and ride the wave.

"I got it," she said as she rolled over and grabbed her purse off the floor, pulling a strip of condoms from inside.

Normally, the sight would disturb me, but not with her. "Planning on getting lucky?" I asked, staring down at her.

She laughed for a moment before her smile faded. "I'm not trashy, Jimmy. They're from the bachelorette party."

# CHAPTER
# NINE

IZZY

I KNOW HOW IT LOOKED. Like I was the type of girl who carried around a box of condoms because I never knew whom I'd be fucking from night to night. It was the furthest thing from the truth. Don't get me wrong. I'm not a prude, and I never put down any woman no matter how many partners they've had. Men can do it without being looked at with disdain, and I wanted to high-five every lady out there getting what she wants.

I had distanced myself from sleeping around. Men were a complication I didn't need or want. Flash was my standby. The one I called when I needed some cock and a quick goodbye. Lately, that in itself had turned into an issue and a fucking headache. I loved him, but as a best friend. We had passion and the sex was fantastic, but the spark wasn't there and neither were the feelings.

Flash was like my favorite teddy bear as a kid, but he ate pussy like a pro. He was comfortable. Maybe a little too easy for me, and I'd grown complacent with just okay instead of fucking amazing. I knew I needed to make a change and kick Flash's ass to the curb, but I had to be gentle about it.

Looking up at James, I didn't see anything comfortable or easy about the man. He stared down at me with such passion and burning that I worried he'd burst into flames before my very eyes.

Sitting up, I tore one condom from the strip and threw the rest on the floor. I'd brought a bunch of them to the bachelorette party as party favors and to throw around at the girls. I'd wanted to make sure every cock was covered and that all the girls were safe. It was something I always preached.

"Must've been one hell of a party."

"Oh it was," I said before tearing open the package with my teeth.

I motioned with my finger for him to step closer, batting my eyelashes at him. I needed to taste him before I covered it. I moved, kneeling on the edge of the bed and waiting for his dick to come to eye level. The glimmer of shiny metal made my insides twist and my pussy convulse. There's something about a man with a piercing in his cock.

I grabbed his ass, bringing him closer to my face as I took in all his glory, feasting on him with my eyes. I opened wide, laying his hardness against my tongue and closing my lips around his length. The velvety firmness mixing with the saltiness made my mouth water. I swallowed around his dick, pulling it farther into my throat, and fought the urge to gag. It hit the back of my throat, cutting off my airway as my eyes watered.

Squeezing his ass, I sucked him deeper before pulling out and repeating the process. I looked up into his eyes, watching his head fall back in ecstasy. Digging my nails into his rock-hard muscles, I flicked the underside of the tip with my tongue. His body trembled beneath my fingertips and my body warmed. I felt powerful with him at my mercy.

The apadravya caressed my tongue and tapped my teeth as I worked his cock. Just as I felt him grow harder and his body shake uncontrollably, I released him, a popping noise filling the room.

His body jerked, his cock lurching forward as if it were searching for my mouth of its own volition. His teeth chattered as he sucked in air and glared at me.

I shrugged and smiled. "Sucks, doesn't it?" I said, and began to giggle.

He pushed me back before grabbing my feet and yanking me to the edge of the bed. I screamed from happiness—his strength had shocked me. I don't know why. The man was huge. He looked like a giant next to me, but I hadn't thought he could move me around like a fucking rag doll. Holding the condom up for him to take, I bit my lip. His cock was red and bulging as it bobbed in the air.

The shiny metal looked like it was ready to pop free on both sides. I couldn't wait any longer to feel it stroking my insides. He slid the rubber over his cock, paying careful attention to the piercing, while I took in the sight of him.

He had strong, broad shoulders covered in tattoos. I wanted to lean forward and get a better look, but I remained in place. If I hadn't known better or had seen a picture of him first, I would've bet money that he was airbrushed. He was too perfect, with all his rippling muscles, hard body, and flawless skin.

He caught me looking, and winked at me. My cheeks turned pink and heated. I don't know why. I was half dressed and had had his dick in my mouth and he'd tasted me. At this point, what was there to be embarrassed about?

He grabbed the bottom of my dress as I lifted my ass and let him remove it. It flew across the room, landing near the door, where we had begun. I held out my arm, looking to touch his skin, and he gripped my wrist and pulled me off the bed. Then I wrapped my legs around his body, trying not to fall to the floor, and instantly captured his lips.

He grunted, grinding his dick against my pussy as I clung to him. Reaching underneath my leg, he grabbed his dick, rubbing it back and forth twice before jamming it inside me.

I cried out, not having expected to feel so full and stretched. But then he stilled, letting my body adjust before he turned and pushed my back against the wall. The rough wallpaper scratched my skin with each thrust. I reached out, trying to grip the wall, and knocked over the lamp. The sound of glass shattering as it hit the floor didn't stop James.

The pictures on the walls rattled as he pounded into me. My tailbone felt like it was being beaten with a bat each time my body slammed up into the wall. With my back on fire, my ass in pain, and my head slamming against the wall, James pummeled me. Sweat trickled from the edge of his hairline, slowly running down his face.

Sweat and I didn't always get along. With him, I wanted to reach out and taste it. See if it had the same salty taste as his dick against my tongue. Just as I leaned forward, going for the wetness to alleviate the dryness inside my mouth, he placed his lips over mine.

Reaching between us, he flicked my clit with his fingers. It wasn't a gentle touch. There were no tentative feels to see if my body was sensitive. Each stroke felt like a slap against my pussy. My insides clamped down, the edge coming nearer as I sucked his tongue into my mouth.

His strokes became harsh and erratic, matching his breathing. I began to bounce off him, my body flying away from his from the forcefulness of his thighs. Slamming back down on his cock over and over again mingled with the flicks, sending me spiraling over the edge and screaming his name until my throat burned. My eyes rolled back in my head, my head slamming uncontrollably against the wall as my entire body went rigid.

He didn't let up his brutal assault on my pussy as I came down from an orgasm that left me dizzy. As he pummeled me over and over again, I gripped his shoulder, letting myself get lost in the moment.

He stilled, his abs clenching harder as he grunted and leaned his forehead against me. Then he sucked in a breath, his body shuddered, and he gulped for air.

"For fuck's sake," he muttered, swallowing again.

I rested my head against the wall, my entire body feeling like jelly. "Yeah," I said, not able to say anything else.

He held me there for a moment before carrying me to the bed and placing me on top of the mattress. He collapsed next to me, his chest heaving as he wiped his forehead.

"Tire you out already?" I asked as I turned to face him.

"Izzy," he said as he pushed the hair that had fallen behind my shoulder. "I'm just getting started, doll."

I rolled onto my back and stared at the ceiling. The room was spinning slightly from the amount of Jack I'd had at the reception. As I was lost in the passion and booze, he'd consumed my entire world and made everything else vanish.

My eyelids felt heavy as I lay there listening to his breathing slow. My mind was cluttered and I wanted to shut it off and drift off to sleep, but my body had other plans—and so did James. The bed dipped and sprang up as he climbed off the bed. A squeak from the shoddy mattress pulled me back to reality. I opened one eye, watching him walk over to the minibar and grab something inside.

"Want a drink?" he asked, dangling a bottle of Jack.

At this point in the night, there were two options. I could either stop drinking and fall asleep or have another and party to the point that, tomorrow, I wouldn't remember what had happened in this room.

"Yes," I said, sitting up on my elbows.

He twisted off the cap, plopped some ice cubes in a glass, and poured the amber liquid inside before handing it to me. I took shallow sips, not wanting to swallow it too quickly. The wetness on my tongue and burn down my throat helped breathe new life into me. We stared at each other, sipping our drinks stark naked. He leaned against the small bar area, while I sat on the bed with my shoulder back, giving him a full show.

Unable to take the silence, I sloshed back the rest of my drink, shaking the glass, causing the ice cubes to clink together. A small grin spread across his face as he placed his cup on the bar and walked toward me.

"What?" I asked before I stared down into my empty glass.

"Gave me an idea," he said as he grabbed his tie off the floor. Then he removed the knot from the silk material. "Lie back."

"Why?"

"Jesus, just lie the fuck back," he growled, taking the glass from my hand and setting it on the nightstand.

The growl had been a little bit scary, but sexy as fuck. A

shiver ran down my spine as I crawled up the bed backward before placing my head on the pillow.

"Give me your hands," he commanded, straddling my body.

I swallowed hard, my mouth feeling dry again as I held up my hands and offered myself to him.

"Hold them together. Clasp them."

"What are you going to do?" I asked out of pure curiosity.

"I'm tying you to the headboard, doll." He smiled, snapping the tie between his hands.

My natural reaction in this situation should have been "fuck no," but since I'd had more Jack than I could remember and James was hot as fuck, I said, "Okay," before clasping my hands together and holding them in front of him without a care.

James twisted the tie around my hands, securing it in a tight knot and drawing them over my head to the headboard. "You okay with this?" he asked, leaning over me with his dick in my face.

"Yes," I said, reaching forward with my lips to lick the tip of his cock.

He shuddered as he fastened the tie to the headboard before grabbing a spare pillow and placing it under my head. "This should help your arms."

"It's not my arms I'm worried about." Really, I wasn't. I knew he wouldn't hurt me. Thomas would kill him, and then the rest of the Gallo men would be in line to revive him and kill him again.

He laughed, nudging my legs apart with his knees. "Wait. Something's missing," he said as he climbed off the bed. He walked to his suitcase, rifled through the contents, and returned with another tie. "For your eyes. Lift your head."

"I want to see," I said, pissed off that he wanted to take away my sight.

"It'll be better."

"I've been blindfolded before, Jimmy. I'm not a virgin."

"Did you like it?" he asked, studying my face.

"Y-yes," I stammered, hating myself the instant I said it.

"Good. Head up."

261

I sighed, lifting my head from the pillow and watching as he drew closer to me before darkness came.

"Comfortable?" he asked as he tied the knot around the back. "Can you see?"

"It's fine. I may fall asleep. Just warning you now," I lied with a smile.

"Impossible," he whispered against my lips, running his tongue along the seam.

I opened my mouth, trapping his tongue between my teeth. Sliding his hand down my torso, he cupped my pussy.

I smiled, still holding his tongue as his hand left my skin. Suddenly, shooting pain radiated from my core, spreading down my legs. The smack of his hand against my pussy sent shock waves through me.

Instantly, I released his tongue and shrieked, "Fuck!" as I tried to free my hands. I wanted to rub my pussy, hold it, and make the sting go away. "Asshole," I hissed.

"Doll, I'm in control. You can challenge me all you want, but I'll get my way."

I grumbled, twisting my body to change the sensation and pulsating heat between my legs. My breathing was fast from the shock of his assault. Laying his hands against my legs to hold them down, he waited for me to calm.

"Can you handle me, little girl?"

"Fuck you," I seethed. "I can handle anything you give." Being full of liquor didn't help with my ability to make rational statements or judgment calls.

I wanted to see his face. Being robbed of my vision made it impossible to read his emotions. The tone of his voice didn't betray his intentions. I hadn't expected him to smack my pussy, and without seeing his hand move, I couldn't prepare for it.

"Does it burn?" he whispered, the bed jostling as he moved.

I nodded, not able to speak without my voice trembling. The sound of something moving against the woodgrain of the nightstand made me turn to the side. I needed to be able to hear what was about to happen, especially if I couldn't see, but how I'd turned just blocked one of my ears.

I faced forward, waiting for the next sharp sting, when I heard the sound of ice against the glass. I cried out as the cold penetrated through the burn. He held the ice against me, letting tiny droplets of water drip between my legs.

The heat of the slap melted the ice, and the sting of the cold gave way to a feeling of relief. I ground my body against it, craving the coolness of the ice against me. Making tiny circles, he moved the hardness around my clit, making sure to keep it far enough away from the one place I wanted it most.

Goose bumps dotted my flesh as he slid the ice cube up the center of my body, stopping at my belly button, dipping it inside, and resting it there. Then I heard the sound of more ice before a second one touched my skin and both started the ascent toward my breasts.

My nipples were rock hard, throbbing with need, and the thought of the ice touching them had me on edge. I wanted warmth, the feel of his mouth sucking on my tit. My body shook as he circled my breasts, tightening the ring until it landed on the center. The ice instantly cooled my piercings, sending the bite deeper into my flesh.

"Your mouth," I snapped, craving the heat.

"You don't call the shots."

Water dripped down each breast, pooling in the center of my chest. My skin felt like it was on fire except for the spots he touched with the ice and the small stream running down my torso.

Suddenly, his warm tongue blazed a trail up my stomach, sucking the water that had collected on my skin. I lurched forward, trying to offer him my nipple, but he pushed me back down with his palm.

"Be still," he warned, holding me against the mattress.

I gulped, trying to find an ounce of wetness in my mouth, but came up empty. After licking a path to my left breast, he sucked it between his warm lips and drew it into his mouth. My other nipple was still being blasted by the cold, the opposite sensations causing my eyes to roll back in my head as I lay there immobile.

Once he released my left breast, he placed the ice back on

my nipple and moved to my right. The sensation overwhelmed me. No longer could I tell if it was water or my own moisture dripping off my pussy.

Squirming, I needed to find something to stop the throbbing and intense need I felt. With the earth-shattering orgasm I'd had minutes ago, I hadn't thought he could have me so close to the edge that fast.

The ice, cupped in his hand, slid down my body to my core and rested against my clit. I sucked in air, the cold more than I could bear without wanting to claw his face off.

After letting the ice slip toward my center, he pushed it against my opening. As he moved his fingers inside me, the ice slid inside too, burning a path as it slid deeper. I hissed as his cold fingers pushed against the ice, filling me completely.

Water started to trickle out between his fingers as he worked them in and out. He adjusted, moving his body farther down mine and lashing at my clit with his hot tongue. I shook my head, ready to explode from the overload of hot and cold. When he added a third finger, a burn settled between my legs and he lapped at my core.

I pulled against my restraints, feeling the need to move, but it was no use. I was his prisoner as he devoured my body, sucking and finger-fucking me.

I began to chant softly, calling his name at first. As my orgasm neared and he curled his fingers inside me, I began to yell, "Yes!" and "Fuck!" over and over again. I couldn't stop pushing myself down on his hand, feeling his tongue slide across my clit. I felt my toes curl as my body grew rigid. Then I held my breath, riding out the wave of pleasure.

Behind the blindfold, my world filled with colors. Vibrant yellows, reds, and oranges danced inside my eyes as I finally gulped air.

I didn't move as he left the bed. My hands were still above my head, growing tinglier by the second. My chest heaved, the hot breath from my body skidding across the droplets of water. The rip and snap alerted me that he was putting on a condom.

He wasn't done with me yet.

Since I hadn't caught my breath, I couldn't speak before he was between my legs again, rubbing the head of his sheathed dick against my cold opening.

"So fuckin' amazing," he growled as he pushed inside.

I mumbled some bullshit even I didn't understand in my post-orgasm haze. He grabbed my legs, placing my knees over my shoulders as he rammed his dick to the hilt. His fingers pulled on my piercings, sending an aftershock from my tits to my pussy as I gripped him tight, milking his cock.

Linking my feet behind his head, I held his body to mine and pushed against his thrusts. The man was a beast. No other way to describe him. There wasn't a moment I felt in control of the situation, and for once, I liked it. Maybe it was the alcohol that had me going against everything I believed in and had allowed me to give up control so easily. I liked to think it was Jack and not James causing me to give in and become complacent.

What seemed like a lifetime passed before his rhythm slowed and his body convulsed against me. His weight crushed me as he collapsed, drawing breath as if he couldn't get enough.

"Hands," I mumbled as I shook them, hoping to give them more blood. The prickly feeling wouldn't allow me to be comfortable.

He lifted off me, untying my hands before removing the blindfold. I blinked and squinted, the light blinding me. I closed my eyes, trying to stop the pain caused by the brightness.

"My eyes hurt," I whined.

He curled his arms around me, pulling my body tight against his. "Sleep, Izzy," he said into my ear.

The warmth and comfort of being in his arms sucked me in. Peace and sleep came to me as the darkness took me.

# CHAPTER
# TEN

MY STOMACH TURNED as I moved. It felt like someone was hammering a nail into my skull. *Tap. Tap. Boom. Tap. Tap. Boom.* I winced, trying to pry my eyes open from their sleepy state. The little construction worker inside my skull didn't relent as I looked around.

I swallowed, not recognizing the room before closing my eyes again. Where the fuck was I? Last night was a blur. I remembered the boring-ass reception line, dinner that had seemed to go on forever, and then drinks at the bar. Not just any drink, but my best friend Jack, sliding back and wrapping me up in his warmth.

I tried to smile when looking back on the evening, but everything hurt—even my cheeks. *What the fuck happened?* I slowly shook my head, trying to clear the fog that clouded my thoughts. My head fell to the side and I opened my eyes to get another look around the room.

I blinked twice, clearing the haze from my vision, and saw *him*. James. My stomach fell as I looked down his body and then to mine. We were naked, our clothes thrown around the room haphazardly. I'd fucked him. My pussy ached, the muscles in my arms burned, and my nipples throbbed at the memory of the night before.

I thought I'd dreamt being awoken from my sleep for

another go, but nope, I hadn't. James was insatiable. Even while asleep, his dick was semi-hard, staring at me as a reminder of the multiple orgasms he'd brought me.

I stared at James, watching him sleep. He looked peaceful and kind and not like the man I'd met the night before. James had a sharp tongue, a commanding tone, and an air of authority about him. Everything that made me run for the hills and hide. My body liked him, though. Fuck, even my mind tried to tell me that he was a great guy.

I knew better than that. No man, especially one like James, would make me change my mind on love and relationships. He'd promised me a night with no strings attached, and that was exactly how I wanted it.

Saying goodbye was overrated. I didn't feel the need to chitchat and thank him for the amazing fuck. Once I had a good grip on the side of the bed, I slowly pulled myself up, praying that the room would stop spinning. Then I turned toward him, waiting to see how heavy a sleeper he was and if I could slink out unnoticed.

I climbed to my feet, holding my head as I collected my dress and panties from the floor. I had to pee like a mother-fucker, but I couldn't risk him waking and finding me in his room.

After placing my panties in my purse, I opened my dress and stepped inside. I zipped it, keeping my eyes locked on him and holding my breath. Then I strapped on my heels, looked around the room one last time to make sure I hadn't left anything behind, and made my way toward the door. Before I turned the handle, I turned and stared at James.

He really was beautiful when he was sleeping. His rock-hard body covered in tattoos, his cock ready for more, and his beauty was enough to suck any girl in, but not me.

A wave of guilt overcame me, but I pushed it aside as I opened the door, trying to avoid waking him. As I entered the hallway, I exhaled and clicked the door closed. I swear, fucking hotels and their loud-ass doors pissed me off more than anything.

A man passed by, looking me up and down, and I felt like a tramp. Dressed in my gown from the night before, my hair a mess, and probably with makeup out of place, but fuck it. I straightened my back, standing tall as I walked to the elevator.

Pushing the elevator button, I glanced back toward his room, silently chanting, "Please don't come out," over and over again.

I couldn't calm my breath as my heart pounded inside my chest at the thought of him finding me in the hallway trying to sneak out.

When the doors opened, I ran to the back of the elevator and held the walls as if they were my lifeline. I'd made it inside without being discovered. I relaxed, almost sliding down the faux-wood walls, allowing the enormity of the situation to hit me.

I'd fucked my brother's friend. I'd fucked him more than once. I'd left without saying goodbye. Would he come after me? Was he a man of his word? There was so much I didn't know about James.

I'd never been the type of girl to sneak out without so much as a goodbye. The night before started flashing before my eyes. Being tied to the bed, the feel of his fingers inside me, the way he'd fucked me, how he tasted—instantly, my body responded. I wanted more, but I closed my eyes and tried to cool off. There was no way in hell I'd allow myself to go there again.

I needed to forget James Caldo.

# CHAPTER
# ELEVEN

JAMES

MY EYES FLEW open as I heard the click of the door closing. Reaching over, I felt the empty space that was still warm from her skin. Groaning, I rolled over and stared at the door. My first instinct was to run after her and drag her back to my room, but I fought it. It wasn't right. Izzy and I weren't meant to have more than a night together… at least not yet.

I'd have my time with her again. There was a connection that couldn't be denied, but she wasn't ready. She still had wildness to her. A rebellious attitude that felt the need to fight against the norm, and that included relationships. Izzy wanted to be the badass chick who didn't need anyone in her life, but that was the furthest thing from the truth.

Her tough shell seemed impenetrable, but I'd witnessed the small crack and peered inside. I could see the fire in her eyes, love in her heart, and the wild animal waging a battle inside. I needed to break down the walls, but timing was key. I couldn't chase after her. I was all about the chase, but not yet.

Her brother, Thomas, and I were tied together through work. We had a mission, and I couldn't do anything that may put his life in danger. Izzy would have to wait until the Sun Devils MC was removed from the equation and Thomas was free from the club.

Throwing my arm across my face, I could smell her on my

skin. Inhaling deeply, memories of the night before flooded my mind. I'd never felt weak in the knees before *her*. The electricity in the air as we touched could've lit an entire house and possibly blown out a few light bulbs in the process.

If I said that it didn't sting a little that she didn't stick around to say goodbye, I'd be lying. Izzy was as affected by me as I was her, and she had to slink away before she would have to confront the feeling I invoked in her last night.

I knew I'd have her again. She couldn't escape the inevitable. The connection we felt was undeniable. I'd let her go... for now. I knew in the end she'd be mine.

A chase would ensue and I'd get exactly what I wanted—Izzy Gallo.

…Continue the Gallo Family Saga with Uncover Me, Thomas Gallo's story. Please visit *menofinked.com/uncover-me* for more information or *menofinked.com/inked-se* to grab the next special edition paperback.

Want a signed copy for your bookshelf?
Visit *chelleblissromance.com* to learn more.

# ABOUT THE AUTHOR

I'm a full-time writer, time-waster extraordinaire, social media addict, coffee fiend, and ex-history teacher. *To learn more about my books, please visit menofinked.com.*

Want to stay up-to-date on the newest Men of Inked release and more? Join my newsletter.

Join over 10,000 readers on Facebook in Chelle Bliss Books private reader group and talk books and all things reading. Come be part of the family!

See the Gallo Family Tree

## Where to Follow Me:

facebook.com/authorchellebliss1

instagram.com/authorchellebliss

bookbub.com/authors/chelle-bliss

goodreads.com/chellebliss

amazon.com/author/chellebliss

twitter.com/ChelleBliss1

pinterest.com/chellebliss10

# *Men of Inked*
# MYSTERY BOX
### DELIVERED EVERY 4 MONTHS

## SPECIAL EDITION PAPERBACKS & EXCLUSIVE MERCHANDISE!

## CHELLEBLISSROMANCE.COM

**CHELLE BLISS**
NEWS, ROMANCE, AND CHAOS

Want a behind-the-scenes look at the chaos of my author life?
Maybe you want early sneak peeks and other kickass treats.

CLICK HERE to join the fun or visit *menofinked.com/news*

…and as a special thank you, you'll receive a free copy of
Resisting, a Men of Inked novella.

MENOFINKED.COM

## MEN OF INKED SERIES

*"One of the sexiest series of all-time" -Bookbub Reviewers* Download book 1 for FREE!

- Book 1 - Throttle Me (Joe aka City)
- Book 2 - Hook Me (Mike)
- Book 3 - Resist Me (Izzy)
- Book 4 - Uncover Me (Thomas)
- Book 5 - Without Me (Anthony)
- Book 6 - Honor Me (City)
- Book 7 - Worship Me (Izzy)

## MEN OF INKED: SOUTHSIDE SERIES

Join the Chicago Gallo Family with their strong alphas, sassy women, and tons of fun.

- Book 1 - Maneuver (Lucio)
- Book 2 - Flow (Daphne)
- Book 3 - Hook (Angelo)
- Book 4 - Hustle (Vinnie)
- Book 5 - Love (Angelo)

## MEN OF INKED: HEATWAVE SERIES

Same Family. New Generation.

- Book 1 - Flame (Gigi)
- Book 2 - Burn (Gigi)
- Book 3 - Wildfire (Tamara)

- Book 4 - Blaze (Lily)
- Book 5 - Ignite (Tamara)
- Book 6 - Spark (Nick)
- Book 7 - Ember (Rocco)
- Book 8 - Singe - (Carmello)
- Book 9 - Ashes - (Rosie)
- Book 10 - Scorch - (Luna)

## THE OPEN ROAD SERIES

Wickedly hot alphas with tons of heart pounding suspense!

- Book 1 - Broken Sparrow (Morris)
- Book 2 - Broken Dove (Leo)
- Book 3 - Broken Wings (Crow)

## ALFA INVESTIGATIONS SERIES

Wickedly hot alphas with tons of heart pounding suspense!

- Book 1 - Sinful Intent (Morgan)
- Book 2 - Unlawful Desire (Frisco)
- Book 3 - Wicked Impulse (Bear)
- Book 4 - Guilty Sin (Ret)

## SINGLE READS

- Mend
- Enshrine
- Misadventures of a City Girl
- Misadventures with a Speed Demon
- Rebound (Flash aka Sam)
- Top Bottom Switch (Ret)
- Santa Baby
- Fearless - (Austin Moore)

**View Chelle's entire collection of books at menofinked.com/books**

To learn more about Chelle's books visit *menofinked.com* or

Made in the USA
Coppell, TX
12 March 2023

14157497R00173